Exes Don't

BOOKS BY LEAH DOBRINSKA

The Mapleton Novels
Love at On Deck Cafe
Good To Be Home
Together With You
Choosing Love

The Larkspur Library Mysteries
Death Checked Out
Mayhem In Circulation
A Killer Hold

The Fall In Love Series
Friends Don't
Enemies Don't
Exes Don't

LEAH DOBRINSKA

3
FALL
IN
LOVE
SERIES

Copyright © 2024 by Leah Dobrinska

All rights reserved.

No portion of this book may be reproduced in any form without written permission from the publisher or author, except in the case of brief quotations embodied in critical articles or reviews.

In accordance with the U.S. Copyright Act of 1976, the scanning, uploading, and electronic sharing of any part of this book without the permission of the author is unlawful piracy and theft of the author's intellectual property. Thank you for your support of the author's rights.

This book is entirely a work of fiction. Names, characters and incidents portrayed in it are either the work of the author's imagination or are used fictitiously. Any resemblance to actual persons, living or dead, businesses, companies, events or localities is entirely coincidental.

Editing: Jenn Lockwood

Cover Design: Melody Jeffries

Library of Congress Control Number: 2024919114

ISBN: 979-8-9885978-2-7 (paperback) | 979-8-9885978-3-4 (ebook)

To anyone searching for their place. You belong.

1
Trope Round-Up

Rose

I peruse the shelf in front of me at Mood Reader with a discerning eye. Here at the adorable book store where I work, we've got books in every genre, but my attention lingers on our romance titles. The trope gang is all here: enemies to lovers, friends to lovers, mutual pining, co-workers. The list goes on and on.

My gaze snags on a new release with a bright, red and green illustrated cover, and I feel a familiar tug of longing. Not, as you might assume, to have a whirlwind holiday romance like the one this story promises to deliver, but to write a book of my own.

Too bad I gave up on that dream a long time ago—about five years ago, to be exact. Right about when some of my favorite romance novel tropes hit too close to home...and blew up in my face.

If—and that's a big if—I ever manage to write my romance novel, let me tell you the tropes that will *not* be included.

Number one. There will be no sports. No professional athletes with chiseled muscles for days and charisma and charm to boot. No swooning, screaming fans and high-stakes games. None of that garbage.

Number two. There will be no royalty or celebrity characters. Talk about making things complicated. No way. My book will include normal, everyday, common people.

Number three. This is a big one. There absolutely, positively will be no spies. No undercover work. No secrets and intrigue.

No cloak-and-dagger shenanigans. It's not all it's cracked up to be...trust me.

Finally, number four. Perhaps the most significant trope I plan to avoid—miscommunication. Lying, hiding feelings, keeping secrets...that's the absolute worst.

"Hey, Rose." Mia, my boss and the owner of Mood Reader pops her head around the New Release shelf I've been organizing, stirring me from my thoughts. "You sure you don't mind closing up for me when you get done?"

"No problem at all." I wave her off. "Get out of here. Patrick is waiting."

Mia blushes, and if I had a normal heart, it would do a little pitter-patter, squeeze in my chest, or take off in a gallop at the sweetness of it all.

Something like that.

Objectively speaking, Mia and her husband, Patrick, are darling. He adores her. We're talking hearts shooting from his eyes, showering her with constant attention as if she's the only person in the room. The stuff of all these romance novels I'm surrounded by.

But even though I recognize the love between Patrick and Mia, I don't have a normal heart. I've got a heart that's been locked down and suffocated under so many layers of deceit I can barely find my own pulse most days.

"I owe you." Mia gives me a side hug before she floats down the aisle toward the check-out counter and retrieves her winter coat. She's so in love she's glowing.

A horn honks from Main Street, and I follow Mia to the door.

"You kids have fun," I tell her.

"Always do. Don't work too hard."

"So bossy." I pout. "It's like you're my boss or something."

"Nah. That's me being your friend. Good night!"

I smile as Patrick hops out of the driver's seat and jogs around the front of his truck to open Mia's door. She climbs in, and he makes sure she's situated before closing it and hurrying around to his side again. They drive off, and I sigh, flicking the lock on the front door before turning around and slouching against it.

Mood Reader is my happy place...my sanctuary in Cashmere Cove. My sister, Poppy, and I moved to this small town that sits on the Wisconsin peninsula, along the Bay of Green Bay, a little over a year ago. Our younger sister, Noli, followed us shortly thereafter. The whole Kasper clan now calls this charming, waterside town home. I never thought I'd find a position like the one I have at Mood Reader. My work is fulfilling, and Mia is the best boss. So much of my adult life has been spent jumping from odd job to odd job, taking whatever is available. I thought coming to Cashmere Cove with Poppy would be more of the same, and my position here would be another in a long line of mundane jobs that serve only as a front. None of them are my real job, after all.

My real job is a secret.

How's that for ominous?

I push off the door and glance at the clock.

I've got about thirty minutes to get things organized before my real job collides with my book store job.

I finish arranging the New Release display, straightening out a stack of library card gift tags Mia and I made to give to anyone who buys a book from us between now and the holidays, when my phone vibrates in the back pocket of my jeans.

I fish it out and find a message from Poppy.

Poppy

> How's everything in the Cove? Miss you guys!

Noli responds before I get a chance, and I find myself nodding along to her message.

Noli

> You're on your honeymoon. Why are you texting? Isn't Mack monopolizing your time?

Poppy and Noli are my best friends, my ride-or-dies. We've faced the ups and downs of life together and lived to tell the tale. Poppy, as the oldest, assumed a mother-hen role, making sure Noli and I had a roof over our heads and graduated high school after our mom died, our dad left us, and our grandmother, who had taken us in, passed away.

When I spell it all out like that, I have to cringe. We've been through it.

So, yeah, while we tease Poppy for being overbearing, we're grateful for her.

> Poppy
> We're getting in plenty of quality time, don't worry. <winking face emoji> <angel face emoji>

> Rose
> Quality time. Is that what the kids are calling it these days?

I send off a GIF of Marvin Gaye singing "Let's Get It On."

> Noli
> TMI. <gagging face emoji>

> Poppy
> <crying laughing emoji> <kissing face emoji>

Poppy and Mack got married last weekend, on the Saturday after Thanksgiving. The wedding was stunning, and the couple was radiant and so obviously in love even someone like me with my nonfunctioning heart could feel the magic in the air. They've been on their honeymoon for all of three days, and I miss them. It'll be different when they get back. They didn't live together before they got married, but now, Poppy will move from the side of the duplex she's been sharing with me to the other half where Mack lives.

Not sure how I feel about sharing a wall with the newlyweds, to be honest. But I'll figure it out. I could always find a new place. It was Poppy who got us the rental when we first moved to town. We affectionately call our half of the duplex "The Downer" because it's been such a fixer upper. But I'm not tied to it in any way. It's been another pit stop on the endless highway of my life. Where am I going, you ask? Your guess is as good as mine.

I don't need to be dwelling on that right now, not when I'm staring down a meeting that I'm dreading in—I check the clock again—ten minutes. I fire off two more quick texts.

> **Rose**
> Quit being such a mom and go enjoy your new husband, Pops.
>
> And spare us the details.

> **Noli**
> Seriously. We're begging you.

> **Poppy**
> You guys are no fun.
>
> You know you love me!
>
> P.S. Noli, tell Collin he better not propose to you for real while we're gone, or I'll kick him in the shins.
>
> And Rosie, don't you go finding someone to fall in love with until I'm back.

A slideshow of images flies through my mind, all of them including a handsome and kind man from my past.

"He's not for you." I say the words out loud to the empty bookstore while at the same time sending my sisters a message.

> **Rose**
> Still planning to die an old cat lady. Thanks for your concern. <cat emoji> <peace sign emoji>

> **Noli**
> Oh my gosh, Pops. Good byeeeeee!!!

I huff out a laugh and busy myself with the books. It's a relief, really. To have the books.

In the past year, my sisters' lives have exploded with happiness and companionship and all the things you'd hope for the people you love. Poppy and Mack nailed the friends-to-lovers trope. Noli and Collin are the picture of enemies to lovers. I'm so glad for them. Truly. But it's only made all the more apparent the shell of a life I live.

There's a single rap on the rear door. It echoes through the long, narrow bookstore, which is much deeper than it is wide, like a car backfiring.

Here goes nothing.

I swing by the check-out counter and turn off our indoor security cameras, mentally apologizing to Mia. I'll make sure the cameras are reactivated when I'm done with this meeting, but I don't need her asking me about the stranger who came in after hours.

The walk to the back of the bookstore has me feeling a little like Wendy, walking the plank. But there's no Peter Pan in my story. Nope. This girl has to rescue herself—or at least grit her teeth, survive, and advance.

I flip the lock, tug my shoulders back, and pull open the door off the alley.

2
Hey, Kids, Spying Is Fun (Not)

Rose

My father steps inside, rubbing his hands against the chill in the late-November air.

I can't help but flash back to a summer day about ten years ago, when I let him into the apartment Poppy, Noli, and I shared. I had just graduated high school, and I hadn't seen him in several years. I couldn't believe he was there—in person. My hands shook with the sheer joy of being reunited. I thought he was coming back so we could be a family again. Instead, he looked me dead in the eye, without an ounce of emotion on his face, and offered me a job. He said he could train me; that I was the type for it. A loner at heart, like him. A fan of physical fitness. A helper.

He also said the fewer people who knew, the better. It would be less complicated and easier to do our job that way.

I could barely process what he was saying, but at the chance to be close to him, I jumped in feet first. I thought I could wear him down over time and bring about a full family reconciliation. But that was ten years ago. I thought wrong.

"You're early." I press the door shut and lock it.

My dad, Lennox, strides forward without a word in response. In one shrewd glance, he takes in the floor-to-ceiling bookcases, the book display tables, the circular staircase, and the second-floor loft. He's good at this—assessing locations, determining threat levels, seeing things other people miss.

I resist the urge to squirm under his evaluation. Dueling feelings wage war in my chest when I'm around him—I want him to be proud of me, and I want him to be gone, all at the same time. I briefly acknowledge that these feelings are stronger here, in my safe space, before bottling them up and focusing on the job. I have to keep my emotions under wraps, especially now, or I'll never get out in one piece.

I trail him into the center of the bookstore, stepping forward and motioning for him to take a seat in one of the overstuffed corduroy chairs Mia has positioned for our patrons to curl up in.

"I'm not thrilled about this," I say as I sit across from him.

I don't know why my dad insisted on meeting in person. He could have passed along the information through my secure email. We could have video-conferenced. I've been doing this for a decade. I'm good at my job. I don't need a babysitter, but it's like my dad can't resist checking up on me. Almost like he doesn't trust me fully with this assignment.

His first words to me are, "You're the best option we have to protect Bates."

So maybe he *does* trust me.

That, or he realizes my history with Anton makes me our best shot at protecting him. My dad knows as well as I know that I'm going to do whatever I can to help.

Secret's out: I'm a security specialist. I work for a private security agency run by my father. We're a team of executive protection officers hired to protect high-profile dignitaries, celebrities, and persons of interest on both American soil and overseas, when the opportunity presents itself—which, admittedly, isn't as often as I'd like. I've been begging my dad to let me establish a satellite team in Europe for years. Because the thing about all the secrets I keep from those closest to me and the double life I lead is that nowhere ever feels like home. I figure I may as well spend my time some place exotic…like the streets of Paris, or the canals of Venice, or the mountains of Switzerland. So far, he hasn't bit on the idea, but I'm holding out hope.

My dad reaches into his bag and pulls out a tablet. After a couple taps of his finger and flicks of his wrist, he flips it around for me, and I'm staring at a photo of Anton Bates.

All six feet, four inches of blond-haired, blue-eyed, star-quarterback goodness.

Remember what I said about sports romances?

Not. For. Me.

I repeat those three words over and over again in my head, even as the skin along the back of my neck prickles. I say a quick prayer that my dad doesn't notice the rush of goosebumps that coat my body. How? *How* does a photograph of the guy I dated all those years ago still have this effect on me? It's pathetic.

I take the tablet and frantically scroll past the image, exhaling when the synopsis of the threats against Anton and our plans for mitigating them appears.

"There's been chatter of an assassination attempt." My dad speaks about the threat against Anton as if he's telling me he had a bran muffin for breakfast. He's detached. Nonchalant. "The palace in Penwick is asking for extra protection. They want our eyes and ears on the ground level."

Not only is Anton a star professional quarterback here in the United States, he's also the prince of a small island nation off the coast of Norway.

Yeah, the royalty trope?

Not. For. Me.

You see where this is going, don't you?

"They've signed off on the cover story we've come up with for you."

And there's the spy trope...no bueno.

I sigh. "Which is?"

"You're a freelance journalist who's been hired to write an in-depth character piece on him." My dad stares me down with one eyebrow arched, as if to say, *It's a good plan, and you know it.*

"You'll have total access to him for the next month, conducting interviews and gathering info."

"Do I actually have to write the article?" I'm a decent writer, but I didn't go to school for journalism.

"If you want, or I can have someone else at the office do it based on the interviews and your notes."

I give a noncommittal nod. I'll figure that part out later. I scroll through the dossier. I know most of this stuff about Anton. I know his family. His mother, Queen Della. His father, the late king consort. A cousin, Duke. That's the guy's name, not his title. Though I guess he could be Duke Duke, which is kind of hilarious.

I know other things about Anton too. Things that aren't listed in the write-up for my job. Like how he listens to Disney music before his football games. Or that he likes his eggs scrambled and on top of whole wheat toast. I know he'll choose chocolate ice cream over vanilla every time. He also hates wearing socks, which I find strangely endearing. He's a great listener, and he makes everyone feel like what they say matters. When he puts his belief in you, you start to believe in yourself.

No.

Not. For. Me.

I get to the bottom of the dossier and blink up at Lennox. "Does Anton know about any of this? The article? The fact that I'm interviewing him?"

"I've been assured that he'll be looped in soon."

He's going to hate this. If he's anything like me, our break up is still seared in his mind. He told me he never wanted to see me again. And now, surprise! A ghost from five years past!

"What about the threat? Is he aware?"

Lennox shakes his head once.

"He doesn't know that extra security is being put in place?" It's a question I already know the answer to, because it was the same five years ago when I went undercover and started dating him.

Here's where I should clarify. I'm not really a spy. Not for most of my assignments, anyway. I'm more like a bodyguard. But Anton has a history of refusing extra security. His mother, Queen Della, hates that. She is who hires us, and it winds up that I'm kind of both spying on him and for him. It's a whole mess.

"Anton refuses extra security measures, so Penwick Palace has stated, in no uncertain terms, that he's not to be made aware of the efforts being made to ensure his protection."

"But—"

"There are no *buts*, Rose. That's it. They've hired us. They trust us to carry out their wishes—which we'll do. Discretion is the name of the game. Can I count on you for that?"

I look away and bite my lip.

I think I could handle the sports and the royalty, but it's the lying to Anton that makes me feel like crawling out of my skin. He's always been so open with me. Deceiving him is like my own personal torture chamber. It's a constant drip of water, splashing on my forehead until I go insane.

"This is how it has to be." My dad's voice takes on a slight edge of exasperation, as if he doesn't understand why I can't reconcile this aspect of the job. To his point, I've been doing this sort of work for almost a decade. I *should* be able to handle everything that comes with it.

But all the lying and the deceit...it's chaffing. I've been keeping pace and outrunning it, but it's gaining ground—reaching out its skeletal hand to grab me around the ankle and yank me down into a heap of dust and self-inflicted destruction.

Not just with Anton.

It's things like shutting off the security system without Mia knowing. Sure, she'll likely never find out. But it doesn't sit well with me.

It's the fact that Noli had a deranged ex-boyfriend stalking her for over a year, and she didn't come to me about it. I could have helped her. I could have done something. But she doesn't know that, because I can't be open with my own sisters.

Heck, I've had to find roundabout ways to help Poppy keep a roof over our heads for years, not ever letting her in on the hefty salary I'm pulling in, because she'd ask questions I don't want to answer. So instead, I've gone behind her back to landlords, worked out deals, and played dumb when I had to. I hate it. But it's what I signed up for.

I could always get a job elsewhere, doing security but not working for my dad. Then I could come clean with my sisters and everyone else about what I actually do. Although, at this point, I've been lying to Poppy and Noli for so long I'm terrified of what they'll say when the truth comes out. And a job with a different agency wouldn't solve my problem where Anton is concerned. Nothing changes how I've lied to him. He'll always be the one who got away…the one I had to let go. If he knew the real me, he wouldn't want me anyway.

"Fine. Yeah. I know." I hand the tablet back to my dad. "To be clear, I don't have to date him again? Just pretend to write the article?"

"Nothing's off the table. If you need more access to him, then…" My dad shrugs as if stringing Anton along, trying to make him trust me again, is such a blip it doesn't even require an explanation.

I swallow away the feeling of sick that's piling up in the back of my throat.

He slides the tablet in his bag. "You start tomorrow. You'll have a meeting at the River Foxes stadium in Green Bay. Then you'll get to work. I'll need daily reports of who Anton is with, what he's doing. That's how we'll identify patterns. You know the drill. Do your job well, and he stays safe. It's as easy as that."

Ha.

That's what I thought too…once upon a time.

3
A Stranger at a Bar

Rose – Five Years Ago

The thick, hoppy scent of beer hits me like a physical force the second I walk into Billy Bob's Bar. I blink, giving my eyes a chance to adjust to the dim light of my surroundings. Billy Bob's is packed, and the place is rowdy. There's a live band playing nineties country music, and between the loud rendition of Brooks and Dunn's "Boot Scootin' Boogie" and the laughter and hollering of the crowd, my senses are overwhelmed. There's an impromptu line dance set up in the middle of the establishment. Tables have been pushed off to the side, and men and women are two-stepping, laughing, and twirling in front of the stage—the picture of general merriment.

I mentally go through the list of things I know about my target: Anton Bates. Blond hair. Blue eyes. Tall. Muscular. Supposedly here with a bunch of his teammates. He can't be too hard to find. I scan the crowd, looking for oversized football players.

My job, should I choose to accept it—and spoiler alert, I have—is to find him, make nice, and establish the foundation of a relationship. Basically, I've got to get the guy to fall in love with me, Andie Anderson style. *How to Lose a Guy in 10 Days*, anyone? Actually, I guess I'm playing the role of Benjamin Barry here. Either way, I cringe. It feels all sorts of icky, but what can I do? Anton is a prince who needs an extra set of eyes and ears around him in case of a threat to his person. I'm the girl for the job. He doesn't know that. He can't know it, according to the queen. And we work for her.

So that's that.

Now, if I could find—

A broad shoulder knocks into the center of my back, sending my arms pinwheeling and my body stumbling forward. I'm a hair's breadth away from falling flat on my face onto these disgusting, sticky floors when I'm yanked upright.

I look up—and then up some more—and into the cerulean-blue eyes of my target. If I didn't already have them memorized from the photos I'd been shown, I would now. I'm struck by the small circle of green around his irises that spills into the outer blue rings like tie-dye. That doesn't show up in photos. Pictures cannot do this man justice, apparently.

Andddd now I'm staring.

"Are you okay?" His voice is softer than I expected from someone who commands offenses—and countries—for a living. It's plush, with a richness to it. Like the fur of a brand-new stuffed animal. I want to nuzzle my nose into it.

I blink and glance down at where his hands still rest on my hips.

He follows my gaze and pulls them away, running one through his hair. It's longer on the top and shaved close at the sides. His cheeks are pink. Wait. Is he blushing?

That's...unexpected.

And adorable.

I smile to put him at ease. "I'm good."

Three guys are laughing and jostling next to Anton. He breaks eye contact with me and nudges the nearest one. "Del, watch it." He points at me. "You could have hurt her."

Del offers me a sheepish shrug, which, given his oversized stature, is more like a giant heave of the shoulders. "Sorry, ma'am. It's just...this song does something to me."

Anton rolls his eyes.

I let loose a genuine laugh. "It's fine. Seriously."

The music changes to the opening chords of Faith Hill's "This Kiss."

"What a banger!" Del hooks his arms around the other two guys. "To the dance floor!" He charges ahead, craning his neck around and calling out to Anton, "Bates, come on!"

"Be right there." Anton turns his attention back to me. "Can I get you a drink? Peace offering for my buddy bulldozing you."

"Sure." I smile again.

He gestures for me to lead the way to the bar. I pull up to the high counter and hear a crunch beneath my boots. I look down and see peanut shells.

"It's my favorite part of this place." Anton drops into the seat next to me and bobs his chin at the ground. "Free peanuts in the shell. You just shuck 'em and toss 'em."

"Isn't that more like littering?"

"Nope." His blue-green eyes dance. "The shells are biodegradable."

I arch a brow. "Look at you, talking all science-y and looking out for our planet."

He pops another peanut in his mouth, holding my gaze with laughter in his eyes. "Is that the type of guy you're into? A nature lover?"

"Well, recycling is one of my favorite hobbies…" I tap my chin playfully. "So, I suppose yes."

"Noted," he chuckles. "I should tell you, then, that I plant trees in my spare time."

"I don't know if I believe that." I furrow my brow. "Were you Johnny Appleseed in a past life?"

He laughs outright at that. "No, but it's one of my initiatives in my home country."

"Your home country?" I cock my head. "I noticed the accent, but I didn't catch your name."

His eyes widen with genuine surprise. "You don't know who I am?"

"Uh, no." The lie tumbles from my lips with ease. "Should I?"

He shakes his head quickly. "I'm glad you don't, actually. It's...nice. Most people recognize me." He shoots a glance around the bar. "That's why I like coming here. I can fly under the radar a bit."

"What are you, like, a spy?" I deadpan.

"I wish." He laughs and pauses before adding, "Why? Are you?"

I almost choke on a peanut, but manage to swallow it. Hard. "Yeah, right."

His shoulders shake with his silent laughter, and I let out an internal sigh of relief. Note to self: no jokes about spies. That one got a little too close for comfort.

The bartender swings by, and we place our drink orders. After she heads off to fix my vodka soda and bring Anton a glass of ice water, he leans his elbow on the bar, turning his whole body so he's facing me. He's the picture of easygoing, and there's an openness to him that I appreciate. He's giving me his full attention, and I feel like I'm the only person in this crowded room.

"I'm actually the quarterback," he says, picking up our conversation. I notice that he doesn't lead with the prince angle, which is interesting. Is he uncomfortable being a royal? Is he prouder of being a pro-football player? I file this information away to puzzle over later.

"The quarterback." I twist my lips to the side, playing dumb. "Is that, like, a secret superhero call sign or something?"

He grins. "No. I'm the quarterback—for the Mobile Tigers."

I drop my jaw, feigning surprised delight. "Are you for real? I was just selected to join the cheer and dance squad for the Tigers."

That's the truth at least. The agency managed to swing this position for me, figuring it would keep me in the same orbit as Anton. I do have a dance background, so there's that.

Anton presses his lips together, like he's trying to hold back a smile. "So you'll be cheering for me this year?"

"I guess so." I look him up and down. "Are you any good? It'll make my job way more fun if the team is decent."

"Oh, I'm good." He leans in. "Don't you worry."

I feel my cheeks heat, but I keep my tone breezy. "I'll be the judge of that." I hold out my hand. "Rose Kasper."

He stares at me but doesn't offer his hand in return.

"What?" I hold my arms out to the side. "Do y'all not shake hands where you're from? Is it, like, a regional thing?"

"Nah. I'm trying to remember the moment."

I let my arms drop to my sides and glance around. "This moment? Here in the loud bar with the peanut shells and the off-key singing?"

"Yeah, and the girl with the smart mouth and pretty eyes." He reaches for my hand. It's hard not to notice the size difference we've got going on. His grip is at once powerful and gentle. He squeezes. "I think I'm going to want to play this back later."

My heart takes off like a stampeding buffalo. It's pounding around in my chest with reckless abandon. The country music goes muted in the background, and the whole bar turns hazy. It's like Anton is the only thing my brain can focus on. Anton with the technicolor eyes and quick compliments. The considerate quarterback. My pulse is out of control, and I've got to get myself together. I cannot let this—whatever *this* is—go to my head.

I squeeze his hand twice in return. "Pretty smooth, Mr. Quarterback."

"I do what I can. And it's Bates. Anton Bates."

My word. The man is like a real-life Bond, James Bond.

Oh, wait. I'm the spy here.

"Well, nice to meet you, Anton Bates." We stare at each other. Anton has a goofy grin on his face, and whatever I was expecting from this prince pro-football player, it wasn't this. This feels easy. Normal. Comfortable.

Maybe *too* comfortable.

Anton grabs a handful of peanuts from the nearby canister and piles them on the bar top in front of me. He takes one and shucks it, popping the nut in his mouth. I mimic his movements, and he watches me as I hesitate before tossing the shell on the floor. He looks inordinately proud.

Is it possible to develop a late-in-life peanut allergy? Would that account for the flip flop my stomach is doing?

"So, what do you like to do when you're not dancing? Or recycling," he adds with a wink.

I reach for the drink the bartender placed in front of me and turn to study Anton over the top of the glass. There he goes again with that openness. His expression is warm, and I find myself wanting to tell him something real. Something true about me. It's not wise. I've had enough experience in this profession to know that mixing my work with my reality is a recipe for disaster, but in this case, I don't care.

"I like to write. I'm working on a novel."

His face lights up. "Are you serious? That's incredible."

"It's nothing yet." I brush off his praise. "I keep stopping and starting. Haven't made it past chapter three."

"Yeah, but I bet you will." His confidence in me makes my heart flutter.

"How can you be sure?" I cock my head. "You've known me for all of ten minutes."

"Gut instinct." He smiles down at me. "I've got a good feeling about you."

Honestly, I've got a good feeling about him too. I've never had such an easy time talking to a guy I just met. In ten minutes, Anton has proven that he listens and he can make me laugh. He's also humble and incredibly attractive. I don't believe in love at first sight, but this feels a lot like *like* at first sight. Like, really like.

That's a problem. Because he's my job. I can't let my real feelings get involved.

The band shifts to a new song, and the energy in the room rockets up another notch when the lead singer starts belting "Callin' Baton Rouge" by Garth Brooks.

"Great song," I say with a smile, grateful to the music for diffusing the intense moment. My knee involuntarily starts bouncing along to the beat.

Anton stares at me and then bobs his head to the center of the bar. "I'm not much of a dancer, but I think we should. You game?"

"To dance? Always." I set my drink down. "Lead the way, Mr. Quarterback."

He grabs my hand and tugs me forward.

I crunch my way through peanuts, trailing him as he plants us directly in the middle of the line dancers. We find Del and the other guys, who Anton introduces as players on his team. I already know their names from the background dossier I received ahead of my assignment, but I act natural.

We start shuffling along with the crowd. Anton wasn't lying about not being much of a dancer. He spins the opposite direction from the rest of us, and the bewildered look on his face when he gets knocked sideways by a woman with a flannel shirt tied above her naval and rhinestone white cowboy boots makes me giggle.

Anton points at me. "Laugh it up."

And I do. So does he. There's something really refreshing about a man who isn't afraid to make a fool of himself and do something he's not great at. Anton Bates has cool confidence in spades, and I'm being sucked into his orbit at an alarming rate.

We stomp and slide in the sea of bodies until he grabs my hand and spins me out of the center of the dance floor to an open patch of peanut-strewn ground. He wraps his arms around my back, and we sway to the iconic fiddle interlude before he drops to a knee and serenades me with Garth's bridge. I fall into the character of Samantha, picking up a pretend phone and listening on the other end of the line.

When the song ends, I throw my hands in the air, cheering in appreciation with the rest of the bar. I can feel my shoulder-length hair fanned out and frizzing around my head. There's sweat pooling above my lip. My shirt has come untucked. I should be self-conscious, but Anton grins down at me, and all I feel is free. And happy.

"Thanks for the dance." I'm a little breathless. High on Garth Brooks, peanuts, and the man in front of me.

I could get addicted to this.

"You got it, Sammy Rose."

Del and the rest of Anton's buddies barrel into us at that moment, but Anton holds my gaze, shooting me a wink.

I'm going to go ahead and choose not to overthink the fact that he's calling me Sammy after the Samantha in the song...the one Garth sings about wanting to spend every last dime calling until he can see her again.

"Come on, man. We gotta bounce. Strength and conditioning in the a.m." Del massages Anton's shoulders.

My stomach sinks at the thought of him leaving. But I check myself. I accomplished what I set out to accomplish tonight. I made contact. Heck, I made more than contact. I've got myself a new nickname. It's probably best to pace myself where this guy is concerned.

"Give me a sec." Anton waves Del and the guys off, promising to meet them in the parking lot.

He comes to a stop, standing right in front of me. We're chest to chest, and I have to look way up into his eyes. He's staring at me like I'm the only person in this bar.

"Maybe I'll see you around?" I don't have to work hard to sound hopeful.

Anton dips his chin, completely serious. "Can I call you?"

I nod, holding out my hand. He fishes his phone out of his back pocket and places it in my palm. I type in my name and number before handing it back to him.

He checks the screen, and a grin spreads over his face.

Was it bold of me to list my contact as Sammy Rose? Maybe. But I want him to remember me.

And not just for the job.

The realization is enough to make me feel a little panicky. But I ignore the tingly sensation in my limbs, focusing instead on the chiseled face of the man in front of me. "Goodnight, Anton Bates."

"Thanks for the dance, Sammy Rose." He leans forward and kisses my cheek. It's quick and chaste, and I should *not* be taking a mental snapshot of the moment, but...too late.

He walks out of the bar, and somehow, I know that this easy assignment just got way more complicated.

4
Biker Gang

Anton - Now

"Alright, gentlemen. Rest up. See you back here next week." Our offensive coordinator dismisses us, and I stand and stretch my arms over my head, trying to work out the stiffness in my neck.

"Gotta love a bye week." Del shoves his chair out and slaps me on the back.

I nod. My muscles are screaming at me from the practice we put in earlier today—and from the first half of the regular season. Our team, the Green Bay River Foxes, is playing well. Really well, actually. But it's late November. We're all a little dinged up. We had a regular week of practice, but now it's Friday, and our coaches have given us off through Tuesday.

Granted, I've got scouting reports I'll pore over and film of our next opponent queued up to watch during my downtime, but a bye week is still a luxury.

"Agreed. It's like the heavens have opened and...do you hear that? The angels are singing!" TJ Wilson, the River Foxes' star running back, folds his hand in prayer formation and makes a celestial *Ahhhhh* sound.

"You know, angels aren't the cute, cuddly little half-dressed cherub creatures we're used to seeing in art and Precious Moments figurines. They're actually terrifying and powerful and something far beyond what the human brain can process—" Lawrence Poe, our resident brainiac and tight end cuts himself off. "You guys don't really care, do you?"

"Bates!"

I turn at the sound of Coach's voice.

"Yes, sir?"

"They need you to stop by Scott's office after the Biker Brigade."

I arch my brows. "What's up?"

"No clue." He shrugs. "Just passing along the message from the GM."

I nod. "Sounds good."

Scott, our team's general manager, is a no-nonsense guy, but we get along well. It's not unusual for me to be called into extra meetings. As the team's quarterback, I'm often shown off as the face of the organization. I don't mind it. I try to do everything I can to give back to the city and the team that's become my home and my family.

Years of training to be in the public eye haven't hurt my efforts either.

I catch up to Del, TJ, and Poe in time to hear TJ ask, "What are y'all up to this weekend?"

"I'm going to sit on my butt and watch other people play"—Del rubs his hands together—"while I eat chips and guac."

"Original," TJ mutters. "What about you, Poe?"

"I've been wanting to read the latest Nora Karl thriller since it came out last month. Going to binge it this weekend."

"Could you guys *be* any more boring?" TJ scoffs.

Poe sticks his nose up. "Well, what do you have planned, Teej?"

"I've got a date." He wiggles his eyebrows.

Del groans. "Tell me it's not with another jersey chaser."

"Hey, there is nothing wrong with a lady friend who appreciates my profession."

"There is when she's just using you," Poe says dryly. "You're better than that, man."

TJ frowns. "It's not my fault you guys prefer guacamole and books to a night out."

Del rolls his eyes. "Let's agree to disagree. What about you, Bates?"

"I've got that thing in California."

The "thing" being a charity gala that my mother demanded I attend. I didn't have the energy to try to talk my way out of it. Sadly, that's become a sort of pattern between her and me. She says jump, and even when I'd rather not, I do.

The guys start heckling me immediately. TJ is singing "California Gurls" by Katy Perry. Del breaks into the song by the same name by the Beach Boys.

Poe smirks. "You get to play prince for the weekend."

"Yeah. My favorite thing to do." I lace my voice with sarcasm. These guys get me. I love my teammates like brothers. They've become the type of close-knit family I always longed for but never had. They know I hate flaunting my royal title, which is really what my mother wants me to do out there. But they also know that, as the heir to the monarchy of a small island nation off the coast of Norway, I have certain hats I'm forced to wear.

I've been able to convince my mom, the queen, that I don't need additional security and special treatment in my day-to-day life—at least not any more than what other pro-football players have. But when I go to events like this, where my royalty is what's on display, I'm forced to have an entourage. I hate it.

Why didn't I say no?

Because I can't stand disappointing my mother. Because I feel like I'd come across as ungrateful for the silver-spoon life I've been allowed to live.

Because I do actually like giving back. Still, I'd rather stay close to home. I much prefer my job as Anton Bates, #4, starting quarterback for the Green Bay River Foxes over His Royal Highness Prince Anton Muriel Bates of Penwick.

"Don't forget about us little guys when you get out there with all those famous people, eh?" TJ mimes tugging at invisible sleeves of a dress shirt.

"Need a date? I'll come with you." Del slings his arm over my shoulder.

"And take you away from your chips and guac? Wouldn't dream of it."

Del covers his heart with his hand. "That's how I know you're a real one, Bates. Always looking out for my best interests."

"You know it." I grin at Del, thoughts of my mother and my royal responsibilities falling away. I got traded to the River Foxes three years back, and Del followed this year, which worked out great for me. It takes a lot to get a quarterback and a center on the same page. Our history together has worked to the team's advantage. The fact that he's one of my best friends off the field is a cherry on top.

We follow the winding hallway that leads us to an exterior wing of the stadium. Several of our other teammates are walking this direction too. It's a team tradition that on Fridays, we put on the Biker Brigade for our fans.

I don't know who came up with the idea or why it has stuck, but young fans bring in their bikes, and then we, the players, ride them in a sort of parade. The kids get to run out and meet the player who's on his or her bike. We sign autographs. Stand for pictures. All that jazz.

It's cute.

Some of us think so more than others.

"I still can't believe they make us do this," Del grumbles as we round the corner and see the line-up of bikes for the day. "Don't they realize I weigh two hundred and eighty-five pounds? I am not built for this madness."

"Buck up, Delly-boy. This is what we do!" TJ takes off in a sprint toward the end of the bike line. "Dibs on the blue mountain bike!"

The rest of us follow on his heels, racing to claim a ride. You never want to be the guy who gets the smallest bike. The smaller the bike, the more uncomfortable it is to ride it. And there's always the risk that you'll break a pedal or bend some metal.

I run toward a solid, sturdy-looking Huffy, but before I can put my hand on it, Caleb, one of our linebackers snags it. "Sorry, 4. Ya snooze, ya lose."

Blast it all. Rules are rules, and the first person to any given bike gets to ride it.

My teammates are like little mice, scattering to the bikes. If we can match this energy on the field for the rest of the season, we'll be undefeated. A quick look around reveals that every other two-wheeled contraption is spoken for except a small purple one with glittery streamers coming off the handlebars and a white woven basket hanging from the front, complete with a brown plush teddy bear resting inside.

I stride over to it, resigned to my fate. I press down on the handle bars, testing the wheels to see if they have enough air in them and if the whole thing will be able to support my weight. When I'm satisfied that it's not going to collapse under me, I swing my leg over and tentatively sit on the uncomfortable banana-shaped seat.

"Lookin' good, Bates!" Poe rings the bell on his orange-and-black mountain bike, walking it forward.

"I can make anything look good." I flick the handle bar streamers for good measure.

"Gentlemen, are we ready?" Ned Norbertson comes to stand in front of us. Ned is the team's VP of Marketing and Fan Engagement. He's sometimes referred to as "Nerdy Ned" behind his back, but honestly, I love the guy. He's smart, super creative, and able to keep a bunch of raucous, oversized football players in line and organized during our weekly Biker Brigade.

We all give varying degrees of affirmative responses, and Ned presses the button on the garage door. It springs open, revealing a long access road that's lined with screaming fans. They're behind barricades and snow piles that have mercifully been plowed out of the way, leaving the quarter mile road we'll pedal down mostly clear.

"Honestly, this is a safety hazard. We really do this all season?" Del rubs his hands over his arms, as if that'll help him ward off the morning chill. "It's freaking winter. There're ice patches up in here."

"That's part of the fun, Delly." Poe rings his bike bell again and takes off to the cheers of the fans.

"I'll show you fun," Del grumbles, pushing off and wobbling on his two-wheeler before straightening it out.

I'm next in line, and I'm mentally applauding myself for handling this lavender sparkly bike like a champion when a familiar face blinds me from the crowd.

No.

I blink.

There's no way.

But...way.

Rose Kasper. In the flesh. Her cheeks are rosy from the cold. Her brown hair still holds its trademark wave. It's cut to chin length. She's three rows back in the line-up of fans, but like magnets, our gazes lock and hold.

I haven't let myself think about Rose in years. She's a memory I leave alone. Anytime a daydream has tried to wedge its way into my thoughts, I've shut it down faster than you can say *heartbreak*. My success rate is fifty-fifty. Maybe sixty-forty, if I'm being completely transparent. What I'm saying is, I'm fighting a losing battle. Rose Kasper is a bruise to my heart that'll always be tender. Here, in the mid-day sunlight, I'm one hundred percent under her trance, and I can't look away...

That is, until I ram my purple, sparkly bike straight into the snow bank and topple off of it into a heap of cold, slushy, wet snow.

The crowd gasps, and my teammates immediately latch on to my faux pax with a chorus of ribbings.

"Man down. Man DOWN!" TJ pedals up from where he was in line behind me. He makes obnoxious siren sounds, as if he's a medic coming to my rescue.

"Ladies and gentlemen, our star QB." Poe rings that dang bell again, circling around and schmoozing the fans. "Much more coordinated on the field than off of it, thank goodness."

Everyone laughs as I get to my feet. I sweep my gaze to where I saw Rose, but she's gone. Did I imagine her?

I grab the teddy bear that went flying and make a theatrical bow as the little girl whose bike I was riding runs forward and picks up her wheels.

"Sorry about that," I tell her.

"It's okay, mister. But momma says I gots ta watch where I'm going. You should try that too."

My teammates burst out laughing, and I look down solemnly at this seven-year-old bearer of wisdom with a missing front tooth. I hand back her bear. "I'll keep that in mind."

"Good. Keep winning this season, mmkay?"

I chuckle. "We'll do our best."

We line up for pictures with the kids, and after signing some autographs and doling out high fives and fist bumps, Ned shepherds us back into the facility.

"Dude." Del shoves my shoulder after we get inside. "We don't need you getting hypothermia."

"What even was that?" Poe asks. "One minute, you're pedaling like a pro, and the next minute, bam! Snowbank. It's like you saw a ghost."

"I thought I did," I mumble.

I think the guys are too anxious about getting out of there to pay much attention to my admission—all except Del.

He falls into step with me, and we get on the elevator together. "You okay?" he asks.

I give my head a slight shake. "Rose Kasper was out there."

"For real?" Del's eyes bulge. "Why?"

"No idea."

"You still hung up on her?" he asks after a beat.

"No. I—" I stop mid-sentence. I what? Am I going to lie to myself and to Del and say that I don't still harbor feelings for Rose? No. But I'm also not going to dredge up the hurt and betrayal I associate with her. "I don't know," I admit. "Seeing her was...unexpected."

Del has a contemplative expression on his bearded face. "You two were great together once upon a time. Maybe there's hope for you yet."

Two thoughts hit me in tandem in response to Del's statement: *I wish* and *Absolutely not*. Call it self-preservation, but I'm leaning toward the latter. Shame on her if she fooled me once. But shame on me if she fools me twice, right?

The elevator dings, and the doors slide open, saving me from having to respond.

"This is me." Del steps off and heads toward the locker room. "Don't have too much fun in Cali without me."

"You know I won't. See you next week, man."

He waves over his shoulder, and the elevator doors close. I ride up to the level of the executive suites. I walk into Scott's office on autopilot. My head is spinning with thoughts of Rose—Sammy Rose, as I used to call her. Knowing she's orbiting in the same space makes me sweat.

"Good, Bates. You made it."

I blink and focus on Scott's face. I nod at him before my gaze pings to Roger, the team's VP of communications, who's seated to Scott's left.

Ned shuffles in the door behind me. "Sorry I'm late. Got caught up with the bikes and a fan who's a taxidermist and wanted to show me some samples of her work. Said she could do up some legit river foxes for us to decorate the halls with."

Ned catches sight of my horrified expression.

"Don't worry," he says. "I let her down easy."

"That's why we hired you, Ned," Scott chuckles and waves us forward. "Gentlemen, take a seat."

I step farther into the office, and Ned follows.

"Dude, you okay? You really ate it out there." He looks me up and down as if assessing for injuries.

I hold my arms out wide. "Not even a scratch. You want me to get the door?" I ask Scott.

He shakes his head. "We're waiting on one more, but we can get started."

I settle into my seat and prepare to get my marching orders. It's as I expected. Scott and Roger outline the plan for me to be the subject of an in-depth personal-interest piece for *Sports Magazine*.

"It's been approved by your people," Scott says.

I hold back my frown. He always says 'your people' in reference to my mother and the palace in Penwick. I don't have anything against my mom and her royal team, but I also don't really consider them my people. I've always had to act a certain way and put on a certain front where they're concerned. My real people are my teammates and the friends I've made here in the United States. With them, I can be myself.

Rose's smiling face pops back into my head. That's annoying, but I guess it makes sense. There was a time when I would have considered her my person. My top person. She knew me better than anyone. We had the best kind of partnership, built on laughter and trust and loyalty and kindness...until it all went up in smoke.

There's a brisk knock on the door jam.

"Good. You're here. Come on in." Scott waves the late arrival forward. "Babs has been getting the journalist that's been selected for this assignment the proper badges for stadium access and security clearance," Scott explains.

I turn to see Babette, the head of the team's HR department. Trailing her is Rose Kasper.

All the oxygen is sucked out of the room. I swear it is. Because I can't get a full breath in to save my life right now.

Rose's gaze sweeps around, and her blue eyes settle on me.

I can't look away.

"This is Rose Kasper." Babette's voice sounds like it's coming from the other side of a tunnel.

Sammy Rose. A fierce competitor with a heart of gold. Not intimidated by much of anything. Gorgeous. Clever. Smart.

Yeah, that's her.

"Dude, you sure you're good?" Ned knocks his fist against my shoulder, and the contact snaps me out of my trance.

"What? Yeah. Fine."

Rose is still looking at me, but she blinks and reaches out a hand to Scott.

"Happy to have you on board for this project, Ms. Kasper," he says.

"It's my pleasure." Rose's voice is low and as silky smooth as I remember. Where's the nearest snow bank? I may as well go ram my head into it. Again. My entire body feels like it's on fire…and not in a good way. How in the world am I ever going to handle this? And since when is Rose a journalist?

I guess a lot can change when you block a person out of your life for five years. Obviously she's made good use of her time if she's who the team is pulling in for this article. Writing for *Sports Magazine* is no small feat. And if she passed muster with the palace in Penwick, that's saying something.

"Bates, here, is a pro, so I'm sure he'll make your job as easy as possible. He's been fully briefed on the scope of the article and given specific instructions that he's to give you insight into all aspects of his life." Roger shoots me a raised-eyebrow look. He's waiting for me to confirm that I'm in agreement with all of this.

I mean, I *was* in agreement. But that was before I knew I'd be giving an all-access pass to Rose—the woman who had that once before and proceeded to take a hacksaw to it.

Rose looks as calm as can be. A classy professional. Like she's totally unaffected by being in the same room as me. Makes sense. She's the one who ended it between us. Why would she care if I'm her subject?

Meanwhile, I can't stop thinking about how gosh darn good she looks in the red pantsuit she's wearing. It screams *power*. She may as well be a Power Ranger, for crying out loud. All the power is on her side. In this moment, I don't stand a chance.

I shove my chair back and rise to my full height. "Yep, fully briefed. I need to run, so…" I say something about circling back and my people being in touch with her people, all without making eye contact with Rose. Truthfully, I sound like I'm talking in gibberish, and I keep making indeterminate noises that are like a mix between a horse's whinny and an automated answering machine.

Then I flee the room.

5
THE ELEVATOR SCENE

Rose

Anton abruptly leaves, and the rest of us sit in silence for a few seconds. Scott and Roger have matching bewildered looks on their faces. Ned is eyeing me with curiosity, and the guy seems about two pieces away from putting together the puzzle that is my history with Anton. He must be the perceptive one in the group. As for me, I'm trying not to take it personally that Anton was so intent on getting out of my presence that he tripped over a mini trash can on his way out the door.

Add that to the fact that he rammed his bike into a snow pile when I saw him outside, and it's obvious I have a terrible influence on the guy. He avoids three-hundred-pound linemen and angry linebackers for a living, and yet one glance from me, and he's a bumbling, stumbling oaf.

"Sorry about that, Ms. Kasper." Scott draws me from my thoughts. "He must be having a bad day. I'm sure he'll come around. Do you have any questions for us about the assignment? It seems like Babette got you taken care of."

I spend the next ten minutes chatting with the River Foxes' head honchos before leaving.

Scott asks me to close the door on my way out, so I swing it shut behind me and grab my cell phone from my pocket. I'm scrolling through emails as I wait for the elevator, trying not to dwell on how good Anton looks these days. I need to get over that—and quickly. I'm going to be spending a lot of time with him, and I can't have his appearance do funny things to my head.

Not just his physical appearance, either, though the mesmerizing eyes, broad shoulders, and amazing hair would be enough to slay me. Seriously, that curly lock that falls over his forehead nearly ends me every time I see it.

But it's more than his good looks.

Anton is and always has been so...so...*cool*. I don't know how to describe it, but it's like he has an intangible aura of confidence and swagger. Case in point: he made plowing into a snow bank on a bike and tripping over a trash can look sexy.

I've stayed up to date on his career, read the articles written about him, and watched his interviews. They all land on one point over and over again: Anton is a leader, and he makes everyone around him feel like they matter and they're cool too. By association to him, sure. But also because of who they are. I don't know how he does it. He's a prince and a professional athlete. He shouldn't come across as relatable. But he does. He is.

Everyone loves Anton Bates.

The elevator dings, and I step inside, nose in my phone, trying not to think about how I could have loved him forever.

Until a throat clears.

I whip my head up to see Anton standing along the side wall with his impressive arms crossed and his eyes narrowed at me. The open, welcoming expression that once drew me to this man like a moth to a flame is long gone. He is not happy to see me.

I immediately take a step backward, my fight-or-flight response kicking in at being in such close quarters. But I bonk my head into the door of the elevator, which has already slid shut. Unfortunately for me, I lack Anton's coolness. Instead of looking sexy or graceful, I stumble forward at the unforeseen contact, and Anton reaches out and grabs me around my upper arms, steadying me as the elevator begins to make its descent. His closeness—the feel of his strong grip on my biceps—triggers a total body reaction. It's like biting into an ice cream cone and having an instant brain freeze. It's painful and all-absorbing, and

I want to whimper against the unfairness of it all. Something that should be, could be, so good it hurts.

I glance up into his eyes and am immediately transfixed by the green ring around his irises that morphs into blue, like a tie-dye swirl. I smell the wintergreen gum he's chewing, and my brain short-circuits. I swallow and open my mouth to say...something. I don't know what, but he beats me to the punch.

"What are you doing here?"

His voice is a bulldozer, and the rumble of it nearly knocks me back again. Goosebumps break out over my entire body. Like I can feel them pop up on the tips of my ears, which is absolutely ridiculous. I allow myself one shaky breath, and then I let a mask of indifferent superiority fall into place. I may not be inherently cool like Anton, but I can pretend with the best of them.

Fake it 'til you make it, babe.

"Um, my job." I force myself to sound condescending. It's a defense mechanism. "I thought Scott made it pretty clear. Or were you too busy coming up with an exit strategy to listen?"

"I heard enough, and you know it. This"—he steps away from me and motions between us—"is not going to work."

"I don't know what you want me to say." I lift an uninterested shoulder, as if my body isn't having a full-blown, meltdown reaction to standing this close to him. "I was hired to write this article, and I intend to do what I'm being paid to do."

Anton shakes his head, and that delicious lock of hair falls over his forehead. I squeeze my fingers together, willing away the urge to reach up and brush it out of his eyes.

"I want you out of here," he growls. "I told you to stay away from me. It's the least you can do," he adds more softly, and the rasp in his voice feels like a gut punch.

I tell myself not to feel it. Not to acknowledge it. I'm here for his own good. He doesn't know that. He might think I'm out to cause him more pain, but it's the total opposite—even if being around him maims me too.

"Get on board with this, Anton. Don't make it harder than it has to be."

"Harder than it has to be?" He gapes at me. "It doesn't have to be anything. It *won't* be anything. I'll talk to Scott and Roger after I get back from California. I'll get out of the article. You may as well return your stadium lanyard and passes to Babs. This"—he waves his hand between us again—"is over. It's been over for years. Now get out of my life, and get out of here."

It's cute that he thinks he actually has a say in this. Also, he's going to California? I need to read Lennox and the team in on that.

I put my hands on my hips. "No."

He takes a step toward me and glares down. Our gazes lock in—blue collides with blue. The stuffy air in the elevator crackles. "What do you mean, no?"

"I mean, I need this job. I'm not going to let you boss me around. So, no. I'm not going anywhere. You can be juvenile about it, but I'm going to stick around. I'll be like a pesky little mosquito, buzzing in your ear, Bates. You can swat me away, try to squash me, but I'll keep coming back for more."

"Really? A mosquito?" Anton's gaze searches my face. "That's the analogy you're going with? An annoying, bloodsucking insect that everyone hates?"

I admit I didn't really think that one through, but I'm in too far to let him see me sweat—at least not visibly. Underneath my jacket is another story. It's like a waterfall is pouring down my back. I've got to get some better deodorant for all the time I'll be spending around Anton. My sweat glands cannot handle this man.

"The point stands." I keep my tone bored, like I'm completely unaffected and unbothered by this elevator confrontation, even though we're chest to chest and my lungs are heaving. Why is he standing so close to me? Doesn't he realize I can't function like this?

"Huh." Anton searches my eyes, and then his lips quirk.

I know what those lips taste like. I know how they feel. I want his mouth on mine.

No.

Not. For. Me.

"What?" I say on a breath, silently cursing my vocal cords for giving out on me and sounding all wheezy.

"Just wondering if you know that mosquitos only bite the people they're attracted to." He clicks his tongue. "They smell the type of blood they like and lap it all up. What, exactly, does that say about you?"

I narrow my eyes at him. I can't tell if he's telling me the truth about this weird fact or what. Either way, I'm not going to answer that question. Instead, I counter with one of my own. "Why do you know that?"

He slips his hands into the pockets of his River Foxes joggers and leans away from me, suddenly looking more like the unflappable and cool star quarterback he's known for being. Dang it.

"Wouldn't you like to know." He smirks.

The elevator door opens behind me, and I look back to see a group of people waiting to get on. I shuffle to the side and out the doors, grateful to put a little space between myself and Anton but somehow feeling colder in the process. The electric charge flowing between us was serving as a warming current, and now that it's gone, the waterfall on my back is turning to ice.

Anton greets everyone who enters the elevator by name, stopping to hold the doors open so people can get on. My senses fire, and my whole body goes from gooey pile of Anton-induced mush to work-mode Rose. I'm watching his interactions with these people using all the skills I've acquired over the years as a trained security specialist. Any one of them could be someone who is going to attempt to hurt him, and I won't let that happen.

The reminder that I have a job to do—a real one, not this bogus article—retrains my focus and gives me a much-needed reminder that I'm in this for the long haul. Anton does a few practiced handshake combinations with a couple guys, and then the doors close, and it's him and me again.

I tap aimlessly on my phone in an attempt to look like a legit reporter. "Want to tell me about the people here? You're obviously invested in the River Foxes organization."

The easy smile Anton wore for the folks getting on the elevator falls, and his face turns stony, completely closed off. I could cry. "Good try. But no. I'm not doing this. Go find someone else's blood to suck."

He spins on his heel and strides off, leaving me in the deserted hallway with my galloping heart and drenched back. But more than that, with a firm resolve to keep him safe...whether I tick him off in the process or not.

6
California Dreaming

Rose

I hop off the plane at LAX with neither a dream nor a cardigan. Nope. I've got a sketchy-at-best plan to get near Anton and a rolled-up formal dress in my carry-on bag. So far, my party in the USA is not nearly as glamorous as Miley makes it sound.

"I hate flying." Noli, my younger sister, puts her hands on the top of her head and closes her eyes. People are scurrying to their gates as we wait in the terminal for Collin, Noli's fake-turned-real husband—it's kind of a long story—to make it up the jetway with their bags.

"You guys didn't have to come," I remind her. Admittedly, I'm glad they did. This assignment is uncomfortable enough. It's nice to have allies...even if they have no idea what's going on with Anton.

"You kidding?" Noli scoffs. "We both have the weekend off, which *never* happens. And Poppy and Mack hook us up with tickets to a literal ball? I'm not going to look my Cinderella moment in the eye and say no thanks. Besides, Collin looks great in a tux."

"I do what I can." Collin winks at Noli as he joins us, tucking her into his side.

They're so cute together. Even me, with the shutdown heart, can't deny it.

The three of us set off for the exit, which takes us a solid forty-five minutes. Noli may hate flying, but I hate this airport. It's an overcrowded maze, and it's keeping me from getting closer to Anton and making sure he's safe.

When we're finally settled in the backseat of our rideshare and on the way to the hotel we've booked for the night—the same one Anton is staying at, and *no* I'm not letting myself think too hard about that—I go through what I know about the weekend's itinerary.

Anton is making an appearance at the pro-am charity golf outing this afternoon. He won't be playing, but he'll be there signing autographs and posing for photos.

Mack's brother, Holland, is a professional golfer. He's our 'in' to this event. Poppy and Mack got us tickets through him, at my request. I need to make nice with Holland because if I can stick with him, I can circulate with the celebrities in attendance, which should give me the access to Anton that I need.

I log in to Poppy's social media account—don't look at me like that...she shared her passwords—and tap on Holland's personal profile. A quick scan of photos verifies what Lennox and the team determined for me. Holland doesn't have a girlfriend, which'll make my job marginally easier. I'll take it.

We pull up to the hotel and pile out of the car. I sling my bag over my shoulder and scan my surroundings. My gaze connects with none other than Anton's—because, of course it does. He's being ushered toward a waiting shiny, black Escalade, which I'm sure will take him to the golf course. A bevvy of bodyguard-looking men in black stand around the SUV, and I take a moment to be grateful for the extra security Anton is forced into having at events like this. One of the guys—the one who's standing with the door open for Anton—says something to him, but Anton doesn't move. He's frozen at the sight of me.

Alright. I can do this. I slip my sunglasses on, as if they can somehow shield me from the hardened blue of his eyes. "You guys go ahead. I see someone I know."

I take off in Anton's direction before Noli and Collin can ask me any questions.

Anton waves off the security guard outside the waiting SUV when I stop in front of him. He looks undeniably handsome and official in tan slacks and a navy button-up with a Penwick crest pin affixed to the collar.

"Well, well, well, if it isn't my own personal mosquito."

I raise a hand and give a jaunty salute. "Reporting for duty."

"Cut the crap, Rose. What are you doing? I told you I wanted you gone when I got back from this trip, so what? You show up here? That's not how this is going to work."

"What can I say? I'm a *sucker* for your blood."

He shakes his head, lifting a hand and massaging the back of his neck. "Just no."

"You're the one who brought up the analogy," I argue, straightening my spine. "I had no intention. I'm a serious professional here."

He rolls his eyes. "Right. I'm leaving."

"For the golf outing. Sure."

He narrows his gaze.

"Yes, I know your itinerary." I tap my bag. "Part of my job. Don't worry. If you don't want to talk to me, I'll observe. Watch you with people. See how you interact with them and how they interact with you."

"Okay, creeper." He scowls at me. "Why are you doing this?"

A bead of sweat trickles down the back of my neck, and I could really use the five-degree air temps we left behind in Wisconsin right about now, because I'm all but melting under Anton's stare.

"It's what I was hired for." Not a complete lie. "Like I told you yesterday, you're kind of stuck with me."

"Whatever. *Observe* all you want. Just leave me alone."

I give him a cheerful wave as he climbs into the backseat. "See ya around!"

When I turn on my heel and head for the hotel, I find Noli standing outside the revolving doors.

"Since when do you know Anton Bates?" she asks, her tone a mix of awe and accusation.

I shrug her off. "I met him when I cheered in Mobile."

Noli keeps her gaze fixed on me, like she's trying to decipher a code that's written on the bridge of my nose. "Did you know him well?"

Yes, and he knew me well.

I keep my expression blasé and ignore the thought. I really wish I had told Noli and Poppy that Anton and I were together five years ago. I could have been honest about that, just not about *why* we were together. But I kept them in the dark because I got spooked by how much he meant to me. I knew when we inevitably broke up, the two of them would have been able to see right through my lies about why I ended things, and I couldn't have that.

I'm paying for withholding that information now, though.

"I mean, our circles overlapped from time to time, so I was around him a bit," I lie. "Why?"

Noli raises a shoulder. "It seemed like there was some history there." She pins me with a look that only a younger sister can give. It says, *I know there's something here you're not telling me, and I'm not letting you off the hook until you fill me in.*

"Did you get that impression because he looked annoyed to see me?" I chuckle, playing it off like no big deal. "Let's just say we didn't always get along."

More lies. We got along great until I broke up with him.

I blink against the memory of *that* horrible night and shrug like it's all no biggie. "I wasn't one of those women who would tell him what he wanted to hear because he was famous."

Half-truths R Us.

Noli shakes her head slowly. "That's not what I meant."

I cock my head, waiting for her to continue.

"Before you caught sight of him and went over there, I noticed him...watching you. He didn't look annoyed. He looked...I don't know."

I bite my lip, and when she doesn't say more, I prod, "What?"

"Like he was longing for you. Is that weird? I don't know. It felt like there was some sort of invisible string that was connecting his gaze to you...and like he didn't want to sever it. He seemed into you."

I toss my arm around Noli's shoulder and lead her into the hotel, dismissing her assessment of Anton's expression without another thought. She obviously got his intense dislike confused with desire.

I click my tongue. "Hate to break it to you, but Anton Bates wants nothing to do with me."

That ship has sailed off into the sunset. More like it's crashed into an iceberg.

"If you say so." Noli drops the subject when she spots Collin coming out of the coffee shop off the hotel's lobby.

"Maple-cinnamon latte for you." He holds out a drink for her. "Rose, I couldn't remember for sure, but I took a guess that you're a cold-brew type."

I greedily grab for the drink, mentally applauding my sister for picking such an upstanding man. One that absolutely nailed my coffee order. A red-eye from Green Bay to LAX was our best option for getting here, but I'm going to need all the caffeine I can get to survive this weekend.

Collin was able to get us checked in while Noli and I were outside, so we take the elevator to the fifth floor and go to our respective rooms.

I toss my bag on the bed and flip on the television, scrolling through the guide until I find coverage of the golf outing. On the screen, Holland is playing with a foursome of his buddies. They're relaxed, dressed in shorts instead of their usual long pants, and they're all smiles. I scan the crowd behind them, and all the attendees seem like they're having fun, enjoying the LA sun. The broadcast switches to a camera angle of a makeshift red carpet, and a familiar black Escalade comes into the frame.

My heart rate spikes with awareness. Anton will step out any second. My body is bracing for another sight of him. I went five years without this sort of exposure. Now it's like my systems are on Anton overload. They aren't handling it well, to be honest. They're all snapping and crackling with long-dormant electricity. It's a fire hazard.

The man in the passenger seat steps out and opens the back door to the SUV. Anton is the first to exit. He smiles and waves at the crowd lining the red carpet. Even through the TV, I can hear the uptick in screams and squeals. Anton's smile is practiced but kind. I know this isn't his favorite sort of event, but he does it for the greater good. I have no claim to him, but watching him work the crowd, I feel a surge of pride in my chest. He's a really good guy.

A guy you have no business swooning over, Rose!

I need to get my head in the game, Troy Bolton style. Anton's safety depends on it.

He turns to shake the hand of someone in branded, pro-am apparel. Must be a big-wig for the charity event. The camera stays trained on Anton, and I'm marveling at his calf muscles when a flash of yellow enters the frame and leaps on his back. It's a woman with long, wavy blonde hair. She's wearing a yellow halter top and white cut-off shorts. She fits in with the rest of the bystanders out enjoying a day on the links, but she's currently got her arms wrapped around Anton's neck, and the next thing I know, she yanks him to the ground.

No.

I dive for my bag and wrench out my phone, all while trying to keep an eye on the TV. The camera is still rolling, and there's a dog pile on top of Anton.

No. No. No.

Guilt rips through me as I speed-dial my dad. I should be there. I should somehow be able to save him from this. What am I good for if not for that?

"Lennox." My dad's no-nonsense tone snaps me out of my spiral.

"Something happened at the golf-outing. Anton went down."

There's a curse from the other end of the line.

I glance back at the TV, and they've gone to a commercial break. I swear under my breath.

"Where are you?" my dad asks.

"At the hotel. I saw it on TV."

"Hold on."

The next three minutes take three years off my life. I pace around my room like a bull in a cramped pen. I grab for my small purse, in case I need to head to the golf course—or God-forbid, the hospital. I have no idea if Anton was hurt in the skirmish. What if that woman injected him with something? What if he's dead? I catch a glimpse of my expression in the full-length closet mirror. My skin is practically translucent.

"It was a crazed fan." My dad's annoyance is clear through the phone line. "Apparently, she's a known issue. This is not the first time she's attempted to get close to him."

I flop onto the bed, breathing for the first time since I saw the ball of sunshine launch herself at Anton's back. All that stress over a crazed fan. Seriously?

"She's being escorted off the premises by security. Bates is fine."

"Good." I release a shaky breath. My heart rate is still accelerated, and I sit on the edge of the bed to collect myself. I'm more rattled than I should be. "That's good."

"Get yourself in a better position to look out for him, Rose. You shouldn't be calling me for information on your principal. You should be there in person. That's what you've been hired to do. Penwick is counting on you. So am I."

As if my own guilt wasn't enough...

"I was planning to head to the golf course shortly, and—"

"I don't need excuses. I need action."

"I know."

"Do you? Because I solidified the plans for Europe."

The silence stretches between us. Is he saying what I think he's saying?

"You're finally ready to set up the satellite agency abroad?" I clarify.

Lennox hums in the affirmative. "You play your cards right, and you'll officially be my pick to get it off the ground."

"Understood." My response comes out sounding noncommittal and sterile. I'm excited, but I'm something else too. Something I don't want to examine while I'm on the phone with my father.

"Good." Lennox matches my tone. "Check in from the gala tonight."

The line goes dead.

I stare at my phone for a second before tossing it onto the bed.

A chance to go to Europe again. This is big news. I'm not surprised my dad is using it as leverage. Nor am I surprised he waited until now to sweeten the pot. He knows what he's doing. Travel has always been a big draw for me. A chance to get out and explore. It was the diversion I needed after everything went south with Anton five years ago. I told my sisters a job opportunity had come up for me to help in an English immersion school abroad, and they didn't ask questions. I've always been nomadic, bouncing from job to job, place to place. It's the nature of the work I do. My sisters think the vagabond lifestyle is my preference—that it's a part of who I am. But I truly have no clue if it is, or if I've just been doing it for long enough that I don't know any different. What do I really like? Who knows?

What I do know is that, right now, I can't help but think of The Downer with something that feels like fondness. There's a pinch in my chest at the thought of packing up my suitcase and leaving

Cashmere Cove—not just for a weekend in California, but for an indeterminate amount of time—to work overseas.

   What about Mood Reader?

   What about my sisters?

   What about Anton? We've just reconnected.

   The thought snaps me out of my spiral.

   Silly, silly Rose. I haven't reconnected with Anton. I've been assigned to protect him. Nothing more. Nothing less. Anton is not a factor here, except for the fact that I need to keep him safe. That's job number one. Everything else hinges on it.

   I dump my carry-on bag out onto the bed next to my phone. I've got shorts and a t-shirt to sleep in, a pair of joggers and a fresh shirt for the plane ride home tomorrow, and an evening gown.

   I shake out the fancy red dress and head to the closet for a hanger. The fabric cascades to the ground, and I pray the wrinkles somehow disappear before I have to put it on later tonight. I'm not usually self-conscious. There's no time or headspace for that in this line of work. But Anton's going to be there tonight. As many times as I tell myself he's nothing more or less than the job, I'd be lying if I said I don't remember what it feels like to have him look at me—and really see me.

7
RIZZ

Rose – Five Years Ago

"It's not a real date. It's not a real date. It's not a real date."

Maybe if I say it enough, I'll get it through my thick skull. I stare at my reflection in the mirror of the small apartment I'm renting near the Mobile Tigers' football stadium. I smooth down my asymmetrical chiffon dress. It hits me slightly above the knee. The sleeveless V-neck halter crisscrosses in the back. It was a beast to get into it myself.

My heart squeezes. I miss Poppy and Noli, and I wish they were here. When I packed my bags and told them I was moving to Mobile to try out for the cheer squad, they were so supportive. They always are. But gosh, I miss them. If we were all still living together in our decrepit apartment in Pensacola, they would be helping me get ready and joking around, making ridiculous comments about falling in love and behaving myself. They'd take my mind off my nerves.

But they aren't here. They don't know that I'm dating—*not* for real, though—Anton Bates. I hate keeping secrets from them. I push the thought of them and the web of lies I've woven out of my mind.

Anton is going to be here any minute. It's been one week since we met at the bar. One week of near constant text messages back and forth. We had lunch together in between his OTAs (organized team activities, in case you, like me, aren't up on your football acronyms) and my cheer practice on Wednesday, but this is our first official date.

"It's not a date." I say it out loud again.

This time with feeling.

A knock sounds. I give the mirror one last look and take a deep breath. I shouldn't be so tense, but someone needs to tell that to my entire nervous system, which is over-enthusiastically reporting for duty.

I swing the door open, and Anton is there.

He drinks me in, and I take a moment to revel in the attention. His appreciative sweep of me from head to toe and back up again makes me feel warm and cherished in the best possible way. It's not a greedy appraisal but a tender one. I love the way he looks at me.

"You look incredible." His soft voice scrapes ever so slightly, like he's a little undone by me. That, coupled with the flicker of heat in his eyes, has me thinking that maybe there's some want to go along with the tenderness. I'm not complaining.

"Thanks." My own voice is breathier than normal. I'm chalking that up to the nerves. I give my dress a swish for good measure. Nothing boosts a woman's confidence like a dress that's good for twirling, am I right? There's something about the feel of the fabric whooshing against your skin. Does something to your psyche. I step into the hallway and tug my door shut, pausing to lock it behind me. I turn back to him and do my own assessment. "You too."

He's in navy slacks and a crisp white button-up. The top two buttons are undone, and his sleeves are rolled to the elbows, revealing tanned, strong forearms and a swanky-looking watch.

"So, you're taking me back to high school tonight, huh?"

He helps me into the front seat of his car and tells me all about where we're headed on the ten-minute drive to Mobile East High School.

When we arrive, he tucks my hand around his elbow, ushering me toward the large glass doors on the front of the school. "I can't tell you how much I wanted a normal high school experience growing up."

"Right, and since you're a prince, that wasn't happening."

His cheeks blossom pink, and he gives me a wincing smile, like he still can't believe I didn't freak out when he told me about his royal background earlier this week. Of course I knew about his prince status before, so I had some time to let it sink in and get used to it in my own brain before I started "dating" him. But even if I hadn't, there's something about Anton that makes me want to make him feel like he's okay, just as he is. He doesn't have to be anything different for me. I'll take him for him.

I briefly wonder what Anton's life will look like this fall. He's earned the job as starting quarterback for the Tigers. He's not going to be able to fly under the radar, so the entirety of the NFL fan base is going to know he's a prince. I wish he'd have more security in place. For his safety. I straighten my shoulders. If I do my job well and keep ahead of any threats, then he'll stay safe. That's what I intend to do.

"My mother wouldn't allow me to go to the common school on the island, so I was homeschooled. Tutors, mostly. Great education. Not so great for my social life. And I felt guilty using the money of the people for my own personal ends. It's one of the things I despise about the setup of the royal line in Penwick. People pay taxes to support our lavish lifestyle. That doesn't sit well with me."

I digest his words, logging them into place as I round out the picture of the man walking next to me. Fun. Hard-working. Doesn't like handouts. I also get the sense that, for as open as he seems, he has a difficult time trusting people. He told me about his friends in Penwick. Most of them were hand-picked by his mom. He never knew who really liked him and who hung out with him because they were told they had to. He tried to be welcoming and unguarded, but he's been burned a time or two.

"Anyway," he goes on. "I got plugged in here at Mobile East when I signed with the Tigers. I started tutoring some of the kids who were struggling with reading."

Be still, my book-loving heart.

"I love it around here because no one cares where I'm from. They've barely heard of Penwick. Most of these kids didn't recognize me as a football player either. Not at first. To them, I was a vehicle for deciphering the Shakespeare they were reading. When someone found out I played for the Tigers, a couple of the kids asked me to help out in the weight room during the off season."

"I'm sure they love having you around." If I were a high schooler, I'd for sure be googly-eyed over him. Heck, I *am* googly-eyed over him.

He shrugs. "Somehow, the kids talked me into this tonight, so here we are, chaperoning prom."

We walk into the gym. It's decked out in maroon and gold streamers. There's a balloon arch and photo backdrop in the corner. It's a typical high school dance scene. I can pick out the "it" couples, grinding in the center of the dance floor. There's also the line of kids standing on one wall, shooting covert glances at the group on the opposite wall. It reeks of teenage pheromones in here.

I beam at him. "I saw your dance moves on Friday. You planning to show these kids up?"

"I think you're misremembering my moves." He does a little shimmy.

I full out giggle. Who giggles these days? Me, apparently.

Anton grins, as if making me smile was his goal, before he surveys the gym. "I never had a prom, what with the whole homeschooled-prince thing." He glances back at me. "What about you?"

I wince but try to hide it.

Anton catches my expression, though. "Looks like there's a story there."

Before I can answer, a squeal comes from across the gym. "Mr. Bates!"

We're swarmed by a posse of teenage girls. I step off to the side as they vie for Anton's attention. They're all talking at once. Anton has a kind word for each of them, complimenting their hair and their dresses, asking about how their AP test prep is going. He seems to really care. It makes my knees feel a little like applesauce.

A group of boys saunters over, trying to look chill, but judging from their fast talking and the way they're all bouncing on the balls of their feet, they're as excited to see Anton as the girls are. He gives them the same sort of interest, answers all their questions, and takes their ribbing in stride. Even as he talks to them, he keeps flicking his gaze to me.

One of the kids bobs his head in my direction. "Yo, man. Who's your lady friend?"

The whole group of teenagers spins as one and stares at me. I hold up my hand and wave awkwardly. Anton steps to my side, rescuing me from their scrutiny.

"This is Sammy Rose," he says.

My heart thrashes. I glance up at him, but he doesn't return my eye contact.

There's a smile in his voice when he pins the kids with a glare. "Or Ms. Kasper to you." He points at them, and then at his own eyes, and back at them.

"Hi, Ms. Kasper," they chorus.

"Hey, y'all. Thanks for having me." I smile.

The kids start whispering among themselves. There's some snickering. Some nudging. I hear someone say, "Bates got rizz. Who knew?"

Anton claps his hands. "Alright, this is your prom, my little minions. Get out there and bust a move."

They stare at him blankly.

"Get jiggy with it." He makes a disco-era step, sticking his pointer finger in the air and tucking it into his opposite hip.

The teens look at him like he's crazy. The guy who mentioned Anton's rizz leans over to his buddy and says, "I take it back."

Anton rolls his eyes, shooing them away. "Go. Dance. Have fun!"

They scatter, tittering as they go.

Anton turns to me. His cheeks are pink, but his eyes are bright.

I tip my chin, assessing him. "You really like hanging out with them, don't you?"

He puts his hand on my back again, escorting me to the table where there are more adults distributing water bottles and sports drinks.

"They keep me humble," he quips. "They're good kids."

I hum. "And you're a good man, Anton Bates."

"Thanks for coming along with me, Sammy Rose." He winks as he hands me a water bottle. Our fingers brush, and a jolt of electricity zips up my arm. I stare at him, and he smiles down at me. What does this man see in me? I'm a nobody to his somebody. And yet...he makes me feel like I belong here—with him. I should go with it, be grateful that he's making my job easier than expected. But the way he's making me feel is about more than this job. It's like someone is finally holding space for me. Outside of my sisters, I haven't had someone care like Anton seems to. I could get addicted to his attention real fast.

I end our standoff by clearing my throat and turning to assess the dance floor. A group of kids peers back at me, but they put their heads together when they see me looking.

"I was afraid of that." Anton's tone is light as he points at the group. "I knew it was a risk."

"What was?" At the mention of risk, my work-mode clicks back into place. Is one of these kids a hitman? Hitwoman?

"Bringing you here. You've got all the teenagers drooling over you. I'm going to have to fend them off."

I burst out laughing, swatting at his arm. "Shut up."

"I'm serious. That dress? Your arm muscles? Your *face*." He lets out a low whistle. "Those poor kids don't stand a chance."

It's official. The face in question is hotter than the surface of the sun. Anton noticed my arm muscles? I think I'm swooning. Fortunately, I can play off my toned muscles as a product of my cheer and dance background. No one needs to know that I stay physically fit so I can keep my clients safe if push comes to shove.

"You're one to talk." I nudge him and can't help but notice the wall of abs my elbow rams into.

"Pray tell." He grins. "Whatever do you mean?"

"You fishing for a compliment, Bates?"

"From you? Absolutely."

I'm suddenly tongue-tied, because I don't think I can stop at praising his arms and face. Is it weird that I'm sort of into his quads? Like, how can they possibly look as good as they do in his dress pants? I don't know, but I'm not questioning it. And more than that, watching him with the kids here? I feel it in the deepest chamber of my heart. The man is in his element among a bunch of hormone-raging, under-privileged teenagers. More than his prince status or the whole professional-quarterback gig, the fact that he's spending his Saturday night at a high school prom, with no fanfare and nothing in it for him, makes him the most attractive to me.

I don't know how to say any of this to him. I've known him for all of a week. I shouldn't be getting my feelings involved in something that's supposed to be fake…at least from my end.

He takes pity on me and my non-answer, holding out his hand. I grab it, and he spins me in a slow twirl under his arm.

"What was that for?" I ask when I'm facing him again.

"Yep. Just checking. I can confirm it's not only your face and your arms. You look good all around." He leans in, his gaze coming to rest on my lips, and my stomach bottoms out. "Don't even get me started on that smart mouth of yours."

I involuntarily lick my lips, and Anton's tie-dye eyes swirl deeper and darker. I gulp. "Okay, charmer," I whisper.

The deejay transitions to an upbeat song, and the whole room screams, snapping the tension that had pulled taut between us. I recognize the song as one that's popular on social media right now. There's a whole dance that goes with it.

Three kids come over and tug on Anton's arm. "Come on, Mr. Bates. You promised you'd let us teach you this one."

"Oh, I would pay money to see this." I smirk at him.

Anton puts up some fake resistance but doesn't stop the students from pulling him out on the dance floor.

He walks backward, looking smoother than silk. "You joining us?"

"Don't want to show you up, Bates." I shake my head and then shrug. "Besides, I can watch you better from here."

"I see how it is." He holds his arms out wide. "You like this view?"

More than I should.

I hold up my hands as if undecided. "That depends on your moves."

He's a good sport about it and gamely makes an effort to learn the dance, even as all the kids crack up at his lack of coordination. I'm woman enough to admit I'm enamored.

When the song ends, "I'll Be" by Edwin McCain comes on, and couples pair off. The crowd parts almost like this is a movie, and Anton is standing there, holding out his hand to me.

I walk forward. I feel the eyes of a bunch of teenagers on me, but I don't even care. Anton is smiling his perfect smile, and all I want is to feel his arms holding me. He sweeps me up into an impeccable waltz.

I'm so shocked that I stumble over my feet. "You said you couldn't dance!"

He chuckles, his grip tightening on my waist. "I may not be able to dance in bars or do weird social media dance moves, but my mother made sure I could dance at balls. This sort of footwork actually helps with football, so yeah, this I can do."

"I'm impressed."

"What? No one waltzed with you at your last prom?" He arches a brow. "You never finished telling me about that earlier, by the way."

"I thought you'd forget you'd asked," I murmur.

He doesn't respond, and when I glance up, he's staring intently down at me.

"I don't plan to forget much when it comes to you." He says it like a promise.

How does he do that? With one simple declaration, he has me feeling like I can fly and like I'm melting into a puddle.

"Not much to tell." I shake my head, trying to keep my growing feelings for Anton from overtaking my common sense. "I went to prom with a friend who was actually into a different friend, but she already had another date. He ended up ditching me for her mid-way through the dance anyway."

"Where is he now? I'll go talk to him."

I laugh lightly. "Not necessary. I didn't want to date him, so more power to him, I guess. But the whole night was sort of...not great. I was wearing a hand-me-down dress from my older sister, Poppy. Our grandma had passed away not long after my mom had died and my dad left us, so it was sort of a weird night."

"I'm sorry." Anton's voice is gravelly and earnest.

A weird tickle of emotion surges up and presses painfully against the back of my throat.

He squeezes my hand where he holds it out in a perfect frame. I squeeze back, letting him know I'm okay. I don't talk about my family a lot, but with Anton, I want to. I tell myself it's to build trust and be able to do my job well, but it's more than that. It's about how safe he makes me feel.

"Poppy, my big sister, tried to make the best of things for me. Both she and Noli, my younger sister, put on a good front, but

I couldn't help but think of what a waste it was that we were spending time and money on a silly dance when we literally didn't know how we'd keep a roof over our heads after paying off my grandma's remaining bills."

I blink against the memory. There have been some lean times when the three of us have had to band together to get through. And, here I am, working with the same father who abandoned us. I feel like a traitor. Then again, it's good work. And it's helped me support my sisters, even if they don't know it.

I give my head a small shake and glance up to find Anton staring down at me with a look of admiration in his blue eyes. Heat rushes into my cheeks.

"You amaze me, you know," he says softly.

I shrug off his praise. "I'm no one special."

"You are to me." He takes my hand and places it over his heart. I can feel it hammering through his shirt. He tucks both of his arms around my waist, and we sway back and forth as the music transitions to something upbeat. The teens start jumping and dancing around us. Anton bends closer to me so I can hear him. "For what it's worth, I will not be ditching you for another girl tonight."

I close my eyes, relishing the warmth of his breath against my cheek. I blink, and his face is so close to mine I could turn my head and kiss him. There's a small scar near the right corner of his mouth that I'm dying to feel under my lips.

"That's a relief." My words come out in a hoarse whisper. I'm attempting to be playful, but the wobble in my voice gives me away, so I tell him the truth. "Because I like you a lot more than I liked that guy in high school."

His gaze drops to my lips again. "I like you a lot more than I like anyone." He lists forward, and my eyelids flutter, but instead of feeling his mouth against mine, I feel his breath along the shell of my ear.

"I want nothing more than to kiss you right now, but it would cause a major scene. I don't want an audience of teenagers who'll be all too happy to interrupt me."

I suck in a breath, my heart a wild horse, thundering around the arid plains.

"When I kiss you—and yes, I said *when*, Sammy Rose. Not if. Because this is happening, right?" He pauses, waiting for my acquiescence.

I think I just fell in love with him a little bit. I nod, and his lips brush against my ear. My whole body trembles.

"Good," he whispers. "When I kiss you, I'd like to take my time with it. Sound like a plan?"

My heart hammers as I squeak out another truth. "The best plan I've heard in a while."

8
Heartbreak Ahead

Anton - Now

I tug at my neckline. My bowtie feels impossibly tight. This entire day has me off kilter. From seeing Rose outside the hotel this morning to being pounced on at the golf outing.

That was no big deal. Poor Paisley Gladwell. I've offered to pose for a photo with her, sign her River Foxes gear, whatever. But my lawyers and the powers-that-be tell me that's not a good idea. Apparently, with crazed fans like that, you give them an inch and they take a mile. I mostly feel sorry for her. I don't understand why someone would be obsessed with me. But what do I know? She's not the first woman to throw herself at me—literally. Too bad the one woman who I'd actually welcome that sort of behavior from turned me down five years ago.

My gaze sweeps across the ballroom and lands on Rose. The fundraiser gala is in full swing. After our dinner, which was several hundred dollars a plate, the tables were cleared and moved off to the side to create an ample-sized dance floor. There's a renowned deejay who's making sure everyone is loose and dancing.

I am neither of those things. I feel stuck and stiff. Like my whole body is merely going through the motions of this event. All I can focus on is Rose.

The dress she's wearing should be criminal. It's a deep shade of red, and it wraps around her curves like it was painted on. It's got long sleeves but a deep V neckline and an open back. Her short hair is swept off her face on one side with an oversized clip that's sparkling in the dimmed lights of the ballroom. She looks like a sweet candied apple, and even though I know she's poisonous, I can't help but crave her.

She's kept her distance from me since this morning, and logically speaking, I should appreciate that, but it's even more torturous to watch her from afar. My Rose Radar has been beeping incessantly in my head, like one of those winter storm warning bulletins that flash across the bottom of the TV to warn of impending dangerous conditions. Instead of blinding snow and ice, my brain has been cycling through a ticker of warnings regarding Rose: *Heartbreak ahead! Steer clear! Maintain adequate distance to avoid further hurt! Ignore her eyes. Ignore her smile. Don't think about her quick wit. Dwell on her at your own risk!*

Beep. Beep. Beeeeeep.

I wish there was a remote I could use to click off my brain—and my heart, for that matter.

I'm standing at the bar, nursing a non-alcoholic beer, when a couple joins me. She's got long brown hair that falls in curls down her back, and he's got broad shoulders and a square jawline. I nod at them, but I do a double-take when my gaze connects with the woman's. I'd recognize the Kasper eyes anywhere.

"Anton Bates, right?"

I set my drink down and hold out my hand. "That's me."

She shakes my outstretched palm. "I'm Noli. And this is my husband, Collin."

"Nice to meet you, man. We're big River Foxes fans." Collin shakes my hand and tucks his arm around Noli's waist.

"Appreciate that. Where are y'all from?" I mask my snooping with a smooth question, but I'm dying to know why they're here too. Are they tagging along with Rose on her assignment, or what's the deal? What, if anything, do they know about me?

"Cashmere Cove. Not far from Green Bay. You know my sister." Noli points across the room. "Rose."

I nod. Noli's expression is mostly neutral, if a little curious, which has me guessing that Rose didn't tell her much about me—or about us. "I do. From my time in Mobile."

"I'm surprised she never mentioned you."

I'm going to try not to take that personally. But it tracks with what Rose said when she ended things. *There's no future here.*

Why would she have told her sisters about me when all I was to her was a guy she used for a casual fling?

"Is she living in Cashmere Cove now too?" I keep my tone casual.

"We've been invaded by all the Kasper sisters," Collin answers with a chuckle.

"Don't act like you don't love having us around." Noli pokes him in the side.

"I would never." Collin kisses her temple.

I'm officially jealous of their comfort level with each other. I've always wanted someone to love me for me. Someone who I can trust enough to be myself and let my guard down around.

Out of the corner of my eye, I see Rose step into a dance with one of the pro-golfers who was part of the event earlier in the day. I involuntarily clench my fists at my sides as I catch a glimpse of her beaming up at him.

"Holland hasn't changed a bit, has he?" Collin is tracking my gaze.

"Who's that?" I glance at him.

Collin tips his chin in the direction of the dance floor. "Holland Bradley. He dated the third Kasper sister, Poppy."

"But then she ended up with his brother, Mack," Noli puts in. "It's a long story. But everyone is happy now, so that's all that matters."

"You think he likes Rose?" Collin asks. It's an innocent question, but I can physically feel my blood pressure skyrocket.

Noli swivels her gaze, pinpointing the pair on the dance floor. "They look good together."

She's right, and I hate it. I don't know Holland Bradley at all, but I hate him too. Even after all these years, the thought of Rose Kasper coupling up with anyone who is not me feels like a needle to my eardrum.

"No wonder she wanted to be here so badly." Noli hums.

"Rose is here because of me," I blurt out, surprising myself with the force of my declaration.

Noli and Collin stare at me with identical slack-jawed expressions on their faces.

"You?" Noli frowns. "Why?"

"She was hired to write an article on me. An in-depth personal interest piece."

Collin arches his brows while Noli glances toward her sister.

"She didn't mention that. Interesting. Very interesting," she mutters. She studies me thoughtfully. "She said you hate her guts."

I punch out a laugh, appreciating the way Noli is a straight-shooter. She and Rose have that in common.

"She's not wrong about that." I push my empty drink farther back on the bar. "If you'll excuse me, I'm going to go talk to her—about the article."

I stalk toward the dance floor without waiting for their response.

Before I'm out of earshot, Noli says, "Something's going on between those two."

I can't tell if she's talking about Rose and me or Rose and Holland, but I don't want to waste time figuring it out.

9
Torture

Rose

I have a smile permanently plastered on my face, and I say a silent prayer it looks genuine enough to make everyone think my feet aren't screaming at me in my heels. That, and that it hides the torture I'm enduring. I'm in the same room as Anton, and he's wearing a tux. All six feet, four inches of him are highlighted by the perfect fit and crisp lines of the fabric. Women have lost their minds over far less.

All night I've been able to feel him shooting daggers at my back, and I've had to pretend like I'm completely unaffected. Like his heavy gaze hasn't made my systems go all wonky. My breathing is erratic. My skin is clammy. I'm a mess.

Torture, I tell you.

"Remind me again why you wanted to come here tonight." Holland's smooth voice has me snapping my gaze to his.

His eyes are dancing in time with the music as he twirls me around the open floor.

"What do you mean?"

"You look like you'd rather be anywhere else."

Note to self: work on my fake smile.

He goes on. "When Mack reached out, he said Poppy told him you really, *really* needed a ticket to this thing. I'm trying to understand your angle here."

"If I tell you, I might have to kill you," I joke.

He laughs, and it's a genuine one—or at least I think it is. I've been around the guy for most of the night, at his elbow as he mixes and mingles with the *it* crowd. He's had people fawning all over him, and he's got the celebrity laugh down pat. It's a little louder and more forced than the one he just let loose, and that's what makes me feel like I got the real deal.

"Try me." He pins me with a gaze, and there's kindness there. I've got to say, as far as ex-boyfriends go, Poppy really hit the jackpot with Holland. She's obviously meant to be with Mack, but Holland is a decent guy. More intuitive and situationally aware than I gave him credit for too. I thought he'd be tied up enough in his own business that he wouldn't think twice about me. But now he's looking at me like he knows there's something I'm not telling him.

"I'm writing a feature piece on Anton Bates. For *Sports Magazine*. It's a big deal."

Holland's eyebrows arch as he spins me out and then pulls me closer again. "Why are you hanging around me when he's your target, then?"

I almost trip at his use of the word *target*, but I pull myself together like a boss. "There's the tiny little problem that he doesn't want me to write the article."

Holland furrows his brow. "Why not? Media and publicity like that…they come with the territory, and Bates has always seemed pretty chill and approachable—at least from what I know about him."

I blow out a breath. I have the sudden urge to tell Holland everything. He's a relatively neutral party, and the weight of all my secrets is so dang heavy. But if I tell Holland, word will most certainly get back to Poppy, and that would be a disaster. I can kiss Europe goodbye if Lennox finds out I've broken the nondisclosure clause of my contract. Still, I settle for a half truth.

"Anton and I have a history."

Holland blinks before a slow smile spreads across his handsome face. "Let me guess. You dated?"

Again with the perceptiveness. "How'd you know?"

He glances over my shoulder. "Because for the better part of this dance, the guy has been staring at me like he wants to knock out all my teeth and then break me in half. Something tells me he might not be over you."

I let loose a practiced laugh. "He's definitely over me."

Holland gives me a pitying look. "Keep telling yourself that. But head's up. He's coming this way."

10

AUDIBLE

Anton

Holland spins Rose, and she catches sight of me. Her eyes widen, and I'm momentarily sucked into their dazzling blue depths.

"Can I cut in?" My voice is firmer and more growly than I intend. But whatever. I'm a man close to drowning, and if sounding angry is my life raft, so be it.

"Sure." Holland is all easy smiles and dimples. I want to punch him in the mouth. "Thanks for the dance, Rosie." He bobs his chin at her, and she smiles back.

I flinch at their evident rapport, at his easy use of her nickname. There was a time when I had a nickname for her. It was my own—between the two of us.

Rose says goodbye to Holland, and as soon as he steps to the side, I grab her hand, spinning her out and pulling her back into me.

I'd be lying if I said I didn't enjoy the rosy color that rushes to her cheeks as I pull her in close. I've surprised her, thrown her off her game.

Good.

I won't let myself think about how amazing it feels to have her back in my arms. I won't let my brain flip through the memories of our first date, holding her close on the high school gym floor, sharing our first kiss later that night, after a dinner of brisket with white sauce, and conversation that lasted into the early morning hours.

We fall into a familiar step. My muscle memory is strong where Rose is concerned, but I can't let myself get pulled under her spell again. I know how it'll end.

We dance in silence, neither one of us making eye contact with the other. I lead her in a full circle around the room before she finally looks at me.

"Thought you told me to leave you alone." There's a challenge in her voice.

I don't rise to it, instead using the music to execute a perfect turn-out, guiding her away from my body and bringing her back. Close. Her breath hitches, but she recovers quicker than I'd like.

"I was doing my part. Observing. Watching from afar. Trying to get my finger on the pulse of Anton Bates's life. It's been riveting thus far."

She's baiting me. I refuse to give her the satisfaction of appearing affected, though I am absolutely dying to know what she thinks of my life. What she thinks of me after all these years.

"Don't you want to know what I've found out?"

I shift my jaw but don't respond.

"Oh, come on, Anton. You're the one who asked to dance with me, and now what? You're giving me the silent treatment."

"Do you talk as a rule while dancing?" The words come out unbidden.

Her response is immediate. She sucks in a breath and then narrows her gaze before a grin slashes across her face.

Dang it.

That smile has more force than the sun. It could power the entire Penwick solar grid.

I'm helpless against it.

I fight against the quirk of my own mouth.

"What did you say?"

"Nothing," I respond too quickly.

"Not nothing." Rose clicks her tongue. "Sounds to me like you're a modern-day Mr. Darcy. Might have to use that in the article."

"There isn't going to be an article," I snap. "That's what I came over here to tell you. Funny enough, I was chatting with your sister"—Rose's step falters—"and she had no idea you were here for work. What gives with that?"

If it wasn't for the acceleration of her breath, she'd appear nonplussed, but I can tell I rattled her. What I don't get is why she wouldn't tell her family about her writing gig.

"Why bore her with the details of my freelance work?" Rose says breezily.

"You saying I'm boring?"

Her gaze locks with mine. "I'd love to find out. Why don't we set up a time for me to interview you, and then I'll let you know."

My hand tightens against her waist. The silky red fabric of her dress feels like fire under my palm, and now that I've locked eyes with her, it's like we're connected by some sort of electrical current.

Her eyebrows arch in a renewed challenge. "Come on, Bates. It's one article. Nothing you haven't done before. Do it for the kids."

I flinch, and she notices. Her voice lowers and softens. "Think of how many of them look up to you and want to know you better. You've always had a heart for them."

She's right. She knows it. I know it. I still don't like it. I still don't want her to be the one to write the article. I'm trying to figure out how to say that to her in a way that'll make her listen, but she changes courses.

"You had a slight incident at the golf outing today. Does that sort of thing happen often?"

I grunt in response. I wish she hadn't seen that. I wish I could say it didn't happen often. "It was no big deal."

"Looked like a pretty big deal."

I laser in on her face. She's chewing on the inside of her cheek. She's holding my gaze, and I'm hit all at once with a new thought. Is it possible she's *concerned* about me? Worried for my safety?

That idea takes root in the center of my heart, and I feel a surge of hope press up against the surface of my chest. Does Rose Kasper *care* about me, after all this time? After she made perfectly clear when she broke my heart that she didn't? That she never would?

I'm not about to let my guard down. Not yet. But the seed has been planted, and I'd be lying if I said I didn't want to give Rose some more of my time, to see if I could make it grow.

Does that make me a sucker for punishment? Maybe. But I'm also a guy who's going to shoot his shot.

Or whatever the football equivalent of that metaphor is.

"I've had a couple encounters with that fan before." I choose my words carefully. "She's harmless."

Rose blinks and holds my gaze for an extra beat before glancing out over my shoulder again.

I let that angle of our conversation simmer, bringing us back to the point. "Most of my life is pretty boring, you know. I go to work with the team. Do the tasks my mother needs me to do for Penwick. If you're desperate for juicy material for your article, you're going to be sorely disappointed."

She whips her gaze back to mine. There's a skeptical crease between her brows. "You're saying there's going to be an article? You'll let me write it?"

I make a show of sighing. "Considering you flew all the way across the country to trail me to this thing, I'm guessing I'm not going to be able to get rid of you. You always were scrappy. I'll let you hang around—under a couple conditions."

"What kind of conditions?" she asks, skepticism coloring her tone.

A loose plan takes shape in my mind. I can see it unfolding like one of the plays on my cheat sheet. I'm going to execute it to perfection. "You have to agree to be a gamer."

"A gamer?"

"Yep, and get a real-deal immersive experience of my life."

"What does that even mean?" She looks wary.

Good. She should be.

I lean in. "Just that I need you to agree to get up close and personal with all things Anton Bates."

I'm feeling all too pleased with myself for thinking of this. If she's going to write an article on me, I'm not going to make it easy on her.

"Is that some sort of innuendo? Because that's unprofessional and unacceptable." Her tone is firm, but she won't meet my gaze, which makes me feel like I have the upper hand. I'll take it.

"I'm not going to date you again, if that's what you're angling for." She says it in such a direct way that I have to fight not to grimace. "Getting back together is off the table."

"That's not what I meant." I mentally cross my fingers. Because if there's even a possibility I can be with Rose again, I'm going to take it. The more I talk to her, the more I find myself watering that seed of hope in my chest. My head is telling me there's no way it'll work—two seconds ago, Rose literally told me getting back together is not happening. But my heart is reading her body language, the way she's leaning in to me, and the investment that I can see in her blue gaze when she holds my stare, and it's screaming, *So you're saying there's a chance.*

I shake my head. "Believe me, you made it very clear that I am not the type of man you see as a long-term partner."

Even with my renewed hope, my voice has an edge to it, one I can't seem to smooth out around her. She cut me deep when she broke up with me.

"Good." She sounds a little disappointed, but I might be reading into it. "As long as we're on the same page."

I arch my eyebrows. "Can it be the same page of one of your romance novels?"

She furrows her brow. "I mean it, Bates. Do not fall for me. And don't try to make me fall for you. We aren't meant to be."

The song comes to an end, and I spin her out before drawing her back in and dipping her.

I stare into her face. Even with five years of time apart, I still could draw the lines of her jaw and the slope of her neck from memory. I've pressed my thumbprint into the crescent-moon-shaped birth mark she has to the right of her eye more times than I can count. So many times that I'd like to think it has the stamp of the lines of my finger etched into it. My adrenaline pumps hard through my veins, and I pull her back upright with a little more force than she's expecting. Her hand lands against my chest as she catches her balance. I gaze at her fingers pressed against my pecs. She's looking at them too.

I half-consider that I should be self-conscious. There's no doubt in my mind she can feel the way my heart is racing, pounding out a rhythm like it's a member of the drum line. But there's nothing I can do about it.

"No falling in love. Got it." My voice is gravelly. I don't agree with her. There's a part of me that'll always believe the two of us are meant to be. But I'll say what she wants to hear…for now. "We have a deal, then?" I ask her.

She furrows her brow. "I don't really know the terms. I'm not too thrilled with this arrangement."

"Now you know how I feel." I smirk. She opens her mouth to respond, but I cut her off. "You'll have to go with the flow." I pin her with a challenging look of my own, holding her gaze as I bring her hand to my lips and place a kiss on her knuckles. "It'll be fun. Trust me."

11
A Roomy Backseat

Rose

My brain feels like it's a murky mixture of split pea soup. I'm jet lagged from the whirlwind trip to California. I put in a full morning of work at Mood Reader. Now I have to go "interview" Anton. How am I supposed to do that? I have no idea.

The trip to California turned out to be mostly pointless. It was nice to see Noli and Collin let loose and have a good time, I guess, but as far as Anton and his safety, nothing remarkable happened...crazed fan aside. If a crazed fan is the worst of his problems, then that's a pretty good day.

I touched base with my dad and the rest of the team late last night. Now my pea-soup mush brain is swimming with intel and the information we've compiled about the threat against Anton. Our sources are pointing to an insider behind the threats. We haven't been able to ascertain whether that means someone from the River Foxes or someone from Penwick. Queen Della is demanding that we stick to Anton like gum to a shoe.

There's a tiny timer that I can practically see up in the corner of my vision—like the ticker on old-school camcorder recordings. It's running a countdown, and there's an end date.

Because that's one thing our intelligence has confirmed: this attempt on Anton's life will happen before Christmas. That means I've got to be on my A-game for the next month. Head on a swivel. Heart under lock and key.

I suppose going to California was good for one thing. It got Anton to agree to letting me interview him, which is my ticket to accessing him while he's at work.

Then again, I'm not sure if I like the determined glint Anton got in his eye toward the end of our dance. Check that. I'm entirely sure I didn't like it. It was like something shifted for him. He went from hating my guts and despising my presence—who can forget the mosquito metaphor, for crying out loud—to holding me in his arms as if I was a rare bird he felt fortunate to stumble upon for only the second time in his illustrious bird-watching career.

Just go with the new analogy.

I tried to head him off, telling him I wouldn't date him again, but I don't know what good it did. Anton is ridiculously competitive when he sets his mind to something. I shiver thinking about him setting his mind on me.

We didn't make any definitive plans to connect back here in Green Bay before he kissed my hand and strode away from me on the dance floor.

And no, I am not thinking about that kiss. I refuse to acknowledge that the two knuckles he hit with his lips have been tingling on and off ever since. Like he seared them permanently, burning the skin right off the bone and leaving my pulse exposed to the air.

I flex my fingers to rid myself of the ridiculous thought. I fumble for my phone, pulling up the text message I received last night. He still had my number, which is another thing I'm choosing not to think about. But his message is the definition of cryptic.

Anton

> Meet me at the Bay at 1:00pm. Dock 117.

What the heck am I supposed to make of that?

I'm fifty percent annoyed by the lack of details he's given me about what to expect, and fifty percent scared he's sending me to some abandoned dock and plans to off me. Not really. Anton would never. Maybe I've been reading too many murder mysteries, though, because his message definitely has that vibe.

I follow the directions from my phone and pull up to Dock 117 at twelve-thirty. Fortunately, it's not deserted or abandoned. There's a whole slew of people milling about and a giant sign broadcasting the annual Polar Plunge, an event held to raise money for athletes with disabilities.

I step out of my car and flip up the fur-lined hood on my parka, zipping the collar all the way up. It's a balmy twenty degrees today, but I'm still thanking my lucky stars I'm not jumping into the frozen Bay of Green Bay. I wonder if Anton is. I wouldn't put it past him, to go all in—literally—rather than to show up at the event for name recognition and moral support.

I stride over to the check-in table, and a woman in giant earmuffs and a Polar Plunge t-sheet worn over her winter coat beams at me. Her sticker nametag reads Lisa.

"Hi there, sweetie. Thanks for coming out. Can I have the name?" Lisa pauses with her finger hovering over her tablet, waiting to check me in.

"Oh no. I'm not—"

"She's here with me, Ms. Lisa." Anton's voice blankets me from behind, and I'm at once ten degrees warmer. I whip my head around to find him striding over from where a group was congregating near the entrance walkway to the Bay.

He makes it to my side, and I offer him a tentative smile, grateful that he saved me from having to explain why I wasn't jumping. "That's right." I turn to Lisa. "Here to document the day. This is such a great event."

"Lisa has been in charge here for...how many years now, Lis?" Anton asks her.

"This is my tenth." Lisa beams back at him. "We're so thankful for all your support, Mr. Bates. Your Majesty."

Anton hits her with a frown, but it's as fake as margarine. "None of this *Your Majesty* business. I'm a plunger like everyone else."

"You're jumping in there?" I eye the Bay. There are chunks of ice floating around in the gray-blue water. I shiver.

"Sure am. You are too." He turns to Lisa. "This is Rose Kasper. She's the late addition I called you about."

What the what now?

I hold up my hands and reach one over to still Lisa's finger as it tap, tap, taps away on her tablet. "There's been a bit of a misunderstanding, Lisa. Can you give us a minute?"

I grab Anton's arm and yank him off to the side of the table. "You signed me up for the Polar Plunge?!"

Anton's voice doing funny things to me aside, my blood has already turned to ice standing out here for the past five minutes. I hate being cold. Absolutely, positively hate it. Anton knows that. Getting into the frozen bay will be the end of me. I won't recover for the rest of the winter. I'll become a permanent ice block.

"I knew you'd be game." Anton crosses his arms. "You said as much in California."

"I did not," I hiss.

"You said you'd roll with what I had to do. *This* is what I'm doing today. What better way to get the full picture of my life for your article than to be by my side as I take the plunge?"

"I can think of about a dozen other ways, starting with standing on the dock and watching you jump." I toss my hands in the air. "I can't do this."

"But you're going to, aren't you?" Anton's smiling at me. "Because the Rose I know doesn't back down from a challenge. The Rose I know wouldn't leave a good cause hanging. And the Rose I know wants to write this article, and I refuse to answer your questions unless I see you leap off the edge of the dock here today."

I huff out a breath, and the air is visible in front of me. Because it's frigging freezing out here. Colder than freezing.

"This is insane." I stomp my foot like a toddler. "Why didn't you tell me you had this planned?"

"Would you have come?"

"I—" I cut myself off because…fair point. But still. "I could have at least come prepared. I don't want to jump in in my jeans."

"Figured you might say that. Come with me."

Anton grabs my hand, and I'm so shocked by the feel of his giant, bear-paw palm engulfing mine that I let myself be led to a four-door truck that's parked over in a reserved parking area. He opens the rear door and points to a duffel bag on the floor.

"You can change in the backseat. Tinted windows and everything. It's pretty roomie in there, anyway," he continues with a flame of humor in his gaze. "Both of us could fit."

I narrow my eyes even as my heart rate jacks up several notches.

"Both of us will not be fitting anywhere, Bates. Especially not the backseat." I climb up into his truck, and as I slam the door behind me, I hear him chuckle.

Curse him and his coolness.

I kick off my shoes and start shimmying out of my jeans, because the sooner I get this over with, the better.

When the driver's side door opens, I yelp and dive-bomb toward the floor. "Anton!"

"I'm not looking. Take it easy."

I hear more than see him slide into the truck from where I'm currently hanging out on the floor behind the driver's seat.

"What are you doing?"

"I'm starting the truck so it warms up for you. We'll be cold enough in no time," he adds, and I hear his grin.

"Whose fault is that?" I grumble.

"No one's forcing you to write the article."

False.

"You can give it up anytime you can't hang with my schedule," he adds.

I chew on the inside of my cheek. I can't say no to a challenge, and he's throwing down a gauntlet here that my competitive nature is lapping right up.

"I won't be giving up."

"That's what I thought."

"Keep your eyes forward, Bates."

I pull on a pair of spandex board shorts. They're slightly big, but I roll the waist and they should work. There's a sports bra in the bag, and I refuse to think about Anton shopping for this for me. He probably sent an assistant or someone from the team to do his bidding. He's a busy man. There's no way he made time between getting home from California and showing up here to go shopping with me in mind. Right?

The mental picture of him in a clothing store, sifting through racks or bins or shelves and hunting down my size, running his hands over the material I'm now wearing on my body, is so startling I suck in an audible breath.

"You alright? Got enough room back there?" A motorized mechanism whirrs to life, and the driver's seat moves forward.

"I'm fine. You didn't have to buy me clothes," I say more quietly.

He doesn't respond right away.

I pull the sports bra over my head and slip on the long-sleeved, water-wicking shirt he's packed. It's got a mock neck and the periwinkle-and-orange River Foxes logo on it.

"Figured you needed some River Foxes gear anyway," he says as I pull on a pair of sweatpants and see that they, too, are stitched with the River Foxes emblem. "Since you'll be around the team and all. You need to look like a fan."

"Shouldn't I stay neutral, for my journalistic integrity?" I contort my body to pull on my fleece-lined boots. "Maybe I should pick up a couple of jerseys from some of your opponents. Make sure no one thinks I'm playing favorites."

Am I messing with him? You bet. The low growl that comes from the front seat tells me I struck a chord. Good.

What I don't say—what I won't admit—is that I own exactly one NFL jersey. Well, two. But they're both his. One from his days on the Mobile Tigers. And a River Foxes one with the number 4 on it. I keep them in my bottom drawer, buried underneath my sweatshirts.

I wedge myself up off the ground and struggle back into my parka, pulling up the hood around my face with a huff. Anton has gone very still in the front seat.

"There. I'm ready. Let's get this over with." When he doesn't respond, I tap his shoulder. "Hello?"

He clears his throat. "Right. Yeah. Let's go."

He hops out of the front seat, and I don't have any time to figure out what sort of cat got his tongue. Because there's a frozen bay waiting for me to jump into it.

12
Polar Plunge

Anton

The thought of Rose wearing a jersey that has anything but my name on the back makes my stomach clench to the point of physical pain.

She climbs out of the back of my truck with a scowl on her pretty face.

"You know, people always romanticize snow globes, talking about how they want to live inside one, but that's a bunch of crap. This is the worst." She peers at the sky as big, fat snowflakes drop down like pillow feathers, and she looks like she wants to shake her fist.

I hide my smile. Do I feel guilty for signing her up for the Polar Plunge without her consent? Slightly. I know she's permanently cold, so this is probably her worst nightmare. But like I told her in California, I'm going to make her work for this interview. More than that, I want to find out if the woman I once knew and loved is still in there, buried under the layer of flippant dismissal she tossed my way when she was breaking my heart outside a beachside bungalow.

So far, and given the determined sparkle in her eyes, all signs point toward yes, and the little hum of hope that's pulsing through my veins is turning into a full-blown song. She's the same Rose—as deadpan as ever and not afraid to share her opinion. Perhaps she has a little more edge to her, some grit that she's acquired, but as time passes, don't we all?

"You asked for a full picture of my life. This is it."

"Right." She rolls her eyes, but the cutting effect is diminished because her teeth are chattering. "Let's get this over with."

We drop our extra clothes and cell phones into the assigned cubbies and walk up to the dock to wait in line.

"Anton Bates!" a woman squeals from nearby. I pause and say a couple words to her before begging off to make it to my jump in time. I feel Rose's gaze on me during the entire interaction.

"You're a natural with the fans." She rubs her hands up and down her arms, shifting from one foot to the other.

I can't help it. My chest puffs up at her compliment.

"They're the reason I have my career. Giving them some of my time is the least I can do."

"Some may say you could do less," she says with a pointed look at the icy water.

I chuckle. "This is one of my favorite events."

"Do any of your teammates participate?" She scans the crowds. "Or anyone else from the organization?"

"Nah. We all have our own things. One of the guys works with a local center for autism. Another does a lot with the homeless shelter. It makes more sense to work in the areas we're passionate about rather than forcing people into commitments. Then they'd just be going through the motions."

Rose stares me down. She looks like she wants to say something.

I give her a second, and when she doesn't speak, I ask, "What's going on inside that brain of yours?"

"Nothing. It's frozen solid and incapable of forming a coherent thought."

"Wait until you go under the water." I laugh. "There's nothing like it. The first time I did it, I figured it wouldn't be so bad. I mean, I sit in ice baths every week. But the bay is a thousand percent colder. Plus, we're outside, and all your adrenaline is pumping. It's such a rush."

Rose's eyes are wide. "Not really selling this, Bates." She darts her gaze around, as if looking for a way out, but we're in the next line of plungers. A guy with a megaphone is calling out the names of the people in the line before us, and then he counts them down, and they leap off the end of the pier. The splash hits our legs.

Rose whimpers, and I grab for her hand.

She drops her gaze to where our skin is touching and then looks up at me. "What are you doing?"

"Making sure you don't run off on me." My voice sounds rougher than I intend. In the wind that kicks up, I can hear the faint echo of the word I left unspoken: *again*.

Rose squares her shoulders, that gritty flicker darkening the blue of her eyes. "I'm not going to bail on you."

The recognition of Rose's determination and competitive spirit stirs a long-dormant feeling of affection deep inside my chest. I tried to bury my feelings for her, but I never got rid of them. They've been lying in wait, ready to rise up like a phoenix. "That's my girl."

The words tumble out of my mouth without a thought, and Rose's eyes bulge.

"I mean…" I swallow. "Not my girl. You're not my girl. You made that very clear." *Goodnight*, I'm babbling. I do not babble. I set my jaw. "Anyway, I appreciate you doing this."

"Yeah, well." She blinks and glances away from me. "I'm signed up, aren't I? Thanks to you." She focuses on toeing off her boots.

I do the same, and we're standing barefoot on the dock. My heart is hammering as I fill my lungs with arctic air, trying to block out the memory of the past fifteen seconds when I made things weird.

"Next up, we have a very special plunger. The starting quarterback for youuur Green Bay River Foxes, number four, Anton Bates!" The announcer's voice as he reads the rest of the names in my line is drowned out by the cheers and screams for me. I frown.

Rose looks up at me. "What is it?"

"I don't like that other people didn't get to hear their names called because of me."

She presses her lips together. "Still as humble as ever, huh?"

I swear I hear a note of respect in her tone. I stare at her, wondering if this is a question for her article or if she's assessing me for her own personal benefit. I hope it's the latter. I'd like to chuck the entire concept of the article into the Bay and get to know Rose again on my own time, at my own pace. All personal. No business.

The megaphone man is telling us to step right up, and then he starts a countdown from ten.

"I'm not going to, like, seize up and not be able to make it out of the water, right? My muscles will still work?" Rose is breathless.

I squeeze her hand, which I'm still holding. "Hang onto me. I've got you."

A horn goes off, and my body moves instinctively. It's best to jump without thinking. Actually, that might be why I like this event. So much of my life is a carefully orchestrated dance—doing what I'm told, when I'm told to do it. Sometimes, it feels good to throw caution to the wind and live on my own terms—of my own volition. Jump in feet first.

My feet leave the dock, and Rose is by my side. We're in the air for all of two seconds before the water engulfs us. The cold makes my lungs constrict, but I kick hard and pop up through the surface.

I'm still gripping Rose's hand, and she surfaces a moment after I do.

The air is stolen from my lungs again when I see her grinning. Her water-streaked face glistens like a diamond, and I'm no longer cold. Rose's smile warms me from the inside out. It's like the first day of blue skies and sunshine after months and months of a dreary Wisconsin winter. I could bask in the glow of her forever. Freezing cold Bay of Green Bay water? Who cares? I've got Rose's happiness to keep me toasty warm.

A splash of frozen lake water pelts my face. I splutter, snapping out of my Rose-induced trance.

She splashes me again, and I turn, dodging the spray, which I swear feels like ice shards against my skin.

"What are you doing?" I ask over my shoulder.

"I c-c-can't believe you made me do this."

I turn to see her wide, glittering eyes and an open-mouthed smile on her lips—which are admittedly turning blue.

"Pretty sure you did that all on your own." I pull her toward the ladder and climb out of the bay behind her. My body is protesting my movements, attempting to shut down and conserve heat, but I force it to cooperate with me.

"You're right. I d-d-did, did-did-didn't I?" She spins around on the dock, beaming at me. Maybe it's the hypothermia setting in, but she looks genuinely happy. Like she's proud of herself. Like she might want to do it all over again. This is my favorite version of Rose. Bold. Determined. Full of life and energy.

The desire to press my lips against hers, to use the remnants of my body heat to warm her up, is so strong I almost give in. But I can't kiss her. Not yet. I need to make her fall in love with me. And then I'll kiss her.

Then I'll never stop kissing her.

13

Secret Tattoo

Rose

It's been three days since the Polar Plunge, and I finally feel like my body temperature has regulated. But now I'm freezing again because I had to hike across a mile's worth of parking lot asphalt to get to the players' entrance of the River Foxes stadium from the visitors' parking lot. I slide my badge in front of the employee entrance and let myself in.

I stop inside the doors and take a deep breath, psyching myself up to face Anton again. Something shifted between the two of us at the Polar Plunge. He was thoughtful and attentive, and the way he looked at me made me feel like I was the only person in the world. Clichéd? Yes. The truth? Also, yes.

But I can't let it go to my head. I can't let *him* go to my head.

After spending the beginning of the week observing practices and sitting at the back of team meetings but not having much direct contact with Anton, I got a text from him last night that said, Meet me in the weight room tomorrow at 3pm. Come ready to WORK.

I was hoping, since we seemed to be on better terms, that he would give up on the whole *be a gamer* shtick. But he seems intent on keeping me off balance. An invite to the weight room? Telling me to come ready to work? He's going to put me through one of his workouts—I'm sure of it.

So much for things getting easier. We used to lift together all the time, and Anton is a beast. I can hold my own, but it won't be pretty. It'll be sweaty.

My phone pings as I'm walking the halls, heading in what I hope is the direction of the River Foxes' team weight room.

Poppy
> Honey bears, I'm homeeeeeee!

Noli
> AH!
>
> Rosie, quick. Hide all the evidence of the rager you threw at The Downer! <beer pint emoji>

I snort.

Rose
> Consider it done. Too bad I haven't been able to patch that hole in the wall yet...

Poppy
> Ha ha. Hilarious. I know you missed me. What's new? What did I miss?

I tap out *Nothing*, but before I can press send, Noli has somehow written and sent back a novel about our trip to California, including details about my freelance writing gig and meeting Anton.

Poppy
> Serious FOMO over here.

Noli
> And something beyond work is going on with Rosie and Anton Bates...

I scoff, but the tips of my ears are burning.

Poppy
> Wait a dang minute. Rose! I told you not to fall madly in love while I was gone.

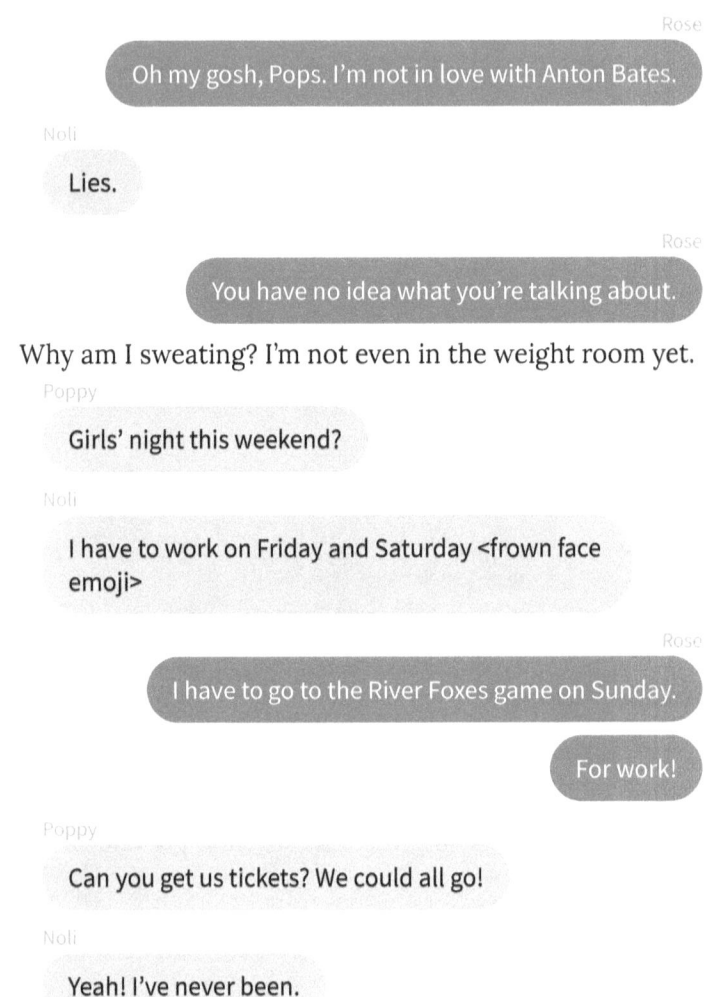

Why am I sweating? I'm not even in the weight room yet.

I consider my options here. If I say no, they'll be even more obnoxious and convinced I'm holding out on them about some torrid affair I'm having with Anton.

I immediately clear my head of *that* visual.

If I say yes, then they'll be around while I'm trying to do my undercover work, which is…not ideal. I don't like mixing my two worlds, and I've always kept my sisters firmly in my normal-life world. But in this case, it might be the lesser of two evils to appease them.

I blow out a breath, toggling over to a text message with the River Foxes' marketing manager, Ned. If anyone can get me extra tickets for Sunday, he's the guy. I make my request and slip my phone into my bag. I set off at a brisk pace down the hallway. I've given myself plenty of time, so even with that ridiculous sister text exchange thrown in, I'm almost a full forty-five minutes early.

By my calculations, the weight room should be straight ahead.

I pull open the door and walk directly into a group of over-sized dudes. They're all dressed in River Foxes gear—gray sweatpants and hoodies emblazoned with the purple-and-tangerine fox logo. They're laughing and talking, but they fall silent at the sight of me. I hold up my hand in an awkward wave, trying to cover my feelings of immense intimidation with a smile.

"Hey there, I'm—"

"Rosie Kasper?" Delany Durgen steps forward. He blinks at me and then smiles so wide his teeth are actually visible from beneath his bushy, overgrown beard.

"Del?" I squeak just before he scoops me up in a teddy bear hug.

"Anton said he saw you, but I thought he was joshin' me. What are you doing here, girlie?" he asks when he sets me down. "Cheerleading?"

"I hung up my cheerleading sneakers a while ago." I tuck a strand of hair behind my ear. I haven't exactly been sneaking around the facilities, but I also haven't been drawing attention to myself. I'm not surprised Del and the guys haven't noticed me. But I'm wondering why Anton hasn't told his teammates about the feature article. Has he not had the chance? Is he embarrassed about it? About me, as the author of it? I look up at Del and sidestep the question, buying myself some time. "I heard you were traded."

Del nods. "This is my first season here."

"The southern boy is still getting used to the weather." One of the other guys gives Del a playful shove. "Introduce us to your friend, Delany."

"She's more Bates's friend than mine." Del flicks his gaze over his shoulder and then back to me, question marks in his eyes. "Or she was."

I imagine the cogs in his mind turning over, trying to figure out what's going on. Del knew Anton and me when we were a couple in Mobile. I have no idea what Anton told him when we broke up. If he painted me in a bad light, which he had every right to do, then why is Del being so nice to me?

"He's actually who I'm here to see." I pin a smile on my face, deciding it's best to get out ahead of it. No need for Del to start asking questions. He might come across as a big oaf, but he's incredibly smart. I hold out my hand to the guy standing next to

Del, who I know is TJ Wilson, the River Foxes' running back. "Rose Kasper. I'm a journalist working on a feature piece on Anton."

I shake the hand of a couple other River Foxes and then turn back to Del. "I should get going so I don't keep his majesty waiting."

I use the formal title intentionally. Because I'm a professional journalist here. But the guys all snort and chuckle. I arch my eyebrows.

"When you've seen a guy in nothing but his skivvies, royal titles sort of go out the window," Poe, the team's star tight end, explains.

"That, and I can torch him at Mario Kart. Dude plays as Toad." TJ rolls his eyes. "Who does that? I'd never trust him to run a country. Yoshi forever."

They all laugh.

"You know," I say when they quiet, "since the piece I'm writing is supposed to be a full exposé, I'd love to get your take on Anton. Would you be willing to let me interview you? Maybe I could sit in on some less formal group hangouts."

Del turns to his teammates. "If Anton's cool with that, sure."

"I make for very good press." TJ winks at me.

"Good." I laugh. "Is Anton here?"

The wall of oversized men separates down the middle, and I get my first real look at the weight room. *Room* is not exactly the right word for the state-of-the-art facility that stretches before me. There are several rows of squat racks making neat lines through the room with large weight discs of every size stacked alongside each. Opposite the squat racks are the bench presses. There's a rack of dumbbell free weights as well as several rowing machines. Speakers are embedded in the walls above the giant, twelve-foot mirrors that ring the room, but there's no music playing right now. It's completely silent, except for the whir of one machine. Anton is running on a nearby treadmill.

He hasn't looked our way, which leads me to believe he's got headphones in. I relish the chance to observe him. His shirt is off and flung over the arm rail of the next machine over. He's not sprinting, but he's keeping a good pace. His strong legs churn as his arms pump in time. His back glistens with perspiration, which seems to highlight his muscles. I'm staring. I can't help it.

This is not the first time I'm seeing Anton shirtless. We used to swim together all the time in the Gulf. I could probably still sketch a pretty accurate picture of the contours and grooves of his upper body. What I can't tear my gaze away from is something new.

There, in the upper corner of his back, directly over his left shoulder blade, is a tattoo. I've never seen it before, and my heart begins to beat in time with Anton's stride. It's pounding so strongly I'm afraid it's going to dash right out of my chest.

Because his tattoo is in the shape of a rose. There's no mistaking it for any other kind of flower. Immediately I'm trying to come up with some reason for him to have my namesake flower tattooed onto his body. Because, *whoa baby*, it cannot be for me.

Maybe he's developed a strong love for Axl Rose and the Guns N' Roses' classic hit "Sweet Child O' Mine." Such a banger, right?

Or maybe he discovered a late-in-life passion for *Beauty and the Beast* and wanted a reminder of the enchanted rose.

Maybe he's into horse racing. Don't they drape the winning filly with a cascade of roses after, like, the Kentucky Derby or something?

TJ makes a finger-whistle that pierces the silence of the weight room and cuts through whatever noise-canceling earbuds Anton has in. He punches a couple buttons on the treadmill and glances over his shoulder as he slows to a jog. His eyes immediately land on me.

I'm standing in the center of a half circle of his teammates, and I don't know what to do with myself. Not after seeing the tattoo. I will not, under any circumstances, draw attention to it. I cannot think about it. I refuse to consider that it could be about me. If I do…well, I don't know what I'll do, but it won't be pretty. It could possibly entail me throwing myself at Anton's feet and begging him to love me and take me back. That cannot happen. He's a prince. I'm a nobody. More than that, I'm lying to him, and Anton deserves better than me.

I've broken into a total body sweat. My chest is tight. Is this what it feels like to have a heart attack?

"You're early." Anton grabs his shirt and yanks it over his head, striding toward us. He eyes his teammates. "Are y'all behaving?"

"We told her she could come to our next guys' night." Del grins at Anton. "For the article."

I nod. This is good. If the focus stays on the article, maybe Anton won't realize I've seen his tattoo.

14
I Work Out
Anton

"What do you usually do when you guys get together?" Rose wiggles her eyebrows at my teammates. She looks completely at ease with them.

Watching her with my friends is opening up a pit of longing in my core. For her. For us. For the way we could fit together. Does she feel it too?

"We keep things pretty low-key." Del shrugs. "We don't have a ton of free time during the season anyway."

"Makes sense." Rose nods.

"Now, don't sell us short. We know how to have fun." TJ crosses his arms.

"If by fun you mean talking us into getting tattoos." Poe rolls his eyes.

"Fun. Adventurous. Meaningful. I'm full of adjectives, big guy." TJ grins. "Don't tell me you aren't happy about that. I've seen you eyeing your ink in the mirror, flexing your bicep to make the poetry on the inside of your arm pop."

"It's a great poem." Poe peels his sleeve up, showing off his tattoo for Rose, who leans in to read it.

"'The only wisdom we can hope to acquire is the wisdom of humility. Humility is endless.'" She cocks her head to the side. "That's deep."

"It's from T.S. Eliot's *Four Quartets*." Poe drops his sleeve back down. "My words to live by."

"So you all got tattoos together?" Rose shifts and shoots me an unreadable glance.

I hold her gaze, even as my heart rate jacks up. The skin on my back feels otherworldly hot.

She saw it. *Of course* she saw it.

"Not me," Del says. "That was before my time."

"We'll do it again sometime." TJ flips his gaze to Rose. "I'm pretty tatted up already and wanted an excuse to get another one, so I made it a whole thing."

Rose isn't breaking eye contact, and I can't look away from her. The conversation the guys are having swirls around us, but it's muted somehow. All I can hear is the blood rushing in my ears.

Poe shakes his head at TJ. "I can't believe you got Anton to go along with that one."

"One of my prouder moments." TJ puffs up his chest. "Anton's tattoo is pretty cool."

I let out a strangled sound, finally tearing my gaze off of Rose.

TJ narrows his eyes at me. "What? It's—" He breaks off, his jaw coming slightly unhinged as he darts a glance at Rose. "Oh." He has the wherewithal to look sheepish. "Never mind."

Rose clears her throat. "We should get started here, right, Anton?"

"Right." I'm not sure how I'm going to work out, since my body feels like it's just run a marathon—and not on the treadmill.

The guys say goodbye to Rose and shoot wide eyes at me over her head.

As they walk out, I hear Poe ask Del, "What gives with her and Bates?"

"Not sure." Del shrugs. "But she's the reason he plowed his bike into that snow bank."

The door snaps shut behind him, and I've never heard silence as loud as the deafening quiet in the weight room.

I've got to say something. Acknowledge the tattoo. It's the screaming elephant in the room. She's making a good show of being super interested in the nearby squat racks, but a person can only stare so long at a metal weight contraption. There's not that much to it.

"So, about the tattoo…" I say.

Rose whips her head toward me, but she's not quite meeting my gaze.

"It's—"

"You told me you never wanted a tattoo," she interrupts me.

I punch out a breath. I remember that. We were lying out on the beach, and she was tracing her finger over the curves and slopes of my back. She started drawing shapes and pictures and having me guess what she was illustrating. We got on the subject of tattoos—if we had any, if we wanted any, where we'd get one. I told her I didn't know if I'd ever find something I wanted to be permanently tied to.

"I did," I say slowly.

She bites her lip. "What changed?"

I consider my answer. It doesn't exactly seem like the time or place to explain that she changed me. She changed everything. She came into my life, and for the first time in my entire existence, I believed I'd found a true partner, someone who had my back—who I could trust. I knew, without a doubt, that I wanted to be near her, somehow, someway. Forever. Even now, when I can't sleep, I close my eyes and imagine the gentle touch of her finger swirling a rose petal pattern against my skin.

So, when TJ took us to the tattoo parlor, it was a no-brainer for me. I wanted a rose.

"I don't know." I choose my next words carefully. "I guess there are certain things I want to hold onto. Certain things I want to hold close. Even after they're gone."

Her blue eyes glisten, and she nods quickly. "Right. Well, that makes sense. I always knew you had a soft spot for *Beauty and the Beast*, anyway."

I arch my eyebrows.

"The rose. It's a great tribute to the movie."

I stare at her. I want to laugh, but I'm afraid she'd punch me, and her fists are surprisingly strong, so I bite my lip. "The movie." I speak slowly, trying and failing to keep the sarcasm from my voice. "Yeah. Let's go with that."

She claps her hands. "So. Working out, right? That's why you brought me here?"

My mouth goes dry when she unzips her parka. She's wearing a navy-blue sports bra and high-waisted workout leggings. She toes off her winter boots and digs into her bag for her gym shoes.

My gaze goes immediately to her arms. She's got the most toned arms of anyone I've ever seen, and they are accentuated by the racerback top she's wearing. Did I intentionally invite Rose to work out with me so I could see her in her athletic gear? No. I'm not that shallow. But I'll admit it's a nice perk.

We used to work out together all the time. She'd go toe-to-toe with me in any of my crazy weight-lifting and endurance regimens. It was how we spent a lot of quality time in Mobile. I thought today, if I can get her back to a place of remembering how good we are together, maybe she'll give me—give us—another chance.

It's a long shot, but it's better than no shot at all. I've completed my fair share of Hail Marys over the years, so why not try with Rose?

My workout today will mostly be light weights and functional movements. We have a game on Sunday, so I'm not lifting anything crazy, but I need to stay loose and fluid.

I walk over to the squat racks I set up for myself and Rose earlier. I guessed on the weight based on what I remembered her lifting in the past. I motion her over.

She studies her rack before wordlessly swinging the cuff lock off the end of one side and adding a ten-pound disc.

I mimic her and do the same on the other side. Apparently, she's gone up in weight since we last worked out together.

"Don't underestimate me," she says coolly. She centers herself under the bar and flexes her hands.

"Wouldn't dream of it. I'm doing three sets of ten. You can do whatever is comfortable."

"Four sets of ten it is." She adjusts her grip. "Spot me."

She says it as a demand. My body reacts to her self-confidence. It's sexy as all get out, and it feels like someone picked me up and dunked me head-first into boiling water. I take a step back, giving her space to do her thing, but I stay close enough in case she needs a hand. Rose has enviable squatting form. Her butt nearly touches her calves as she goes through her set. I'm not trying to look at her butt, I swear. But it's difficult to miss. She's strong and graceful, and my own limbs feel a little like rubber, watching her completely own her workout.

I try my best to unstick my tongue from the roof of my mouth. "Feel free to ask your questions while we work."

She grunts and finishes her last rep of the set. She follows me over to my bar, and it's my turn. "I see what you're doing here...bringing me into your space. This den of masculinity."

"Den of what now?" I huff.

"You're trying to rattle me," she says from where she's standing behind me. "But I am un-rattle-able. Like a baby toy without the beads inside of it."

"With a spot-on analogy like that, you're really making your point there."

"Thank you. I thought so too," she says. "Now, tell me about how a prince from Penwick came to be a professional football player in the United States."

I power through my reps. "Don't you already know the answer to that?"

"Humor me."

"Fine. I've always loved football. American football. I came to play here for university. It's a tradition for Penwick royalty to study abroad—broaden our horizons, learn from the outside world, so to speak." I bucked tradition a bit when I *stayed* abroad, but no need to go into that. "I had a good college career, and I got some interest from NFL scouts. Since I don't have to assume full-time duties at the palace until I turn thirty, I took the opportunity to do what I love."

"What do the Penwickian people think of you being a pro football player?"

I rack the bar and spin around to face her. "You'd have to ask them."

"Sure, I'll just call all my contacts in Penwick right up," she says. We walk back to her bar, and she unracks her weight and starts in on her next set. At the top of one of her reps, she says, "Seriously, Anton, give me something to work with."

I keep my focus on her back. "The River Foxes have some fans across the pond, yes."

"What about your mother?" She finishes and faces me.

"You already know the answer to that too." I cross my arms and stare at her. "I'd rather you didn't ask me to humor you about this particular subject."

I go back to my bar and speed through my next set. She stands silently behind me for all ten reps, and I rerack the bar with a satisfying clatter. When I turn around, she's nibbling her lip.

"I didn't mean to—" She cuts herself off, as if she's not certain exactly what she didn't mean to do. "I'm trying to—"

"Do your job. I know." I run my hand through my hair, walking past her and waiting for her to set up. I don't speak again until her back is to me and she's four reps into her set. "How about this? It's a challenge to balance the two worlds that I straddle. But I give my all to the project that's in front of me, whether that's my home country or my team here. My mother...understands that."

Rose racks the weight and spins around. She, of all people, should know that my relationship with my mother is a complicated one—one I don't appreciate dredging up and discussing. Back when we dated, when I thought we were going to be together forever, I told her about how I feel like a puppet. How I can't say no to my mom, even when I want to, because duty has been so ingrained in me. Rose knows it all, and right now, I hate that I let her in—hate that I let her see me vulnerable. It feels unfair given how everything ended between us.

I turn toward my platform, but Rose catches my arm. I freeze at the soft yet firm contact of her skin against mine. I slowly raise my eyes to hers, waiting for her to pull away. Surely she feels the snap, crackle, and pop at the physical contact. It's a dangerous thing to feel so combustible. The thin line between love and hate and hurt and help blurs.

She holds firm to my bicep. "It's not personal, bringing up your mom." I glance away, but she presses on. "It's a logical question."

I flick my gaze back to her. "Doesn't mean I like it."

She nods. "That's fair."

She releases my arm and steps back. We each finish our squat reps in silence before I lead her over to the exercise balls. I start in on my rollouts, and she does some sort of ab workout. We go through our motions in silence.

I'm lost in thought about my mom. She's never been warm and fuzzy toward me. I respect her, and I wish she would extend me the same courtesy. She's always treated me as if I'm a pawn in the game of her life. There have been several moments where I should have been bolder. More confrontational. Stood up to her and made my voice and my desires heard. Maybe if I had, I wouldn't be floundering now to share with her what I really want for my future. I haven't breathed a word about it to anyone. I don't know if I can.

Instead of thinking about my mother or the massive decision I need to make, I latch onto something much more pleasant, and that is the way Rose looks with a focused, even expression on her face as she contorts her body into a sequence of bicycle kicks and crunches. I've always admired her fluidity of motion. It's the dancer in her. But there's something deeper than that too. Her bearing and the grace with which she carries herself—in everything—is just purely her. It's who she is.

She catches me staring.

I blink, my face immediately flooding with the heat of embarrassment. It really sucks to have feelings for a person and not have them reciprocated. Can we get that out in the open? "Sorry," I mutter, averting my gaze.

"It's fine." She shrugs. In my periphery, I see her move to stand. She crosses her arms and waits on me.

I close my eyes, focusing on my form as I finish out my own reps. When I'm done, Rose is staring at me intently.

I grab for my water bottle. "What's the hard look for?"

"Nothing." Rose shakes her head slightly. "I just… I remember her. Your mom," she adds quietly.

15
THE FIRST MEETING

Anton – Five Years Ago

I stare down at my phone, where an ill-fated text message glares up at me.

Mother

> I'm at your house, if you can even call it that. Where are you?

I swallow and turn to the side on my beach towel. Rose's profile comes into view. She's got her eyes closed and her face turned up to the sun. The waves of the Gulf crash into the shore, creating a giant sound machine. We're on our own swatch of beach, and it feels like God made this day just for me. The water. The sunshine. The warm Gulf-front breeze kicking up Rose's choppy hair, tossing strands against her cheeks. The gentle rise and fall of her chest as she breathes easily.

Her.

It's been three months since I ran into her at the bar—well, since Del ran into her. But that's a technicality. It's been the best three months of my life. I read somewhere that, in relationships, you should know if you want to be with a person after three months. It's enough time to get the necessary information about your partner to make an informed decision about next steps. Plow ahead or break it off.

What do I know after three months with Rose?

Everything I need to know. She's smart and quick-witted. She works hard and is humble. She's always looking out for those around her.

The other week, I was waiting to surprise her after her cheer practice. She came out of the building with a woman around our age. The two talked for another ten minutes. The other woman was crying, and their conversation ended with a hug. When I asked Rose about it later, she said one of her teammates was struggling through dental school, and since she wasn't from the area, she was having a hard time finding enough people to serve as her patients. Apparently, they had to find their own patients who were willing to be their test subjects, for lack of a better word.

"She's afraid she's not going to have enough clinical hours to pass the class," Rose had told me. "I tried to rally some of the other girls on the team, but they aren't too excited about having a novice tinkering with their mouths." She'd scoffed, and I could tell she hated the vanity on display. "I'm going in for a cleaning. Know anyone who needs a root canal?"

She proceeded to recruit half my teammates, several of her neighbors, and a couple of random people off the street. We had her friend's schedule filled in less than three days. She didn't have to do that. She could have stayed in her own little world, her own little bubble. But she saw something she could help with, and she helped.

I love her for that.

I love *her*. I haven't told her yet. But I do. And I can't wait to see what happens next.

I glance back at my phone, which is burning up in my hand. I think it's because of the scorching Alabama sunshine, but it also could be from the sudden pressure cooker I'm about to ask Rose to step into.

I glance back in her direction, and she's swiveled her head so she's staring at me.

"What's going on?" She tents her eyes with her hand, shading her face. "You look like you sat on a pinecone."

"Gee, thanks." I snort before turning serious again. "It's nothing major. Totally not a big deal at all. Nothing to be concerned about. Truly. I just have a slight favor. A bit of news."

Rose scooches up on her elbow so she's facing me fully. The muscles in her arms flex, and her abs are on full display in the two-piece, athletic-looking swimsuit she wears. I keep my focus on her face because as much as I want to pull her into my arms and kiss her senseless, letting the ocean waves drown out the reality of my life, I can't do that. She's waiting for me to continue, and she grabs the football we were throwing back and forth earlier and tosses it to me. "Tell me, Bates."

I catch the ball with one hand. "I don't want you to freak out."

She rolls her eyes. "All of this"—she motions her hands in a circle in my direction—"is making me freak out. Just say it."

"My mother is in town." I sigh. "She's at my house. Right now."

"Your mother." She blinks slowly. "As in the queen of Penwick?"

I nod and grimace.

"Is at your house?" She flicks her gaze over my shoulder. "As in the house that's right up the beach?"

"I wasn't expecting her. I had no clue she was going to be in the States, or I swear I would have prepped you more. I feel terrible springing her on you like this." I drag a hand through my hair, rising up to a seated position. "Are you okay meeting her?"

Rose sits and crosses her legs so she's facing me. "I mean, she's a queen, so I'm intimidated, not gonna lie. But you really want me to meet her?" she asks.

There's no hesitation in her voice. That's my girl. Never one to back down from a fight—or in this case, meeting my mother. But she sounds almost surprised that I would want to introduce her to my mom.

I hold out the football with an end pointed in her direction. When she wraps her hand around it to take it from me, I hang on. "I want you in every aspect of my life, Rose. If I haven't made that clear, I'm going to have to up my game."

Her eyes search mine, and I swear I can see her thoughts in the tidal waves of blue. Then they take on a flirty glint, and she cocks her head to the side. "You've got game?" She squeezes the football and tries to pull it away from me. "I didn't realize it."

I yank the ball in my direction and her with it. She topples into my lap.

"What's that now?" I wrap her up, pinning her to me with one arm. I toss the ball up in the air, catching it with my free hand.

"Show off."

I bend and speak right into her ear. "I'll show off my game for you anytime, any place. You name it."

She shivers and snuggles closer to me.

This here is everything I've ever wanted. I wish I could freeze time. I dip down and kiss her, trailing my lips up her neck until she shifts in my arms so she's looking at me. Strands of her hair whip in the wind and flutter over my jawline. "Do we need to go now?"

I sigh. "Yeah, we shouldn't keep her waiting."

We stand and roll up our towels, stuffing them in the beach bag we packed a couple hours before. I toss the football in on top of where Rose tucked the rom-com she was reading. We had fixed a picnic lunch, expecting to stay out all afternoon. I hoist the cooler up off the sand, and I swallow down a mouthful of annoyance at my mom's timing. I want to spend the day with Rose. I cherish the time we get together, and I'm trying to stockpile as many moments with her as I can before the season starts in the fall, and we both get busy.

But I haven't seen my mom in seven months. I need to put on a good face and play host.

I'm sweating as we start the hike back to my small, beachside bungalow—and not just from the sun. I might have played it cool with Rose, but the meeting of these two women—the most important women in my life—is not something I take lightly.

I glance to my right, and Rose is surveying me. She wiggles her shoulders. "Relax, Bates. I can be very charming."

I feel my own shoulders drop. If she's not making a huge deal out of this, then I sure as heck shouldn't be. I'm a little shocked by her lack of nerves, but I don't overthink it. I'm mostly grateful. If Rose can handle my royal status—and the ostentatiousness of my mother—then she's even more perfect for me than I thought.

"We should hurry, though, huh?" she says.

"I'm not really in a rush to share you." I reach out to wrap her in my arms again, but she side-steps out of my grasp.

"Good try. But I need to make a solid first impression. Race you up to the house." Rose takes off in a sprint, the beach umbrella she's carrying bouncing along at her side.

I'm weighed down by the cooler and beach bag, but I tear off after her. My legs churn through the sand as I gain on her. I feel the grain and dust getting stuck to my sweat-covered calves and my lower back, but I dig deep and pull even with her.

She's beaming as she races ahead, and I match her pace as we push all the way back to the steps that come down off the back deck of my tiny bungalow.

We're both gasping for air as we drop our gear. Rose places her hands behind her neck to catch her breath. "I win," she says between gulps of oxygen.

I shake my head at her, my own hands on my hips. "You had a head start."

She beams. "Gotta keep you on your toes."

I step toward her and scoop her into my arms.

She squeals as I lift her off the ground. "What are you doing?"

I flip her so I'm cradling her, with one arm around her back and the other under her knees. "You keep me on my toes, so I'm sweeping you off your feet."

She throws her head back and laughs. When she meets my gaze again, her eyes are dancing. "That was terrible."

I take the opportunity this position grants me to kiss the column of her neck again. She sucks in a breath, and I pull back, studying her eyes. The blue is like my own personal ocean.

Rose cups my cheek and leans forward in my arms. I kiss the birthmark on the edge of her eye, then the bridge of her nose, and then the dimple on the other side of her cheek before bringing my mouth to hers and kissing her slowly and deeply.

Until the screen door off the back of my house bangs open, and we spring apart.

There, standing in all her intimidating queenly glory, is my mother.

Rose sucks in a sharp breath and frantically taps the back of my shoulder where her hand is resting. I get the *put me down* message loud and clear.

I dip her toward the ground, and she slides out of my arms. I miss the closeness immediately, but I clear my throat and stand to my full height. I will make this a good first meeting between these two women, no matter what it takes.

"Mother. Welcome." I take three steps forward and meet her as she descends the stairs and comes to a stop right in front of me.

She leans in, and I give her an air kiss on each cheek. It's formal, and I cringe. After my dad passed, it was as if my mom shut off the part of her brain that controlled her affection.

I turn and beckon Rose forward.

"Mother, I'd like you to meet Rose, my girlfriend." The word *girlfriend* seems so insignificant for what Rose is to me. Confidant. Friend. Teammate. *Love of my life.* But I can't say any of those things. Not yet. I smile down at Rose before flicking my gaze to my mom, saying a silent prayer that she'll play nice.

My mother's left eye twitches slightly as she assesses us. I wouldn't think anything of it, except I've read countless articles in the Penwick media, and all the talking heads are convinced that's my mother's tell. Her eye twitches when she's holding back or when she has something on her mind that she's not saying.

Before I can dwell on what that might mean, Rose takes a step forward and thrusts out her hand. "It's a pleasure to meet you, Your Majesty."

My mom takes the proffered hand and gives it a lackluster squeeze.

Rose rolls her lips into her mouth in a moment of uncertainty before masking it with a smile. "I'm sorry we weren't around to greet you properly."

My mom waves her arm dismissively. "It's my own fault for popping in unannounced. Though, in my defense, even if I would have tried to contact this one"—she gestures to me—"to let him know I was coming to the States, the chances of him responding to me would be slim to none."

She's not wrong. I'm a busy guy, yeah. But I also tend to avoid my mom's communications like they're a contagious virus, and I'm trying not to get sick.

"I know the feeling. Anton will leave me on *read* sometimes too. I have to resort to calling him...like some sort of heathen." Rose chuckles and squeezes my side to let me know she's joking.

"That was *one* time," I argue, grateful to her for lightening the mood and getting me out of having to respond to my mom's critique.

Truthfully, I kind of like when she calls me. Texting is great and all, but I'll take any chance I can get to hear her voice.

"Anyway," Rose says, smiling up at me. "We're sort of a mess. We were out at the beach."

"I can see that." My mom looks down her nose at us, and I can imagine what she's thinking. *I let my royal son live abroad, and all sense of decorum flies out the window.*

She snaps her gaze from my sand-covered legs to my eyes. "Anton, why don't you get cleaned up first and let us ladies have a little chat. Then, while Rose is getting ready, we can get some plans together for a suitable dinner."

I open my mouth to respond, not wanting to subject Rose to any one-on-one time with my mom unless it's absolutely necessary, but I catch Rose's eye, and she gives me an encouraging nod.

"Okay," I agree. I place a quick kiss on Rose's temple and bound up the stairs and inside.

I manage to get myself together in less than ten minutes. I pause at the door to the porch, observing the two women for a moment before making my presence known.

Rose and my mom have moved to the set of chairs I have in the far corner of the fenced-in porch. They have their heads together and appear to be in deep conversation. My mother has her back to me, and she seems to be doing most of the talking. Rose is facing the door, so I can see her nodding. Her brow is furrowed like she's putting a lot of thought into whatever my mother is telling her.

Hopefully not anything that'll scare her off.

I push open the door, and my mom glances over her shoulder. "Ah, Anton. Good. You're back."

"How's it going?" I stand near Rose's shoulder, placing a hand on her upper back in a show of support.

"Good, good. Rose was telling me she's a cheerleader." My mom glances at Rose and then up at me again. "How positively charming."

I stiffen at the condescension that's laced in her compliment. If I can hear it, I'm sure Rose can. I feel her tense under my hand, and I want to come to her defense, but I don't know how to call my mom out for her arrogance without opening up a whole can of worms about Rose's status and mine. I don't really want to have that conversation now, so instead, I do the half-baked thing and say, "Did she tell you she's a writer, as well?"

"A woman of many talents, no doubt." My mom's eye twitches again.

Rose places her hand over mine and squeezes. "I'll give you two a chance to catch up."

She smiles at me, and it looks genuine. I exhale a small sigh of relief as she heads inside. Rose can handle herself. I don't doubt that. And she's strong enough to handle my mother.

I drop into the chair she vacated.

"Rose seems like a very nice girl." My mom crosses her leg and pins me with a calculating look.

"She is," I say cautiously. And then, because I'm all in here, I add, "I'm in love with her."

My mom's eyes bulge, and then that left one twitches again, ever so slightly. "Nonsense, Anton."

"I'm serious. She's it for me. I've never been surer of anything."

She presses her lips together, and I glance over her shoulder to make sure Rose isn't standing at the door. When I tell her how I feel, it will be romantic and direct—and not with my mother present.

"You're from completely different worlds. It'll never work." My mother flicks a piece of lint from her pantsuit. "Besides, you'll need to marry a woman from Penwick, preferably someone of our status."

I roll my eyes. "An arranged marriage? I won't be doing that."

My mom arches her eyebrows. "You'll do what's expected of you because of the crown you were born wearing, Anton. There are certain things that are non-negotiable."

I shake my head. "There's nothing in Penwick law that forbids me from being with an American."

If there was, that would be another item to add to my ever-growing list of reasons to abdicate. It's mostly a silly little game I play, or a dream I have. What my life could be like if I wasn't beholden to the crown. If I didn't have to go back to Penwick at age thirty and live the life I was born into. But it's merely a game. There's no way I could shirk my responsibilities.

My mom waves me off. "It's all but implied. And it's for the best. I mean, my word, Anton, you think a *cheerleader*, even one who writes," she adds with a scoff, "is going to be able to help you run our country? That's preposterous. You need a partner who is established in politics and understands the social norms of Penwick. Someone who can step into a room and demand respect. Like I said, Rose seems like a very nice girl, but she's not for you—at least not forever."

I gulp down the wave of nausea that's building up in my esophagus. As much as I know Rose is the woman for me and as much as I believe she's the exact type of person I want by my side, I have to concede one thing about my mom's point. We're from different worlds, Rose and I. I have no idea if she'd be willing to uproot her life and move to Penwick—to give up everything she's ever known, the familiarity and luxuries of American living, to come and live on a small island where half the population is grumpy about the royal family and the drain they believe us to be on the resources of the country. If I'm being completely honest, I sort of side with the people on this one. I want to make my own way.

All of this is a conversation I need to have with Rose, but it's not one I'm going to have with my mom at the table, looking down her nose at us.

My mom takes my lack of response as my acknowledgement of her rightness, and I don't have the backbone to correct her. "Glad we had this talk. You know, this really is a charming little spot. Not at all like Penwick."

Maybe that's why I like it so much.

I can't sit still anymore. Thirty minutes and I already need a break from my mother and the stifling weight of my future. I stand and take two paces across the porch. I hear a small, barely audible intake of breath and catch sight of Rose inside the door. She steps out onto the porch in a simple green sundress. She's put on gold hoop earrings and has her hair braided across the front like a headband. Our eyes lock, and she smiles at me, even as my heart sinks. How much of this conversation did she hear?

My mom stands, in all her royal grandeur, and beams. "Oh, good. Rose, darling, you're here. Now, let's eat. I'm starving."

16
IDENTITY CRISIS

Rose - Now

Anton and I are both subdued as we finish up our workouts. I had to ask about his family and Penwick. If I want to make this *Sports Magazine* article credible in any way, those are subjects I need to cover. But it's a delicate topic where Anton is concerned. My mind spins with memories of my one and only in-person meeting with his mother. When she got me one-on-one, she called me a tart. She told me she didn't think I could adequately do my job if I was, and I quote, "too busy snogging her son to keep an eye out for him."

Basically, she put me in an impossible position back then. I was hired—by her—to get close to Anton so I could ensure his safety, but then she told me I was getting too close to him.

I reminded her I was just doing my job and that I was good at my job, so she had nothing to worry about. But truthfully, she called me out on something I didn't want to admit to myself—Anton was more than a job. He was everything to me. I wasn't sure how to stop falling for him, so I doubled down on my intention to keep him safe. I told myself I could do that, and even do it better because I had actual feelings for him, but then I overheard what Queen Della said to Anton about how I would never be the type of woman who he could end up with.

There she went, being right about something else I didn't want to believe.

Anton and I were destined to fall apart. It was that meeting with the queen of Penwick that spelled out the beginning of the end for us. Sure, we stayed together for another three months—three months when I let myself be deliriously happy in his presence, when I soaked up his kindness and his kisses like a sponge.

I never let Anton know that I heard his mother call me a nobody. I wished he would have stood up for me, but it really didn't matter. Queen Della was right. I'm not who he needed—then or now—and I knew it wouldn't last. It couldn't.

The final thing the queen told me was, "I hope you're thinking as hard about how you're going to end this little dalliance as you are about keeping up appearances. Because when your work is done, I don't want my son to have any hope that this relationship can continue. It's up to you to convince him that you two aren't meant to be."

Convince him I did.

Little did the queen know—heck, little did I know—she'd need my services again.

Here we are.

Guilt at bringing up his mother—at *working* for his mother without Anton's consent, twice now—gnaws at me, shredding my carefully constructed outer shell like a cheese grater to a block of sharp cheddar. I keep the rest of my questions surface level. Anton's polite, if a little distant, in his responses. I can't help but wonder if his mind is on the past like mine is.

After we change out of our athletic gear and into street clothes, I manage to convince him to show me around the stadium under the guise of wanting to have a full picture of the place for my article. Truthfully, I'm scoping out security cameras and envisioning where a potential attacker could be lurking if he or she was going to make an attempt on Anton's life.

"That about covers it. Pretty much your basic NFL stadium." Anton stops and turns to me. "Now I need to go and get some rest."

"Yeah, sure." I adjust my grip on my purse, my pulse kicking up. I'm not his full-time security. He doesn't have that because he's refused it all these years. I get that. It's not my job to be with him 24-7, but I don't like the thought of leaving him alone with the looming threat. I pull up a mental picture of his high-end apartment complex. At least it's secure, with a manned desk and locked doors. I'm sure he'll be fine at home alone. Or maybe he's not going home alone. My pulse accelerates even further. Maybe he has a date.

I blink and find him staring at me. I immediately rearrange my facial features, attempting to mask my thoughts and the displeasure they're causing.

Without waiting for me, Anton turns and heads down the hallway. "I'll walk you to your car," he says over his shoulder.

"What? That's not necessary." I jog to catch up with him.

He spins around, and I collide with his chest. I suck in a breath as he sticks out a hand and catches me on the elbow, steadying me.

"Where are you parked?" he asks.

"Right outside."

"Right outside? As in the visitors' lot that's practically in the next county?" He rolls his eyes. "I'll walk you over there."

"I'm perfectly capable of getting to my car on my own." If he knew that I was professionally trained in defensive techniques and take-down maneuvers, this would be a non-issue.

"I know you are." He sighs, flicking his gaze to mine. "I'm trying to be a gentleman here, okay? Let me have this one thing."

I swallow down a retort and nod my head. He pushes the door open, and we walk into the cold winter air. The change in temperature from inside to outside momentarily snatches my breath. I fold my arms across my chest to conserve body heat and lean into the wind.

"Feels like Penwick here." Anton has his chin tucked into his coat. He glances over at me, and I remain silent. "Much more so than it did down in Mobile."

"Do you miss it?" I slide along a patch of ice, shuffling my feet to keep my balance.

"Mobile? Or Penwick?"

"Either. Both."

He tips his chin up. "I learned a ton playing for the Tigers, and I'm so grateful to them for taking a chance on me right out of college. But I feel like I've hit my stride here. My teammates are like family."

It's a good response. Honest yet very politically correct. I can tell he means it about his teammates too. Judging from my earlier interaction with them, the feelings go both ways.

"As for Penwick," Anton continues, "it's a beautiful country. I wish I could visit more, but..." He shrugs.

"It's still a lot of pressure when you're there, huh?" I say quietly.

He nods. "More so now, with my thirtieth birthday looming. Back home, there's a spotlight on my every movement. The press churns out stories about how I act, what I say and do, and all the pundits weigh in on what type of leader I'll be. Everything is picked apart and analyzed. I want to live and do my work, but it's paralyzing with that amount of pressure and publicity."

We walk on in silence, the only sound the crunch of leftover snow beneath our feet.

"You probably think that sounds like a sob story." Anton chuckles bitterly. "A poor, miserable royal, unhappy with his silver spoon and privilege."

"That's not what I think. You know that." I'm surprised by how fierce I sound. After a beat, I add, "I can keep that off the record."

He curses under his breath, reaching up and raking a hand through his hair. "I wasn't thinking about the article." His eyes hold a pleading gleam when I meet his gaze. "You really won't publish any of that?"

"Of course not. We're just a couple of old friends, catching up." My voice hitches on the word *friends*. I look away, grasping for a way to deflect. "Speaking of friends, you'll invite me to guys' night?"

"They won't let me get away with *not* inviting you."

We stop outside my car. "Alright, then. Let me know the details. I'm going to head home."

"To Cashmere Cove, right? Noli mentioned that's where you're living these days."

Darn him and his open-faced interest in me. He's not supposed to care. The fact that he does makes it harder for me not to want him.

"Yeah. It's a small town—"

"Up the bay. I know it." He nods thoughtfully. "It's wild you've been so close, and I had no idea."

"Yeah. Same here. I sort of stopped following the league after getting out of cheering." That's a bold-faced lie, and I chew the inside of my cheek to keep from saying anything incriminating. No one knows he's the reason I was so willing to follow Poppy to Wisconsin. It's pathetic of me, really, but somehow being in the same state as him eased the pain of our break up, which still ate at me, even years later.

He studies me, a whole slew of questions scampering across his unfairly handsome face. "You still writing?"

"No." I shake my head briskly. "I don't think I'll ever come up with something good enough to publish."

He frowns. "I don't believe that."

I shrug. "It is what it is."

"But you loved writing." He sounds almost accusatory, like he can't believe I had the audacity to quit.

I tap my bag. "I'm still writing, aren't I? That's what I'm doing here."

"It's not the same thing." He crosses his arms. "You told me writing makes you feel the most like yourself—writing fiction," he says, as if I don't know exactly what he's talking about.

It's my own fault he knows this about me. I opened up to him and shared the real, true parts of me all those years ago. I'm paying the price now. But if I'm being honest, deep down, it's nice to feel known—scary too.

"Yeah, well, life happens." It's a cop-out response, but I don't have a better one. I've dabbled with different story ideas over the years, but I can't seem to stick on one.

"What else have you been up to?" Anton looks like he's settling in for a heart-to-heart. How is he not freezing? It's going to take three large cups of cocoa to warm me up after this.

"If you insist on giving me the third degree, get in." I unlock my door and get behind the wheel, turning the car on and cranking the heat in one swift motion.

Anton jogs around to the passenger side and slides in. Slide isn't exactly accurate in this case. He folds himself in, but his knees go up to his chest in the cramped space.

"Uh..." He feels around on both sides of the chair for the lever to move the seat back.

"Sorry, it's right here." Without thinking, I reach toward the lever directly in front of him. My hand grazes the inside of his thigh.

Do not dwell on his muscular legs. Do. Not. Dwell.

I pull up on the lever, and he shifts back. The movement sends me careening into his lap, but I lunge back to my own side of the car as quickly as possible, like an unhinged jack-in-the-box. One of those creepy ones.

"Where are you parked?" I grab the steering wheel to give myself something to focus on that isn't the warmth of his body. "I'll drive you to your car."

"Head that way." He points me forward, and I feel his gaze on me and hear the smile in his voice. "You were about to tell me what else you've been up to."

"I'm the one who's supposed to do the interviewing."

"Humor me." He throws my own words back at me.

I make a face at him. "Nothing exciting. I worked abroad for a while, then lived down in Florida, and then followed my big sister up here. The three of us all live in Cashmere Cove now. I work at Mood Reader, the bookstore in town."

"That's fitting for you," he says. "Nice to be close to your family, I'm sure."

He directs me to a side lot. He has to hold out a badge to get the gate to go up so I can get in. That's good from a security standpoint, but it won't help him if it's someone within the River Foxes organization who has it out for him. But why would they? He's their star. Who would want him out of the picture?

I make a mental note to look into the backup quarterback. Maybe he's dying for more playing time or something? It's a weak motive, and I know it, but I need to cover all my bases.

"What about when you're not working? What's your favorite way to spend your time?"

I *have no clue.*

It's the sad reality of my life. I truly don't know what my own interests are these days. I do what my job tells me to do. I live in the deceitful bed I've made. I don't even know who I am. I have no passions of my own. It's a sobering reminder that I'm a shell of a person.

"I-I don't really know."

"What do you mean?"

"I mean I don't know," I snap, trying and failing to keep my voice level. I'm not angry at Anton. I'm angry at myself. Why couldn't I have come up with something? Said I liked yoga, or badminton, or making bread, or *anything.*

It's because something about his presence chips away at the bricks of my carefully constructed walls.

I blow out a breath. "Sorry."

He's watching me closely. "You don't know what you like to do these days? That's what you're saying?"

Tears prick at the backs of my eyes, but I blink them away like a champ. I will not break down about this. Not now. Not in front of Anton. If I can stay focused on my job, then I can keep this identity crisis at bay.

"I just…I don't know. I haven't done a lot in my free time lately, so I guess I don't know how to answer your question." *Understatement of the century.* "I'm mostly busy with the bookstore. And my freelance work." Another cop-out answer. Shocking.

"I see." Anton sounds like he has fifteen follow-up questions, but he doesn't press. I'm grateful for that. "There's my truck."

I pull in next to it.

"Thanks for the lift." He opens the door. "I'll text you about getting together with me and the guys."

"Great. Thanks." I attempt to slip back into professional mode. "I'll be around at practice tomorrow, the walk-through on Saturday, and your game too."

He bends down so he can see me. The wind whips his hair, tossing it into his eyes. "You're coming to the game this weekend?"

"Ned got me hooked up with a sideline pass and everything."

Anton looks almost stricken, and I can't quite figure out why. He plays in front of thousands of people in person every week—millions more, if you count the TV broadcast. What's the big deal if I'm there? Is it a big deal to him? The thought makes my breath come in shorter bursts.

"Is, uh…that okay with you?"

Anton swallows. "Yeah. Sure. That's good. Okay, then. 'Night, Sam—" He breaks off and clears his throat. "'Night, Rose."

I'm so stunned by his slip-up that I almost don't notice that we're not alone.

17

DUKE IT OUT

Rose

I let myself be lulled into a false sense of security. But I make up for it. I move fast enough to make freaking Usain Bolt look like a tortoise. In less than a millisecond, I'm out of my front seat and positioning myself between Anton and a figure dressed in black who materializes out of the darkness.

"Who goes there?" I hold up my hands, prepared to fend off this attacker—whoever it is.

Anton steps up next to me, and before I can shove him backward, he says, "Duke?"

"Duke," I repeat, dropping my fists. "Like your cousin Duke?"

"I see my reputation precedes me." Duke chuckles.

"Or at least your ridiculous name," Anton chortles. "Good to see you, man."

Anton steps forward, and the men embrace. I take the beat to compose myself and come up with some sort of excuse for why I went all medieval knight with my, '*Who goes there?*' pronouncement.

"Rose, what were you doing?" Anton turns to me, looking bewildered.

"I thought he was paparazzi." My excuse is weaker than a square of off-brand toilet paper. "I have the exclusive," I add, as if that makes it any better.

"Right." Anton shoots me a befuddled look before turning to his cousin. "Duke, this is Rose Kasper. She's my...exclusive interviewer."

I shoot daggers at his teasing face.

"Pleasure to meet you, Ms. Kasper." Duke extends a hand, and I shake it. "Thought maybe Anton had hired some attractive personal security."

I laugh, but it's overdone and manic-sounding to my ear. Anton looks at me funny. Gosh, I am blowing this tonight.

"I don't need security," Anton says. "That's the best part about living here. Normalcy."

I glance between the two men, keeping my face neutral even as my mind flies to the question of why Duke is in town. The royal family isn't expected to arrive for a couple weeks, when they'll celebrate the holidays together.

Anton must be wondering the same thing. "What are you doing here? Why didn't you tell me you were coming?"

"Where's the fun in that?" Duke cracks a grin. "I came early for family Christmas."

"Brilliant." Anton turns to survey the parking lot. "Wait. Where are you parked?"

"I got dropped off."

It's a dodgy answer, and my senses immediately fire to life. What if Duke is the one who has it out for Anton?

I'm grasping for a reason to stay in their company, but Anton is oblivious. He's directing Duke around to the far side of his truck. "Hop in." He turns back to me. "You good?"

"Um, yeah. Great."

"Thanks for attempting to rescue me from the paparazzi."

"You betcha." I salute. *Why, Rose? WHY?*

"Okay, then. Bye."

"Toodle-oo." *Oh my gosh.* The cold is turning my brain to ice. That, or the terror I suddenly feel for Anton's safety is making me incapable of stringing together a complete thought.

There's only one thing to do.

I hurry around to my driver's side, and the second I'm in my car, I call my dad.

He picks up on the first ring. "What's going on?"

"Anton's cousin, Duke, appeared out of the darkness in the parking lot at the River Foxes stadium. Did we know he was coming to town?"

Lennox curses, and I hear typing on the other end of the phone.

I glance out my window to where Anton is parked. He motions for me to go first out of the parking lot.

I attempt a casual smile, but I feel anything but casual or smiley right now. I was hoping he'd pull out first so I could discreetly tail him, but of course he's being a gentleman.

Dang it, Anton. There's a time and a place for being polite, and the moment when your life may be hanging in the balance isn't one of them!

In his defense, he has no idea he's in danger. Because I haven't told him. Neither has anyone else. No wonder he despises his status as a royal. How's he supposed to trust anything?

I pull out of the parking lot and pretend to head toward Cashmere Cove. When Anton goes the opposite direction, I crank my wheel.

"I can follow them back to Anton's place if need be," I say into the phone.

"No, no. Stand down. It's not your job to be Bates's bodyguard."

"It's my job to keep him safe. What's the point of what I'm doing if not that?"

"You're the eyes and ears on the ground, not the last line of defense."

I frown. I don't like the sound of there *being* a last line of defense. If someone gets to the last line, then it means they've slipped through the cracks.

Is that what Duke has done?

Instead of arguing, I say, "Run me through what you know."

"Duke was in Washington D.C. He's been the liaison between the U.S. government and the palace in Penwick. We knew that. We just didn't know he'd arrived in Green Bay."

"Do you have any reason to believe he'll try to harm Anton? Could he be the insider that our sources are picking up on?" I ask.

"That was my immediate thought. One hypothesis is that Duke is trying to stage a coup. He's the spare heir, so if Anton is out of the picture, then he inherits the crown when it passes out of Queen Della's hands. Penwick policy states that when the heir turns thirty, the crown turns over. It's their country's way of keeping fresh blood in a position of power and not letting leadership grow stagnant."

I know all that from Anton. I also know about his relationship with his cousin.

"Duke and Anton were always close," I muse aloud. "I can't imagine he'd try to harm his own cousin."

My dad scoffs on the other end of the line. "Don't be naïve, Rose. You know as well as I do that people have killed for less."

I grit my teeth. "So, what? Do we have eyes on Duke and Anton? Or should I go after them?"

"I patched a message through to our contacts at the palace in Penwick. They have a direct line to Duke's personal assistant, who's also a member of the Penwick Security Force. He'll be on guard. Duke will have no idea, but he'll be under constant surveillance."

"We're sure that security agent can be trusted?"

Where was he tonight?

"He works for the queen herself, one of her most trusted men, so yes. He's already been watching from a distance." My dad types something on the other end of the line. I hear the clicking of the keys on his laptop.

"Where?" I instinctively check my rearview mirror.

"He dropped Duke in the lot at the stadium, according to the palace. He's in constant communication with them."

"Duke really has no idea?"

"I've been assured this agent is the best of the best."

I exhale. "Where does that leave me?"

"Your role hasn't changed. We still need you around Anton and the River Foxes organization, listening in and keeping track of anything out of place. It isn't out of the question that Duke would connect with someone who has access to Anton at work in order to get the job done."

"Understood. Any other updates?"

"None except to say good work. You were on the ball tonight. Continue to prove yourself like that and show me that you're the right person for the foreign affairs job, and it's all but yours. I'll be in touch."

Lennox ends the call, and I drop my phone into my lap.

I spend the twenty-five-minute drive back to Cashmere Cove turning over the events of the day. It takes the entire drive for me to get my heart rate settled. Instead of going straight to The Downer, I pull onto Main Street. I let the sights of the quaint small town soothe me. The road is lit with a romantic glow emanating from old-fashioned streetlights. Christmas decorations were put up, so now, on the upper end of every streetlight pole, there's a wreath of fresh greens. All the businesses lining Main Street are done up too, with lights tacked along rooflines and window frames.

I pull into the small alley parking space near Mood Reader and make the quick walk around the back of the bookstore, letting myself in through the rear door. The scent of paper and books immediately soothes me. I keep the lights off inside, enjoying the twinkling from the outside Christmas lights. I drop into one of the comfy chairs at the front of the store. I tap my foot on the ground and stare around the darkened bookshop. Eventually, I stand and start wandering through the rows of shelves, running my fingers over the spines of our books and pausing to straighten tipped copies and line up the titles on the nearest endcap.

I don't know what's the matter with me or why I'm so fidgety after the call with my dad. It's good the team has a lead. It's good they're onto Duke. I should be grateful we're two steps ahead of the person who's likely at the root of Anton's issues. I *am* grateful. It makes my job easier if we're up against a known enemy. And that's good because I want the position abroad. At least, I think I do.

So why does the thought of leaving Cashmere Cove and the bookstore make me feel like crying?

My phone buzzes where I stashed it in my back pocket, and I pull it out, expecting a follow-up message from Lennox with further intel.

Instead, it's a text from Anton giving me the details for when I can come and hang out with him and his buddies. I enter the information into my phone, including the address to Poe's place, where they're meeting up on Friday night, and type back my response.

Rose

> Thanks. I'll be there. Should make for some good information for the article!

> How's Duke? Tell him I'm sorry I almost attacked him. I take paparazzi and the exclusivity clause in my contract very seriously. <winking face emoji>

Better to address my weird behavior head on. That, and I'm not above prodding Anton for more information about Duke.

Anton

> Clearly. Thought it was going to come to fisticuffs there for a minute.

I smile down at my phone. Every once in a while, Anton will use super formal, old-fashioned speech patterns and vocabulary words. It's the most charming thing. When we were dating, I teased him about it relentlessly, but I secretly love it.

> **Anton**
> Duke's good. He left to check into his hotel. I'll let him know about your mosquito-like tendencies…always buzzing around.

> **Rose**
> Hardy har.

I fiddle with my phone's case as tiny bubbles pop up on the screen and then disappear. I picture Anton at his house, composing a message back to me. I wonder if he's leaning over his kitchen counter, shoveling in a bowl of pasta like he used to do.

When his message pops up, it's an attachment. I furrow my brow and stare down at my screen. He's shared a Note with me that's titled *Sammy Rose*.

I bite my lip and click on it. It populates with some sort of a list.

I read through it once, trying to make sense of what I'm seeing. Staring back at me are a bunch of things I like—or at least a bunch of things I used to like, once upon a time. My coffee order—large iced latte with oat milk and two pumps of caramel. My favorite Mexican restaurant in Mobile with an asterisk next to it. Down below, there's a note that says:

- prefers flour tortillas to corn tortillas and the spiciest salsa possible.

Beneath that, he's made a notation about how I hate being cold. He's written, *Possible birthday gift idea - rice heating pad?* below it, and my heart shatters at the sweetness of it all.

My favorite books are typed out in order. He's got my favorite board game marked down as Yahtzee! with cribbage listed as a close second. There's a note about how I prefer mini golfing to watching movies, and in parentheses, he's written (*likes to be active rather than sitting still*).

He's got a section about himself too. He's titled it, *Her Taste in Me(n)*. And there, he's listed:

- Likes my hair longer on the top.

- Prefers when I'm clean shaven.

- A scruffy beard irritates her skin.

I remember the moment I told him that. I felt so stupid saying it, but we were kissing, and the way his whiskers felt against my cheek was taking me out of the moment. He never let his facial hair grow after that.

Come to think of it, I don't think I've seen him with a beard or anything resembling scruff in the years since.

Surely that can't be because of me.

Can it?

My heart, the shriveled up, dysfunctional tiny lump of coal, sparks and begins to glow red as a warm ember inside my chest. My vision blurs with unshed tears, and before I can think twice, I tap the call button.

Anton answers on the second ring.

"What is all this?" My voice is watery, and I attempt to swallow down my emotion.

He's quiet for a beat. "You said in the car you weren't sure what you liked to do these days. You sounded sad about it, so I figured I could help. You liked these things once upon a time. Maybe you still do."

The fact that he made this list at all, much less still has it after all the time that's passed and the way I left things with him… "I-I don't know what to say."

"You don't have to say anything." Anton's low, steady voice rumbles over the line. I want to curl up in his baritone. "It's nothing."

"It's something to me."

"Are you…crying?" His voice is strained. "Shoot, Rose. I didn't mean to make you cry."

"No." I wipe my nose and force my voice to be even. "I, uh…swallowed a bug."

What's one more lie?

"It's the dead of winter. Bugs should have migrated south by now."

"Bugs migrate?"

"Yeah, Poe loves butterflies, and he was telling me about how—wait. Are you deflecting?"

I chuckle in spite of myself. "I'm fine, Anton."

"If you're sure." He sounds hesitant. "I just thought this could be a starting point if nothing else. Maybe your tastes have changed, which they're allowed to do, obviously. I mean, I know nothing about your taste in men these days, but...yeah."

He's fishing so hard I can hear him cast the line from here.

Something about that makes my chest ache, because I can hear what he's not saying. *Your taste in men is allowed to change.*

What he doesn't realize is I lied all those years ago when I broke up with him and told him he wasn't my type. My taste in men is one thing that hasn't changed. My taste in men is him. Always has been. Always will be. It's the one thing I know for certain about myself.

But I don't say that.

Instead, I whisper, "Thank you."

18

GUYS' NIGHT

Anton

TJ steps in front of me and holds up his hand. "Dude, would you stop pacing? You're making me nervous."

"Actually, it's proven that pacing helps the brain process and sort information," Poe pipes up from the kitchen where he's putting together a snack board. The man's charcuterie is the stuff of legends.

"Which begs the question…" Del sets down his bottle of water on the coffee table and holds his arms out to the side. "What needs so much processing that you're wearing a hole in Poe's hardwood floors?"

I sink down into an overstuffed chair and bury my head in my hands.

We're all gathered at Poe's place for our weekly guys' night. We rotate houses during the season, but every week, we get together on Friday night. It's a good way to keep focused ahead of game day. Saturday nights, we're all together at the team hotel and in bed early anyway, but Friday nights, there's the temptation to burn off some steam after a long week. Going out on the town, drinking, and staying out late would not help the team's cause on Sunday, even with a day in between to recover. So, Friday night guys' nights became a thing.

"Yeah, come on, man. Are you finally going to tell us what's really going on between you and Rose?" TJ grabs the football Poe has sitting in the corner and starts tossing it to himself.

Poe walks into the room and sets down a platter of food on the coffee table before snatching the ball out of midair and taking it away from TJ.

"Hey!"

"I just got that new vase." Poe points to the table inside his front door. "It's a legit antique."

"You don't trust these hands?" TJ holds up his palms, flipping them back and forth.

Poe holds the ball out and points the tip at TJ. "On the field? Sure. But around my vase? Nope. No offense."

"I am completely offended. I have great hands."

"Shut it, you two. I want to hear what's going on with Bates." Del stares me down.

I sigh. "Rose will be here any minute."

"That's exactly why you need to tell us what's the deal with you two…so we don't do anything to embarrass you." Del bats his eyes at me, and I narrow my gaze back.

"You wouldn't."

"Not intentionally, but how are we supposed to know?"

"I'm guessing I shouldn't hit on her." TJ sounds nonchalant, and I know he's messing with me, but every muscle in my body clenches involuntarily at the thought.

TJ chuckles. "I'll take that as a sign to keep my hands…my perfectly capable hands"—he scowls at Poe—"off."

My blood pressure has now skyrocketed from thinking of anyone's hands near or on Rose. I stand and start pacing again.

"Dude. Relax. We'll be cool." Del reaches forward and pops a grape into his mouth.

"We're always cool," Poe agrees. "We're here to make you look good."

"Like on the field," TJ adds.

"So, tell us what's going on so we can help," Del finishes.

"Fine." I sit back down and lean forward, resting my elbows on my knees. The guys crowd around, and I feel like I should have some sort of white board or something. It's like I'm drawing up a play in the huddle, when in actuality, I'm outlining the greatest love and loss of my life.

Not to be dramatic or anything.

"I loved Rose once. She broke my heart. Having her come back into my life has made me realize that my feelings for her never went away. But I don't know where she stands, and I don't want to put myself out there if she's going to trample on my heart again. It's a complicated mess, and I don't need y'all making it weird."

TJ lets out a whistle. "So, this is your second chance at love…if you want it. But you're not sure that you want it?"

"Basically. Mostly, I'm not sure if *she* wants *me*."

TJ rubs his hands together. "It's easy, then."

"What is?" I frown.

"Use your time together to figure her out. You can start tonight."

I glance around the room. Poe is nodding slowly, like he's tracking what TJ is saying. I don't follow at all, and I narrow my gaze at Del. "Dude, are you crying?"

Del blinks at me with watery eyes. "I really like the two of you together. I want this to work out."

"For crying out loud, Del."

"Literally." He sniffles.

"Focus." TJ claps his hands. "Let me tell you how this is going to go down."

I lean forward. "I'm listening."

"Tonight, when she gets here, you're going to act like you're on a date with her."

I scowl. "This isn't really a date-like atmosphere with you goons along for the ride."

"We're your wingmen." Poe puffs his chest up. "Good thing I planned the perfect activity for us." He glances around the room. "Just need to call in a reinforcement."

"What?" I frown. I don't want anyone else witnessing my attempts to rekindle the fire with Rose. "Why?"

"We need an even number," Poe says cryptically as he taps out a message on his phone.

I roll my eyes. This is a train wreck. I love these guys, but they are incapable of not making a huge deal out of all the things. It's how we are with each other. I know it's because they care, but right now, I'd love for them to turn it down several notches.

"Can you play it cool when she gets here?" I try to put the brakes on the runaway train. "What are we even doing tonight? Tell me it's something normal."

Poe huffs and looks offended. "Normal is subjective. Normal is no fun. Normal is heartbreaking."

"Dude. That's deep." Del looks impressed.

A knock on the door echoes through Poe's condo.

"That's her. Would everyone act natural? Don't say anything about my feelings for her." I stand and point at them. "And don't embarrass me."

"Aye-aye, 4!" TJ jumps up from his chair and turns toward the door. His eyes are wide, and he looks like an overeager golden retriever puppy. There's no way he's going to play it cool. I'm in for an absolute circus tonight. I can feel it.

"I'll get it. It's my house." Poe cuts me off on the way to the door.

Del joins the rest of us. "She knows me. I should be the one to welcome her."

"We can't all get the door." I'm trying to use my body to block out my teammates. "We'll look ridiculous. I should be the one to greet her. She's writing the article about me."

"And you're in loooove with her." TJ wiggles his shoulders.

"None of that!" I hiss. "I'm not in lo—"

Another knock sounds, cutting me off mid-lie.

TJ ducks under my outstretched hands and makes a break for it. Del wraps his arms around my stomach and lifts me off the ground.

"Durgen, put me down!"

Poe scoots around us and gets to the door as TJ is swinging it open.

Rose stands on the other side, looking like an absolute athleisure vision in black leggings and an oversized fleece zip up. Her eyes go wide at the sight of us. I imagine the scene from her perspective: four, two-hundred-plus pound football players crammed in the foyer of a condo, one being hoisted off the ground by another, and two looking at her with their tongues practically hanging out of their mouths.

"Uh, hi? Do I need to give you two a moment?" She gestures to where Del is still holding me in his arms.

I push off of him, and he sets me down. He's grinning.

"Good to see you again, girlie!" He steps forward and wraps Rose in his arms, lifting her up.

Jealousy lances through me, even though I know Del's feelings for Rose are like that of a sibling. What I wouldn't give to wrap my arms around her and hold her that close.

She's smiling as he sets her down, and I need to remember to thank him later. Because for as over the top as his greeting is, it has totally put her at ease. The lines on her face have fallen away, and her eyes are sparkling with good humor.

"This is quite the welcome," she quips. "Thanks for having me."

She holds out a slim, wrapped package and hands it to Poe.

"What's this? You didn't have to get me anything."

Rose waves him off. "You're letting me into your home and allowing me to crash your guys' night. It's the least I can do." She digs into the bag at her side. "And here." She hands out packages to each of us before slipping out of her winter coat. "I didn't want any of you to feel left out."

TJ greedily rips into his. Del reverently unfolds the wrapping paper. I'm the last to retrieve my gift from her, and when I do, our fingers brush. Her gaze darts to mine, and I offer her a tentative smile.

I don't know where we stand since I shared my list of things about her. Maybe she thinks it's creepy. Maybe she thinks it's pathetic that I had a list at all. It was buried deep in the archives of my phone, but I never could bring myself to get rid of it.

"This is the coolest." Poe holds up his opened gift. It's a butterfly. A dead one. But it's in a clear case, and its wings are fanned out and pinned back. There's some sort of write-up on one side of it. It's very Poe-ish.

"Anton mentioned that you like butterflies, so I took a chance." Rose looks suddenly shy.

"I love it! It's going to go right here." Poe sets it next to his vintage vase. "No tossing the ball around here, you got that, Teej?"

"Yeah. Yeah. Look at this!" TJ pulls out a Super Mario Bros. figurine. "Yoshi. My favorite—and the best player, obviously."

I gape at Rose. "How did you know that?"

"He mentioned it in the weight room." She shrugs.

My jaw is hanging on the floor. How did she manage to find gifts for my friends—specific, perfect gifts—with minimal notice?

Del lets out a laugh. He holds up a Christmas tree ornament that's a pair of cowboy boots, spinning it around to see it from all angles.

"To remind you of the first night you met me." Rose bats her eyelashes in an overdone way.

She's teasing, but I'm immediately transported to the bar, and the peanuts, and the seamless conversation, and the Garth Brooks, and nicknaming her Sammy Rose. On top of all those old memories, I'd like to think we're making new ones—jumping in the frozen Bay of Green Bay, dancing in California. Here, tonight.

My breath hitches with anticipation about what's going to come. It could be a disaster. It has been before. But I can't live in fear of that. I want to go all in with Rose. Past Rose and present Rose and future Rose. I want them all.

If only I knew she wanted the same.

She's staring at me as I delicately lift the tissue paper out of the small gift bag she brought for me. Inside is a little notebook. There's a hand-drawn cover, and I can't help but grin the second I see what she's written—also, because no one else got a homemade gift.

"How the Mosquito Wins the Day," I read. "A true story, written and illustrated by Rose Kasper. I love this."

She exhales when I smile at her, almost as if she was afraid I wouldn't like it. I flip though the notebook to see she's written an elaborate and rhyming poem all about how a mosquito's persistence helps her win her ultimate prize and sink her teeth into just the thing she's always wanted. It's cheeky and self-deprecating and adorable.

And I've never wanted to be bitten by a mosquito more in my life.

19
Chosen Family

Rose

What does it say about me that a bit of praise from Anton sends me spiraling into a tornado of happiness? I don't know, but here I am, sucked into the eye of the storm. My chest feels lighter than it has in days, and my cheeks already hurt from smiling so much at Anton and his friends.

My gifts were a hit, and they effectively broke the ice for me, just as I'd hoped.

"What gives with all of this?" Anton holds out an arm, stopping me in the foyer as the rest of the guys shuffle back into Poe's impressive living room.

"A small host gift for Poe." I keep my voice breezy. "I didn't want to have the rest of y'all feeling left out, so I brought a little something extra for everyone."

Truthfully, people always soften up when presented with a gift, so I bring stuff along when I need an in. My success rate is sky high, and it's one of the oldest tricks in my book.

"You know you don't have to buy our affection." Anton's voice is low.

How does he do that? How does he know that in most rooms—in most scenarios—I absolutely feel like I do?

"I mean, it's really thoughtful of you," he adds. "But we're glad you're here, er, happy to have you here, just you." He presses his lips together, as if he's annoyed with himself for not being able to string together a coherent thought. "What I mean to say is thank you."

I bite back a smile at how off his game he is. "It's nothing."

"It's something to me." He holds my gaze, and I can't deny that with him, I feel like I belong. I've never needed a gift to break the ice, because it's like his deepest thoughts and feelings somehow mesh together seamlessly with mine. It's a wonderful sensation, to be truly known.

Dangerous, too. I can't let myself rest in it, no matter how good it would feel to let him love me again. I have a job to do, and he's not for me. Not like that.

Anton is studying me, and I'm afraid the tug-of-war going on inside my brain is plainly visible. But fortunately, he keeps things light. "Have you considered publishing your mosquito masterpiece? Could be the next bestseller."

I make a face at him. "That's for your eyes only."

Those eyes darken and take on a flirty spark in the lamplight of Poe's living room. "I like the sound of that."

Walked right into that one.

My mouth is dry as dust. I clear my throat and turn to the rest of the guys who are doing their best to look like they're not listening to every word Anton and I exchange. Their acting skills are seriously lacking.

The second we round the corner toward them, Poe ducks into the kitchen. TJ tilts his chin up in the air and starts whistling. Del opens a book that was sitting on the end table and pretends to read it. Anton walks over to him and snatches the book out of Del's hands.

"Hey! I was just getting to the good part," Del complains.

Anton knocks him on the head with it. "It was upside down, you fool."

Del's cheeks blush hot pink beneath his beard.

"So, Rose…" TJ plops down on the end of Poe's sectional. "About this article. What can we tell you about Anton? I'm ready to spill all his secrets."

"Hey now. I—"

"I'm so glad you asked." I grin at Anton, talking right over the top of him as I settle myself in a side chair and retrieve my tablet. Anton mutters something about payback and how TJ better watch his mouth. I smile. "Before we get into that juicy stuff, I'd love to hear about the River Foxes and your team dynamics. Then, I'm here to observe y'all as friends. You can forget I'm even around and go about your usual time together."

If I'm not mistaken, Anton scoffs. I shoot him a questioning glance, but he doesn't make eye contact.

Del has his gaze fixed on Anton, and then he pivots it to me. "Speaking as a new member to the team here, I can say that this group of players and coaches really gels. We're like a well-oiled machine. A lot of that has to do with Anton as our fearless leader."

Poe walks in carrying a stack of painting canvases, which is…unexpected. Before anyone can ask a question about it, he says, "I'd agree with that. We all respect each other, and that starts from the top. Anton puts in longer hours than everyone else, so you know when he demands something of the rest of the team, he's right there with us. He's not asking us to do something he hasn't done or isn't willing to do."

"Yeah," Del chimes in. "He's so personable too. He gives everyone his attention. Some people may think that, because he's a prince, he's high maintenance, but Anton is one of the most down-to-earth guys I've ever met. Would give you the shirt off his back. Though, it wouldn't fit me." He pats his belly.

I smile. It's reassuring, hearing them talk about Anton. What they're telling me is in line with the man I knew. He always showed up for his team, his friends, and his charities. I admire that about him. How our friends speak about us is a true sign of our character. These guys are genuinely pals, and it warms the cockles of my shriveled, broken heart to know that Anton has them in his corner.

"You guys. Stop." Anton is blushing furiously.

"Can't," Del says.

"Won't," Poe adds. "It's all true, 4."

"What about you?" TJ wiggles his brows at me.

"What about me?"

"Have you gotten the same vibe from Anton? We hear there's a history between you two. What's your endgame here?"

"Teej." Anton sounds threatening. "Don't."

"What?" TJ crosses his impressive arms. "You know we're gonna look out for you. Not going to let her write some sort of blasphemy."

"Excellent word choice," Poe says, pointing at TJ. "Blasphemy."

TJ doffs a pretend hat. "Learned from the best, my man."

They both look to me. I flick my eyes to Anton, who looks decidedly uncomfortable, and back to them.

I'm not about to discuss our relationship history with his friends before I discuss it with him. And really, there's nothing to discuss. The past is the past. Right? Right.

"I respect the way you have Anton's back. It says a lot about him and about you. I'm not going to publish any type of smear campaign, if that's what you're afraid of."

I hold their stares, shifting only to make eye contact with each of Anton's friends. I want them to know I have no intention of hurting him. My heart balloons at their care for him. It's something he never got within his given family, but it seems like he's found it with his chosen family.

"Alright, then." Del blinks first. "We good, fellas?"

"I am if you are." TJ nods, but then he points at Poe. "But I'm slightly terrified of what's going on over here."

Poe holds up a blank canvas. "What's so terrifying about portrait painting?"

20
Picture Perfect

Anton

As it turns out, portrait painting *is* terrifying.

"Dude. You're making Kennedy look like Sasquatch." TJ clucks his tongue at Del, who's currently painting Stephen Kennedy, our team's star wide receiver. He showed up ten minutes after Rose, and now I understand Poe's thought process. Del is painting Kennedy and vice versa. TJ and Poe are painting each other. Which leaves Rose and me as partners. The six of us are facing each other, two by two at Poe's dining table. TJ and Del are sitting across from Poe and Kennedy. Rose and I are staring at each other. We've got canvases set up on easels and a rainbow of acrylic paint arching between us. Poe has even provided multiple sizes of brushes.

As if that would help our cause.

I stare at my portrait of her. How am I ever supposed to capture her essence with acrylic paint? How can I possibly do her justice? I don't know, but I'm giving it my best effort. For the first time in my entire life, I'm grateful my mom made me take private art classes as a kid.

I've spent an inordinate amount of time trying to paint her mouth. Probably because I can't stop thinking about kissing that smile off her lips. She told us we should carry on and forget that she's even here. Fat chance. I'm hyperaware of her. Every shift in the chair. Every intake of her breath. The way she tips her chin when she's concentrating. The subtle smell of rose water that's always been her signature scent.

"Am not!" Del huffs, glancing across the table at Kennedy. "Don't listen to him, K-man. You look bomb."

"Guys." Poe dips his brush in some black paint and swipes it across the top of his canvas. I think he's trying to paint TJ's hair, but I can't be sure it's not some sort of impressionist snake or something. "Quit it. We're supposed to be vibing."

I glance to my left, where Kennedy is attempting to paint Del. "If it makes you feel any better, it's giving Abominable Snowman over here."

"I resent that," Kennedy says with a scowl.

Rose snickers from where she's sitting across from me. She taps the bottom of her paint brush against her chin, bobbing her gaze up at me and then down at her canvas. A lock of hair falls over her cheek, and I want to reach out and tuck it behind her ear.

"Hey." Poe lightly punches my shoulder, drawing my attention. "Don't give anything away. The grand reveal at the end is the best part."

"Says who? Have you had painting parties with people other than us?" Del pouts. "If you say yes, I'm going to be jealous."

"Saw it online." Poe shrugs. "I wouldn't paint with anyone but you guys."

I look over at Rose, who is eating this up. She's trying and failing to press her lips together and swallow back her smile, but it keeps breaking free. She clears her throat when she spots me staring at her.

I want to say something witty and impress her, but I can't come up with a line. The guys and I have been joking around, but it's like I'm so aware of Rose and so aware of how I don't want to mess anything up that I can't seem to string together a decent sentence where she's concerned. I just keep staring at her. Like an obsessed puppy, waiting for her to give me a treat.

Am I panting? Is my tail wagging out of control? Probably. I'm a mess. A slobbering, foolish, gone for her mess.

We paint for another thirty minutes, lobbing fake insults and jokes back and forth. Rose asks the guys some questions about the team, but she doesn't seem too worried about getting information for the article.

"Alright. It is time." Poe sets down his brush dramatically.

TJ makes a face. "Okay, Rafiki."

Del starts humming the instrumental chorus from *The Lion King*.

Poe rolls his eyes before holding up his painting of TJ for everyone to see. "Well, Teej, I promise I love you more than my painting suggests."

We all cackle. TJ shows off his painting of Poe, which looks like a cross between a LEGO figure and Frankenstein. Kennedy and Del go next, and we have a good laugh at the Sasquatch and Abominable Snowman lookalikes.

When it's Rose's and my turn to share our portraits, she starts by saying, "Painting has never been my gift," before turning her canvas toward me.

I can't help but grin at the curlicue of hair she's painted over the top of my forehead. She's made my jaw extra square, which I secretly love, and she's painted me with a wide smile. I like seeing myself like this—through her eyes.

"It's really good." I take the canvas from her, studying it up close.

"There's something about your eyes. Don't think I could ever get them exactly right, even if I tried all night," she mumbles, almost to herself.

I flick my gaze to hers, and we're locked in like the snap of two magnets. She's studying the eyes in question, and I'm doing the same. For the life of me, I can't get words out.

"O-kay." Kennedy slaps my back, severing the moment. He doesn't know the backstory here, so I can't blame him. "Show her yours, man. It's good."

I set down Rose's painting of me and hold up the one I did of her. I spin it around for the other side of the table to see.

Rose's jaw drops.

Del and TJ gape.

"Dude. What the heck? Are you good at everything?" TJ scowls at me before swiveling to glance at Rose. "It looks just like her."

"Thanks," I say. I don't take my eyes off her.

She reaches over and grabs the canvas. Our fingers brush, my whole hand heats at the electric pop, and she sucks in a breath, but she doesn't take her gaze off the portrait.

"Nice, man." Del nods approvingly.

I dip my chin in response.

Finally Rose meets my gaze. "It's beautiful."

"You are."

Rose's cheeks turn scarlet.

Well, shoot.

Did I say that out loud?

"I mean..."

TJ jumps up from his seat. "I'll help you clean up, Poe."

"Let's wash the brushes in the laundry room sink." Poe takes his cue from TJ, and all of a sudden, the guys are like a cleaning tornado. And then we're alone.

"I should probably get going," Rose says, her eyes on me.

"Sure. Okay. Yeah." I'm stumbling over myself like a man walking around in the middle of the night.

She lets me lead her to the door. I rest my hand on her back and keep it steady, even though the feel of the curve of her hip is enough to make me want to pull her fully into my arms. It's at once familiar and new, and all I want to do is hold her.

I help her into her coat in the foyer, and she bobs her chin in the direction of the dining room. "Your friends are great. You're lucky to have each other."

Don't I know it. The very camaraderie I was always missing in Penwick, when I had everything being handed to me, I found in the middle of Wisconsin, working my tail off. Go figure.

I peer over my shoulder to see the four of them peeking around the corner. They're like four oversized members of the neighborhood watch. I shoo them away.

Rose chuckles. "Good luck on Sunday, guys," she calls.

I turn back to her. "You'll be at the game, right?"

"I'll be there." She grimaces. "Actually, so will my whole family."

My eyebrows fly up. "Your sisters?"

"And Mack and Collin, yep."

"I'll do my best to put on a good show." I wink.

"You always do." Her response is so immediate I think it surprises even her. She blushes furiously. "I mean, I'm sure you do."

"Rose Kasper, have you been following my career?" I cross my arms.

She crosses hers right back. "No comment."

I grin. "If you want to bring your family down to the players' entrance after the game, I can show them around."

Rose's eyes widen. "You'd do that?"

When will this woman realize there isn't really anything I wouldn't do for her?

"It's not a huge deal. Besides, Ned loves getting footage of us being interactive with the fans."

"A win-win, then." Rose shifts her weight between her legs. "Hey, uh, will Duke be at the game?"

"I think so. Why?"

She blinks before meeting my gaze again. "It might be nice to get his perspective for the article—if that's okay with you," she adds. "You guys were close as kids. He'd be a good Penwick source, right?"

"Sure. Duke loves the spotlight. He'll be all for it. Bring your family around, and you and Duke can talk then."

"Great. It's a date. I mean"—Rose blanches—"*not* a date with Duke. Or you. It's a plan. A good plan." She steps back. "See you Sunday."

She's adorable when she's frazzled. And thank goodness I'm not the only one who's off my game.

"Bye, Rosie." I close the door behind her and turn around.

Del, TJ, Poe, and Kennedy are standing side by side, like a wall of muscle, with their arms crossed and serious expressions on their faces.

"Who died?" I quip.

"No one except your rizz, man." TJ shakes his head.

"I don't need your opinion on my rizz."

"What you need is a full-fledged intervention. That woman is still hung up on you, and you're obviously in love with her."

"She's the reason for your tattoo." TJ blows out a breath. "I mean, *hello*."

"But you hardly said two words to her tonight. And no goodbye kiss." Del plops down on the sectional. We all follow. "What gives?"

"She makes me nervous—in a good way," I admit. "But I'm still nervous."

"It's time to put yourself out there, then. Go big or go home." Poe sounds like he knows what he's talking about. How, I'm not sure. I've never seen him in a serious relationship.

"Poe is right. You got to level up." Del rubs his hands together.

"Flip the script." TJ nods slowly.

"How am I supposed to do that?"

"Dunno, but between all of us, we can work out a solid game plan." Del shrugs. "Just like on the field."

Kennedy glances around. "No clue what's going on here, but you know I'm in."

TJ and Poe nod seriously, and I figure *what the heck*.

"I can use all the help I can get."

"Excellent. Let's get ready to rumble," TJ says with a TV announcer inflection to his voice. We all lean in, and as silly as we probably look, five football players devising a game plan for my romantic future, I can't help but be filled with gratitude for these guys who love me enough to want to see me happy.

"Operation Help Anton Get Rose Back has commenced," TJ says.

"That's way too long of an operation name," Poe argues matter-of-factly. "All the good operations have titles that roll off the tongue. Look at the World War II history books."

"Let's not compare my potential relationship to a world war." I wince.

"We'll workshop it," Del says, bringing us back to the point. "Now here's what I think. She brought you a gift tonight. You should return the favor."

"I was already planning on it." I outline my idea for them.

"That's good, man. A good start." TJ points at me. "After this weekend, I also think you should meet her on her turf for a change."

"Go on."

TJ, Poe, and Kennedy start tossing around ideas, but Del catches my eye and turns serious. "You sure you want to go all in with her again, Bates? I like Rose, but I'm not the one with my heart on the line here."

Del is right. Can I do this again? Or maybe the better question is, how can I not?

21

The Breakup

Anton - Five Years Ago

Rose paces half a block away with her phone pressed against her ear. I'm waiting for her to end her call so we can go on our Monday night walk. It's become a tradition of ours. We stroll through my neighborhood and circle around on the beach, talking through the highlights of the weekend's game and anything else. Sometimes, we walk in silence too. Her presence makes me feel completely at ease in my own skin. Completely safe. What more could a man want, really?

We've been dating for six months now, and for the past two weeks, I've been talking to my mom about getting my great-grandmother's engagement ring out of the safe in Penwick. Yep. The family ring. I mean business.

My mom is not on board. She's holding fast to her opinion that an American cheerleader isn't the type of woman for me. I'll wear her down eventually. As soon as she acknowledges that I know what I want and what I want is Rose, she'll have no choice but to give us her blessing. If she won't, I'll buy my own ring. But I'm trying to honor and respect the royal lineage I was born into.

I've already started dreaming up proposals. I've got about four different scenarios I'm considering, one of which is to simply drop down on one knee during a Monday night walk.

Rose pockets her phone and strides toward me. Stress lines bracket her mouth.

I grab for her hand. "Everything okay?"

"Fine." Her voice is tight.

"So no, then." I nudge her shoulder. "What's going on?"

"Nothing, Anton. Leave it."

"If you tell me, maybe I can help."

She looks away from me.

"Hey. I don't like that." I stop walking, pulling her back when she tries to keep going. I reach over and tip her chin in my direction. She won't meet my gaze. I frown. "Sammy Rose?"

She flinches, and when she finally looks at me, an avalanche of emotion thunders through her eyes. I'm startled by the pain and agony I see, but even more than that, what terrifies me is the look of determination in the depths of her baby blues.

"I don't want to do this anymore."

I swallow. *Don't panic*. Surely this doesn't mean what it sounds like it means. "Don't want to do what?"

"This." She pulls out of my grasp. "You. Me. This relationship. It's stifling. It's not what I want. I'm out."

She spins on her heel, and I'm reeling. Where is this coming from? Earlier today she texted me a photo of a page of her manuscript and asked me for my thoughts. Nothing about her behavior makes any sense.

Stunned as I am, I'm not letting her walk away from me without more of a conversation. I jog to catch up with her, coming to a stop directly in front of her, cutting off her exit strategy, at least for now.

She lets out a frustrated, dismissive huff. "Get out of my way, Anton."

She makes a move to go around me, and I don't stop her, but I keep pace so we're walking side by side. Waves are coming off of her, but I can't tell what the emotion is. Sadness? Anger? Regret?

Add in some desperation, and maybe I'm describing myself.

"You're ending what we have with no explanation. I won't let you do that."

She stops abruptly. "You don't get to control me. You want a reason? Fine. I was trying to spare your feelings, but here you go." She sucks in a breath. "This was fun, but we were never going to be anything more than a fling. We're from different worlds. I ran into you in that bar, and I got to have a whirlwind romance with a football player and a prince. But dating you long term is way more pressure than I would ever want. There's no future here."

I'm trying to digest all of this, but it's like taking insults through a firehose from a person who holds my heart in her hands. I'm shattering.

"I mean, my gosh, Anton. I have no desire to deal with the baggage that comes with a real relationship with you. I was going to go along with it for a bit and try to let you down easy, but then you kept pressing me, so now you know. I'm done. It's over."

"I—" I cut myself off because what do I even say? "I don't know what to say."

She presses her mouth into a flat line and glances away from me.

I'm so hurt. I don't think I can breathe.

It's like I'm back in third grade, overhearing a conversation between one of my so-called friends and his mother when she was dropping him off at the palace for a playdate.

"But, mum," *my friend had whined, "I don't want to stay. I don't even like him. He always wants to look at American football trading cards. He's such a nerd, and it's so stupid."*

"Nonsense, Alexander. You'll stay, and you'll like it. Best to keep the palace happy, and it'll pay off to have a friend in high places someday."

My mind flashes forward, and I feel like I'm that awkward sixteen-year-old boy standing in front of Scarlett Monahue on the bluff overlooking the Atlantic Ocean, having just had my first kiss, only to lean away and find her sneering. She cocked her head over her shoulder to where a gaggle of girls had their hands covering their mouths in an attempt to quiet their laughter.

"What's...going on?" *I spluttered.*

Scarlett looked at me with pity. "Oh, Anton, you didn't actually think I liked you for real, did you?"

That's exactly what I thought.

"My friends just bet me I couldn't get you to kiss me by tonight, but I won. See you."

She skipped off to join her friends, leaving me standing there feeling all of two feet tall.

A means to an end.

Not unlike how I feel now. I've been used and tossed aside by someone I trusted. Again.

Rose meets my eyes, and the avalanche of emotion is gone, replaced by a gray hue to her blue tint.

Something inside me locks shut tight. "I don't ever want to see you again."

It's a cliché if I've ever heard one, but I don't care. I turn away from her and walk toward the beach.

If I hear what sounds like a whimper of anguish, I'm sure it was the wind, mocking me. I don't turn around. I don't look back.

22

Gameday Best

Rose - Now

I love the way the morning light filters in through The Downer's front windows. I sit with my legs curled up on the green, crushed velvet couch Poppy and I splurged on when we moved to Cashmere Cove and sip my coffee, shifting so the winter sunlight hits me smack across the face. It's not much, but it's something, and my Vitamin D stores are sorely depleted, so I'll take it.

I don't often have quiet, slow mornings like this. I'm either at the bookstore early or doing something for my other job. I hit up church last night because I knew I needed to work this morning ahead of the game. I went over the dossier my dad and the team sent me about Duke. I'll see him again today, and I need to be prepared. I am prepared. Except, Anton's case is...different.

I don't understand why he's being nice. I don't deserve it. It's making it way harder to do my job. It's making it nearly impossible not to fall madly in love with him.

My mind keeps leaping back in time and replaying the night I broke up with him in Mobile. I'd gotten a call from my dad saying my services with Anton were no longer needed. I was being sent immediately overseas for a job serving as the personal assistant slash security for a dignitary from Sweden. In the blink of an ill-timed phone call, I went from looking forward to one of our regular Monday night walks around town to being required to break up with a man I had real and true feelings for. I could have put it off, but it would have only made it worse, so I handled it then and there. I shut my emotions down and told him the only thing I knew would keep him from trying to win me back.

I pretended like I used him. I was cruel and cold, and I've hated myself for it ever since.

I stand and start pacing the worn, wood floors of The Downer. It's quiet living alone, but I kind of love it. Poppy and Mack are right next door, in their half of the duplex, and I physically pinch my eyes closed and sing a mental *la la la la* to stop myself from thinking about how two newlyweds likely wake up on a Sunday morning. But it's nice having them nearby. Noli, too, is just across town with Collin. I love Cashmere Cove.

It's going to be hard to leave it all behind. But if all goes as planned, I'll have a one-way ticket to Europe with my name on it in the New Year. It's everything I've ever wanted. But this morning, looking around The Downer, seeing the way the December sun hits the dust particles in the air and lights them up as if they're interior snowflakes, the thought of leaving makes me melancholy.

When I glance out the sidelight of the front door, I do a double-take. There's a long, brown-wrapped package laying on the porch. I'm not expecting anything, so I'm instantly suspicious.

I open the front door slowly, sucking in a breath as the chill of the morning air invades my cocoon of warmth. I glance left and right. No one is around. I nudge the box with my toe and then roll my eyes at myself.

Real high-quality investigative work there, Rose.

What do I think, it's going to jump to life?

My name is written on the brown wrapping in black Sharpie marker. I narrow my gaze because I'd recognize that handwriting anywhere. What is Anton doing dropping off a gift here? How does he know where I live?

I bend and grab the package, pulling it inside and slamming the door against the chill.

I cross to the kitchen and set the box on the counter, going to the junk drawer for a pair of scissors.

"Hey!"

The sound of a voice behind me has me screaming and whirling around, wielding the scissors as if it's a javelin I can use to pierce the intruder.

"Poppy!" I work to get my breath back under control as my big sister walks into my living room. "What the heck? Ever heard of knocking?"

She shrugs, tucking her hands into the pockets of her fleece robe. She's wearing matching slippers too. "Since when do we knock?"

She's right. We've always come and gone freely from each other's spaces.

Her eyes are on my package as she walks into the kitchen. "Whatcha got there?"

"Nothing." I say it too quickly, and I can tell she's even more interested by the way her eyebrows rise up under her bangs. "Actually, I'm not sure what it is."

"Open it!" Poppy pulls out a stool.

"Don't you have something better to be doing right now? Something with Mack," I add pointedly.

"Rose Marie Kasper!" Poppy's cheeks flush.

"What? I'm just saying."

"Well, he had to run out to the job site to check on something this morning."

"Ah, so I'm a consolation prize."

"No." Poppy eyes me carefully. "You've never been that, and I hope you know it."

"Yeah, yeah." I brush off her concern. This is not the first time I've sensed Poppy trying to work out what I'm really thinking. Too bad for her, I'm a professional liar at this point—so much so that even I don't know what I'm thinking.

"You know how much I love a good present." She rubs her hands together. "Let's see it."

"Fine." I use the edge of the scissors to slice into the packing tape that's securing the creases of the box.

"Who's it from?" Poppy stands and walks around to the coffee carafe, helping herself to a mug.

I debate lying, but there's no way I'll be able to pull it off. Not when she's looking over my shoulder.

"Anton."

"Anton? Anton Bates? As in the man whose football game we're going to see in a couple hours?"

"You know another Anton Bates?"

"I don't know *any* Anton Bates." Poppy takes a sip of her coffee, waggling her eyebrows at me. "But it seems *you* know this one...quite a bit more than you let on. Spill."

I peel back the flaps of the box. "There's nothing to spill. I knew him in Mobile—briefly. I was hired to write an article on him here. I'm sure this has something to do with the job."

Then again, maybe not.

I pull away the tissue paper, and there, folded neatly in the box, is a winter jacket. Not any winter jacket, though. This one is periwinkle and branded with the River Foxes logo. I lift it delicately out of the box, and directly over the heart, there's a number four patch. Turning it around, I feel my cheeks flush. Bates is spelled out in a curve along the back in letters that mimic the team's official jerseys. Actually, it's almost like someone took a jersey and transposed it onto this jacket to make a one-of-a-kind masterpiece.

"This is the coolest thing I've ever seen." Poppy reaches forward and feels the sleeve. "Looks warm and cozy too."

I swallow around a lump in my throat, because it sure does. There's a white envelope sitting at the bottom of the box, and I lift it out, thumbing my finger underneath the seal. I turn so Poppy can't read the note.

Dear Rose,

I've made you cold enough this week with the Polar Plunge, so I wanted you to have something warm to wear to the game today. I know you said you might pick up some of the opposing team's jerseys to wear, but the thought of that made me want to die. So, I had this made for you. One of the guys' wives does this with jerseys. She custom-made it yesterday. I hope you love it. I hope it keeps you comfortable. Thanks for coming...means a lot to me, even if it is for the article. I'll look for you.

Always,

Anton

I read his note three times over. Poppy, mercifully, stays silent, and she turns back to the coffee maker and gives me a second to compose myself.

Because this is all too much. Too thoughtful.

And the *Always, Anton* sign-off? What am I supposed to make of that? Always, what? My mind spins with possibilities I don't dare let myself dream of.

Always mine.

Always there.

Always has been and always will be.

Always and forever.

I blink through tears that have pooled in the corners of my eyes and catch sight of something in the corner of the box. It's a brown paper bag with the top curled in on itself. I lift it gingerly and inhale a sharp breath at the scent of what I can already tell is inside, my mind flashing back to a Mobile bar and the beat of country music pumping through my heart.

"Are those peanuts?" Poppy is facing me again, looking like she's dying to ask a million other questions but, instead, has narrowed it down to one, practical inquiry. I'm not naïve enough to think she's going to let me off the hook without explaining myself here, but again, I'm grateful for her discretion right now. I'm a fragile little birdy, and I'm about an inch away from falling out of the nest and crashing onto the sidewalk below. She gets it, and she's not making any sudden movements. A surge of affection for my sister wells up in my chest, along with a renewed pang of guilt for all the ways I've lied to her over the years when all she's done is take care of me and be there for me.

"Yeah." I clear out the wad of emotion in the back of my throat. "Yeah, they are."

Inside the bag, along with peanuts, still in the shell, there's another note. I pull it out and read it to myself.

A snack for the game. Peanuts will never not make me think of you. Hope that's not weird! ~A

I clutch the bag to my chest. If I'm being honest, the peanuts mean even more to me than the fancy new coat. I love them both for different reasons. His thoughtfulness is so disarming. It makes all the little hairs on my skin spring to life.

I need to shut my feelings down. I should be working on securing the walls around my heart. Battening down the hatches. Diving into the storm cellar. The man has obviously fixed his attention on winning me back. I'll be putty in his hands if I'm not careful. I can't let that happen. It's not fair to him—even if it's all I want.

Poppy huffs from the other side of the kitchen. "Okay. What gives?"

I try my best to put on an innocent expression, but she narrows her gaze at me.

"There's something going on, Rose. Noli sensed it in California, and I know she's right, judging solely by the fact that you've been speechless for the past five minutes. No snark. No quick commentary on any of this." She swirls her hand in the direction of my package. "Are you and Anton involved?"

Loaded question.

I need to be careful here. I absolutely cannot give Poppy the wrong idea. But the closer I can stick to the truth, the better. "We dated in Mobile. Briefly."

Poppy shrieks. "Why didn't you tell me?"

"It was nothing. A fling."

Lies. Lies. Lies.

"Not to him. Clearly. He's sending you gifts. What's the deal with the peanuts? I'm guessing there's a story there."

"We, uh...had peanuts the first night we met." Apparently, my ability to fabricate stories is lacking this morning. I allow myself this one moment of honesty with my big sister, and then I swear to myself I'm locking this down.

"Oh my goshhhh, Rose." Poppy grabs my wrist and squeezes. "He still has feelings for you."

I wince. "I don't know, Pops."

"Well, I do." Poppy huffs. "I want to meet him. I'll be able to give a more thorough assessment of the situation when I get an in-person feel for him."

I shake my head. "Can you not make a big deal out of this?"

She bites her lip, studying me. "Why? Because it's not actually a big deal, or because it is, but you don't know how to handle it?"

I drop my face into my palms. "The latter."

She starts rubbing my back, staying quiet and waiting for me to continue.

"I just..." I look up at her. "I am not the woman for Anton, whether I want to be or not. It didn't work out back then. It's not going to work now. It's better for both of us if we don't delude ourselves into thinking we're meant to be."

Poppy frowns. "That's a terrible attitude to have about this."

"Pops, I—"

She holds up her hand. "I'm not going to make you talk about it right now because I can tell you're an inch away from shutting down on me."

True.

"But," she continues, "I'm here for you, okay? Whenever you're ready to talk."

I nod and swallow. "Did you, uh, need something?"

She gives me a side hug. "Nah. Just wanted to see you."

My heart swells as she skips back to her side of the duplex, calling over her shoulder that she can't wait for the game.

Gosh, I love my sisters.

"I don't want to leave them." The words tumble from my mouth, spoken to no one but my empty duplex. It's the first time I've acknowledged that.

But what will I do if I don't go abroad? What is my life without my undercover work? I'm buried under so much of it, how will I ever dig my way out?

These are esoteric thoughts for another time.

I pull my jacket and peanuts to my face and bury my head in them.

I've got a football game to watch and an article to write. Not to mention an ex-boyfriend whose literal life is in my hands. Those are my priorities right now.

· · • • ● • ● • • ·

Two hours later, I'm standing on the sidelines of the field, watching the River Foxes warm up. That's not entirely true. I'm really only watching one player: Anton.

The man is locked in. He's throwing warm-up passes to his receivers and tight ends like he's firing surface-to-air missiles. It's slightly terrifying and, yeah, totally hot.

"Bates looks like he could break a guy's finger if they aren't careful." Collin is standing to my left, with Noli.

Poppy leans forward from where she and Mack are standing on my right. "Maybe he's trying to impress a certain journalist so she gives him some good press."

She wags her eyebrows at me, and I roll my eyes. "Very funny."

All around us, the stadium vibrates with pre-game energy. Jock jams emanate from the speakers, and the smell of snow mixes with the smell of fresh grass. Here in Green Bay, the field isn't lined with turf. Thanks to the snow that fell last night, we get to experience the heady mixture of the frozen tundra. By the game's end, the field will be a muddy mess, but for now, it's picturesque, the green and the white.

I tuck my chin into my coat from Anton. Physically, it's keeping me toasty warm on the outside, and knowing that he was thinking about me is heating me from the inside. A win-win.

"We should probably head to our seats." Noli glances over her shoulder.

My family is going to be in the stands for the game. I'll be here on the sidelines so I can get a full gameday experience for the article. *Read: so I can keep a closer lookout for anyone trying to hurt Anton.* All our intelligence is pointing to a more muted attack. Whoever is out to get him doesn't seem to want to make a big splash. They're more concerned with taking him out than they are with drawing attention to themselves. So, I doubt they'll hit at a game, when the entire general public has the potential to witness it.

Still, as I hug my sisters and fist bump my brothers-in-law, my head is on a swivel.

"We'll find you after the game." Poppy releases me from a hug. "Where should we meet?"

"I've got to connect with Anton in the locker room."

"Why? Does he need you to towel him off?" Noli pokes her chin up and rests it on Poppy's shoulder. "Rub down his muscles?"

"Oh my gosh. Stop it." I dart a glance around to make sure no one overheard her. I spin back to them and pin Poppy with a warning look. "You told her?"

Poppy shrugs. "There are no secrets among sisters."

If she only knew. I blink away my guilt.

"If you must know, I'm meeting Anton's cousin after the game so I can get a couple quotes from someone within the Penwick royal family—for the article."

Poppy sucks in a breath. "Isn't it crazy? Anton is actual royalty, and there he is, right out there playing football with a bunch of American commoners."

We all turn to watch him. He's doing some sort of calisthenic stretching, and I'm honestly here for it. He can do butt kicks for me any time.

"He prefers the commoners, actually."

I don't register that I've spoken out loud until I hear my sisters giggling—legit giggling like they're eleven years old.

"I'm sure he does." Poppy smirks. "One commoner in particular."

I feel my cheeks heat in spite of the air temperature.

"I still can't believe you're dating a prince and didn't tell us, Rosie." Noli shakes her head.

"I *was. Was* dating a prince," I grind out. "Past tense. Anton and I are not together. Would you keep your voice down?" One of the assistant coaches jogs toward us to retrieve some of the spare footballs. "I don't need anyone to know about our history. I've got a job to do."

Poppy mimes zipping her lips as Noli mutters, "Sorry. Can you blame me? This is a lot of new information to take in. I mean, I knew I should have been suspicious when you said you wanted to be a cat lady, but I didn't realize you were out there brushing shoulders with famous people."

I sigh. "I'm sorry, okay? I didn't want to make a big deal out of it."

The play-by-play announcer starts talking about the upcoming coin toss, and the players warming up on the field make their way over to the sidelines.

"You guys should hurry so you don't miss kick off." I'm not trying to get rid of my sisters—truly I'm not. But I need to focus. "Anton said you could come down after the game too."

"Seriously?" Noli pumps her fist into the air, and Poppy starts jumping up and down. "I can't wait to meet him!"

"Don't make me regret this," I mutter.

Poppy laughs and gives me a finger wave. She loops her arm with Noli's, and they skip off to find their seats.

I blow out a breath and turn my attention back to the field.

Anton is jogging to midfield with the other team captains for the coin toss. My pulse picks up. He's out there like a sitting duck. My gaze skitters around the stadium, but in a crowd of sixty thousand, how am I supposed to pick out any threats?

I don't take a breath until he's back on the River Foxes sideline. He won the toss, and the team deferred, so the defense will take the field after the kick off.

Anton stalks over to the bench, looking completely in control. He's the perfect mix of fierce football player and adorable boy next door—and yes, as my sisters so dutifully reminded me, a prince. He's the definition of the whole package. He pulls on a stocking cap that's River Foxes orange with the fox logo stitched on the front. I'm trying to keep my composure while I stare at him, but I suck in a hard breath when he glances over and our eyes lock. It feels like I've swallowed a shooting star. My throat goes dry, and my whole body tingles.

His game face is in place, but when he spots me, the edges of his mouth hitch upward ever so slightly. His gaze sweeps over me from my head to my toes and back up again. I'm a chocolate candy bar that's been left out in the sun—gooey and melty and kicking myself for feeling so sickly sweet about his attention.

What do I do? Nod? Smile? Ignore him?

He lifts a hand, and I think he's going to wave at me, but he swirls one finger around in a circle. He's asking me to twirl.

Do I feel slightly ridiculous? Yes.

Do I feel completely cherished? Also yes.

I do a slow spin so he can see the jacket from all angles.

When I make it around to be looking at him again, his eyes hold a darker glint than usual. I'm in a giant piece of outerwear. Not even something figure-flattering or objectively sexy, and yet, under Anton's gaze, I feel beautiful.

I gulp. I should not be enjoying this as much as I am. I need to ward off his attention and his affection, but it's hopeless. He makes me feel like I'm the only other person in this crowded, loud stadium.

I'm saved from doing something stupid like walking over to him, sitting down in his lap, and kissing him for all he's worth when the backup quarterback and their QB coach step in between the two of us, severing our stare-down. They move to sit on the bench next to Anton, and the coach shoves a tablet into his hands. He glances down at it, but he looks back up and meets my gaze.

And then, as if this were a romance novel, the man winks.

23
Someone to Play For

Anton

I'm not sure if this is the best football game of my career—you'd have to ask the stats guy—but it's got to be pretty dang close. I've thrown for four touchdowns and run for another one. The crowd in the River Foxes stadium is electric. We're completely crushing our opponent, the team from North Carolina, which is why, with eight minutes left in the fourth quarter and our offense on the field, I'm sitting on the bench.

I'm not complaining. I don't need to pad my stats. They're plenty cushioned. I also don't need to get a stupid injury when the game is well in hand.

Also, the view of Rose is better from over here. She looks incredible. She's trying to pay attention to the game, and she's making a good effort—I'll give her that—but her gaze keeps bouncing in my direction. Exactly where I like it. I'm flying high. Higher than I've been in a long time.

I wasn't sure how she'd react to my gift, but all signs point to it being a good idea.

TJ saunters over to me and plops down on the bench. "Heckuva game, 4."

"Back atcha."

"It looks like Operation Beauty and the Beast is firing on all cylinders." He looks pointedly in Rose's direction.

"It would seem so."

"Told ya the gift idea was a good one."

I nod.

Rose is looking down at her tablet. Her head pops up, and I hold my breath, waiting for her to look my way. She's been able to sense me staring at her all game, and it's like we've got our own little form of communication going on. I'm loving it.

My back-up takes a knee to run out the clock, and, as I hoped, Rose snags my eye. I can tell that she's trying—and failing—to fight a smile. I keep her in my periphery as I shake hands with the other team. She trails Ned, who pulls me to an open spot in the corner of the end zone.

"Can I...?" I motion back to Rose, but Ned gives me an apologetic look.

"Interview first here, then with her."

I grit my teeth but nod. I glance at Rose, but she's frowning down at her tablet.

Erin Thomas, the sideline reporter for KNOX NFL Sunday saddles up to me. "Anton, great game. Thanks for giving us some of your time."

"Happy to."

We make small talk for thirty seconds until her cameraman is in place, and she grins at him, nodding and obviously listening to the commentators from the booth in her ear. "Thanks, Jim." She turns to me. "Anton, you were on fire today. You've looked good all season, but what went especially right for you out there this afternoon?"

"The guys and I continue to find our stride as the season goes on. We were firing on all cylinders today. It's almost like we can read each other's minds. That comes from putting in the reps. There's stuff we'll continue to work on, obviously, but I like what I'm seeing."

"Your QB rating was nearly perfect. Did you do anything differently today to have such a standout performance?"

I *re-fell in love.*

I bite back that initial thought, though it's the truth. Ned and Rose are standing off to the side of the camera. Rose is looking at me now. Her eyebrows are arched, like she's waiting to hear my answer. I stare straight at her, and, like she knows exactly what I'm thinking, her cheeks flush a tantalizing pink. My chest puffs up because *my* attention did that to her.

She doesn't break eye contact, and I love her a little more for that. She's not about to back down from me, and it's invigorating. There's palpable tension between us, the good kind, like when someone tugs on the ends of a loose braid, drawing the strands together so they're snug and perfectly entwined.

You know who I'd like to be snug and perfectly entwined with? I'll give you three guesses and the first two don't count.

I hold Rose's gaze as I deliver my response, letting a sly grin spread across my face.

"I had someone here who I was trying to impress."

Rose's eyes widen and flicker with a hint of heat. I want to dive straight into the furnace, but then she shakes her head, smirking at me. She schools her features when Erin turns to try to follow my gaze off camera.

"Care to share who you were playing for?" Erin doesn't bother to mask her curiosity.

I'm acutely aware, in this moment, of how much I prefer having Rose ask me interview questions. Erin is good at her job, but it feels like she's out for the next big story. Rose has never once acted opportunistic with her questions, and she almost looks pained when she has to probe. A point in her favor, to be sure. I'm not about to spring the spotlight on her right now, not when the new relationship I'm painstakingly trying to build with her still feels so fragile.

"My cousin is here from Penwick. We used to play ball together as kids. I had to show him how far I've come from the days when he would kick my butt in the backyard." I grin.

I can't tell if Erin buys my answer, but she's a professional about it. "If he's your good luck charm, I'm guessing River Foxes Nation is going to want him in attendance for the rest of the season. Best of luck next week."

"Thanks. Go Foxes."

"Back to you, Jim."

The cameraman gives us the all-clear, and Erin thanks me for my time.

"Your cousin is a royal too, then, huh?" Erin's eyes dance. I bristle. She doesn't even know the guy. He could be a complete tool. He's not, but would she still be so keen to meet him if he was a regular Joe?

"Yep." I turn to go.

"Want to introduce me?"

"Sorry, Erin. I've got to get to the locker room for the team meeting and then the presser."

"You've got my number." She gives me a finger wave and turns to leave.

Finally.

Ned is next to me again. "You're all set to head to the locker room, Bates."

"Thanks, man."

He moves aside, and I fall into step with Rose.

I glance over at her. She's even more stunning up close. "Nice coat."

"This old thing?" She swings side to side. "Nice game."

"Eh. It was average."

Rose rolls her eyes. "So humble. But seriously, thank you for this." She holds out her arms, hands tucked under the sleeves of her jacket. "Unnecessary, but totally appreciated. This thing is like an oven. I've never been warmer." She tucks her chin into the high neckline.

I'm aware that there are cameras everywhere, so I'm careful not to let my emotions play across my face. I don't knock my shoulder into hers, like I'm dying to do. I don't smile. I keep my expression completely neutral, even though all the adrenaline that's coursing through me from my good game and from having Rose here, next to me, in a coat with my name on it, makes me want to scoop her into my arms, throw her over my shoulder, and take her someplace where I can kiss her without an audience.

Caveman much, Bates?

I spot Duke in his seat near the tunnel. He waves, and I grin at him. I'm looking forward to spending some more time with him this week, before my mom shows up for our family Christmas celebration.

I turn my attention to Rose. She's looking up toward Duke too.

"I've got to shower and do press. I can meet you right after that, though. It'll probably be another hour." I wince, hating when I'm an inconvenience to other people.

Rose doesn't seem fazed. "Sounds good. I'm going to collect my sisters. They really want to meet you."

"Yeah?" My heart rate kicks up. If I can impress Rose's family, that'll be another win for today.

"Yeah, for some odd reason," Rose deadpans. "It's like you're the star of the team or something."

She's teasing me. She's sort of flirting with me. This is good. This is very good.

"I'll go fast," I tell her as we split off, me to the locker room and her to corral her guests.

"I'll be here."

And dang it if I don't wish she means always.

24
DO YOUr JOB

Rose

Poppy is tittering about, talking a mile a minute about the game and about Anton and how incredible he played. "I'm serious, Rosie. Your man's out there like a real-life Superman."

"Poppy, if you don't stop calling him *my man*, I'm not letting you meet him," I scold. "We are co-workers. Less than that. I am interviewing him. He's my subject material."

"We can all imagine how you'd pore over him." Noli wags her brows.

"With attention to every single detail." Poppy grins.

"A fine-tooth-comb style treatment."

I look to Collin and Mack. "Can't you two do something about them?"

The men glance at each other and then back to me. Collin shrugs. "They're not wrong. Even I have a little bit of a guy-crush on Anton."

"Think he'll sign my jersey?" Mack asks.

I tip my head back.

My spy world and my real world are on a collision course, and it's got me completely off balance. I can't even blame my sisters. I was lulled into a false sense of security. I got caught up in watching Anton play as a fan of the game—as a fan of his—until I got a text message from headquarters during Anton's post-game interview, saying that Duke had given his assistant, aka the man put in place to keep an eye on him, the slip. Fortunately, another text came through shortly thereafter, giving the all clear.

Still, it was a sobering reminder that I need to keep my focus. I'm about to meet Duke in person for the first time, and I need to be on my game. I'm not sure how I'm supposed to do that with my sisters all but planning my wedding to a man I absolutely cannot fall for (again) and my brothers-in-law wanting to be his bestie.

The door to the team's private area swings open, and Anton appears, trailed by Duke and his good-for-nothing right-hand man. Seriously, the guy has one job. How does he lose his mark?

Anton's eyes sweep from Poppy, who's standing starstruck, to Noli, who gives him a small wave, to Collin and Mack, who chin-check him, and then they settle on me. His practiced smile melts into something more natural when his gaze connects with mine.

I, for one, have to work to keep breathing at regular intervals. Anton looks incredible. He's dressed in a perfectly tailored black suit coat and slim-fit trousers. He's got on a simple white V-neck t-shirt that's stretched to dangerous lengths across his broad shoulders. His collar bones seem to glisten. It's weird that I find his clavicles attractive. I get that. But here we are. There's something about the fact that all this muscle and bone coalesce to make a man who is so fully capable on the field and so willingly kind and helpful off the field. It's a deadly combination. One that apparently has me salivating at the mere sight of his collar bones.

His hair is damp from his shower, and it's curling on top, with that one strand dangling over his forehead in a perfect curlicue. My fingers itch to reach out and twirl it around. I drop my gaze. His feet are bare beneath snake-print loafers, and I bite back a smile. I make a mental note to ask him if his sockwear preference has changed since moving to a colder climate. Somehow, I doubt it, judging from his elected footwear tonight.

"My face is up here, Ms. Kapser." Anton's deep voice holds a smile.

I spring my gaze up to meet his laughing eyes.

"I know that." I sound defensive.

"Just teasing you." He grins at me. "Though, I have been told I've got excellent taste in shoes."

"You definitely do." Poppy steps forward and tucks her hand under my elbow, reaching out her opposite arm toward Anton. "Poppy Bradley. I'm Rose's older sister."

"Pleasure to meet you, Poppy. I've heard nothing but good things."

Poppy smiles, shooting me a look as if to say, *He's heard of me, and until today, I had no idea you two were ever a thing?*

I ignore her, motioning instead for Mack to step forward. "This is Poppy's husband, Mack. And you remember Noli and Collin from California."

Anton greets them with his characteristic warmth. They chat easily, and I try to ignore how well he fits right in to the group of us by turning my focus to Duke.

Also known as public enemy number one—to me, at least.

"Nice to see you again, Duke. Anton said you might be willing to talk to me for a feature piece I'm working on about him."

Duke smiles cordially. The resemblance between him and Anton is uncanny. They have the same ninety-degree-angle jaw and blond hair. Duke's eyes are brown where Anton's are blue-green, and he wears his hair shorter than Anton does, but they could be brothers.

"It would be my pleasure, Ms. Kasper. Anton says you're an excellent interviewer."

I refuse to be charmed by his kind eyes and friendliness. But I also need him to think I like him, so I smile back. "I'm sure he's embellished."

"No, I haven't." Anton pulls himself out the conversation he's having and winks at me again. "Why don't I give you guys the tour of the facilities here, and you can talk as we walk?" He looks to me and Duke to make sure we're okay with the plan.

I nod, and Duke sweeps his hand out in front of us, inviting Anton to lead the way.

Anton slips easily back into conversation with my family, and I tell myself I'm being ridiculous for the way my heart squeezes with jealousy. He's not paying me much attention. He's in full-blown host mode. He's good at it. But I would be lying if I didn't admit that I prefer when his attention rests solely on me.

See? This is another reason why Anton and I could never work. He's going to have a whole country who's looking to him for his attention. I'm too small a person to be able to handle that and not feel insecure.

"So…" Duke draws my attention. The two of us have fallen into step toward the back of the group. "What sorts of secrets can I tell you about my dear cousin Anton?"

"You tell me. He said y'all are close."

"Very." Duke nods. "Neither of us had siblings, but we had each other. We grew up together." Duke gets a faraway look in his eye. "Anton is the best of us, that much I'll tell you. He's always had the charitable heart. Sometimes to a fault."

"Go on."

"I worry that he's always giving of himself, never saying no. He needs to rein it in, or he's going to burn out. Look at what he's been doing for the past couple of years, juggling a high-profile job here in the States and the demands that come with being a professional athlete." Duke holds up fingers to track Anton's commitments. "Then there are his personal charities, the Penwick Palace charities, his duties as a royal. His obligations are enough to make a normal man dizzy."

I can't say I disagree, but I don't say anything in response, and Duke continues.

"I always wanted to be more like him, but I had a bit of a wild streak." Duke says this with the perfect mix of affection for Anton and self-deprecation.

I've got to hand it to the guy. He's definitely charming.

"I've only gotten Anton to break the rules with me on a couple of occasions. Some of my proudest moments," he adds with a grin.

"This sounds like the sort of thing I'd like to hear about for the article."

"Nothing so salacious," Duke assures me. "We did take one of the palace security vehicles for a joyride in the middle of the night before we had our licenses. I don't think Anton enjoyed one minute of it. He was so worried we were going to get caught. He drove ten miles under the posted speed limit the whole time. He didn't want to wreck the car or hurt someone. No matter that we were in the middle of nowhere in the middle of the night. That's Anton for you. Conscientious to a fault."

"Conscientious is a good word for him," I agree. "That seems to be a theme I've picked up on in my interviews with those who know him. How do you think he'll be as a ruler of Penwick?"

Duke glances ahead and stares at the back of Anton's head. "He'll be the best—if he makes it that far."

I nearly stumble over my feet, my guard flying up faster than a rocket being launched into the Texas sky. "Excuse me?"

Duke blinks and stares back at me, a sheepish expression passing over his features. "Look at him. He's happy here. I don't think he wants to be in Penwick. Do you?"

I feign composure and stare at Anton. I can't argue with Duke. Anton always has seemed more himself when he's talking football and dealing with personal charities as opposed to when he's with his mother or doing official Penwick business. But I never considered that he wouldn't go back to his home country.

"You said he's conscientious, sometimes to a fault. Won't that translate to undertaking his duty to Penwick?" I ask.

Duke tilts his head back and forth. "You're probably right, unless something comes up that forces his hand," he adds quietly.

Is that a threat? Is it a warning? Is it a premonition? Duke stares directly in my eyes, and the skin twists at the back of my neck with the full force of his appraising gaze.

Alarm bells blare in my ears, but I still don't have anything concrete linking Duke to any sort of attack on Anton. Out of the corner of my eye, I catch sight of his assistant, Charles, who I don't have much faith in anymore. He's been listening to our whole conversation, and it seems he, too, is poised and ready to step in or make a move if Duke lets anything slip about his plans to harm Anton.

We're a good distance back from where Anton has taken my family through the doors of the weight room. At least I can breathe easily knowing nothing's going to happen to him with them. I trust those four people implicitly.

If only Anton could say the same about his family. If only he *knew* that his cousin can't be trusted. I turn my focus back to Duke.

"You're the spare heir if I'm not mistaken." I'm impressed with my ability to keep my cool. Duke is an imposing figure, and in spite of all the charm he wields, there's something about him that feels off. Call it intuition. "How would you feel if…something came up and prevented him from taking his rightful position as leader of Penwick?"

Duke doesn't remove his penetrating gaze from my face for what feels like an obscene amount of time.

"That depends," he says finally.

"On what?"

"Whether it was his choice to abdicate or something else entirely."

"What else would it be?" I've stopped walking now, determined to get some real intel. My dad would tell me I'm pushing too hard, but I'm throwing the rule book out the window here. Anton deserves my best effort, and dang it, that's what I'm going to give him.

Duke shrugs and blinks, as if he's done with this conversation. "Your guess is as good as mine. I'm merely saying that I've considered the possibility. I'd be ready if I needed to step in. I love Penwick, and I would be proud to serve our people. That's another way Anton and I have always differed. I like the confines of our small island nation. It's comfortable to me. A safe place. I feel like we can make a difference right from our little corner of the world. But to Anton, Penwick feels like a prison. He's always wanted to get out."

I want to pound my head into the nearest wall. Nothing about this conversation has provided any clarity.

"If you'll excuse me for a moment, I need to use the restroom." Duke ducks into the bathroom, leaving me with Charles.

I turn to the man, who is nearly a foot taller than me. He rivals Anton in size, and he's got a hard look on his face.

"Is he always so forthcoming but not really forthcoming at the same time?" I ask.

Charles chuckles. "Basically. Duke is an enigma. That's why I'm here."

"You have any information for me?" I ask, my voice low.

He shakes his head once. "If I did, I'd share it through the proper channels." He glances around. "Not here, out in the open, where anyone could overhear."

I make a point of glancing around the deserted hallway, because give me a break. I'm done with this guy. "Stick close to him."

Charles's jaw clenches. "I don't take orders from you."

"Me telling you to do your job isn't an order. It's an expectation."

25

THE MATH WORKS

Anton

Rose hugs Poppy, Noli, Mack, and Collin goodbye before they leave the stadium.

"We'll see you tomorrow for book club," Noli calls over her shoulder. "Don't miss it."

"Seeing as how I'm running it, I think I'll be there," Rose says with an eye roll. "Sisters," she mutters.

I fight back a smile, even as the pit of longing in my chest turns into a Grand Canyon-style gorge. I envy the easy way the Kasper siblings interact and the love they extend to their family's newest members, Mack and Collin. There's obvious affection there.

As two-thirds of the Kasper sisters and their partners are in their car heading home, I am three-thirds confident that I want to be the final third to their family pie chart.

Don't question that. The math works.

"I hope they were alright." Rose draws me from my thoughts with a smidge of trepidation lacing her tone. "They can be...a lot."

"They're great," I assure her. "Did you get everything you needed from Duke?"

"Yep." She smiles brightly as he approaches with his assistant, Charles.

And I'm officially jealous of my cousin. I want Rose's smile pointed at me.

"I'll be in touch if I have follow-up questions," she adds with a glance in his direction as if to make sure that's alright.

"Sounds good." Duke looks at me. "We still on for tonight?"

I nod. "I'm going to finish up with Rose, but then I'm free."

"Good." Duke stifles a yawn. "I'm going back to the hotel to take a nap. I'll see you later."

We say goodbye. Charles gives me a long look before he trails Duke out into the parking lot. I've got to remember to ask Duke what gives with that guy. I saw him peering at Rose with a hard expression earlier. Something about him feels off.

I don't have much time to dwell on Charles. I promised Rose I'd answer some more of her questions in exchange for her letting me drive her back to Cashmere Cove. Not a bad tradeoff for some more time with her, if I do say so myself.

I lead Rose through the maze of hallways toward the players' exit.

Before we walk out into the arctic air, Rose tugs the front of her jacket together to zip it up.

Wait a minute...

I zone in on the jersey she's wearing underneath her coat. It's one from my days on the Mobile Tigers, when I wore number 8. How did I not notice it until right now?

She catches me staring, and her cheeks go pink.

"You kept it." My voice is barely above a whisper.

"Yeah, well." She looks away. "It's the only jersey I own," she says after a while.

My heart thumps up into my throat. I remember gifting it to her. Must've been only a couple weeks before she broke up with me. She pulled it on over her tank top, and it draped down to her knees, covering the shorts she was wearing. There was something heady about seeing her in it. Like it was a physical representation of blanketing her with my love.

Honestly, there's something heady about seeing her in it now...after all this time. "Means a lot to me that you still have it. That you wore it."

She lifts a shoulder, like it's no big deal. We walk out to my truck, and she explains, "Poppy needed something to wear, so I gave her my River Foxes one. I figured since I was wearing the coat over the top, it wouldn't matter if my jersey was dated."

She climbs into the passenger seat, and I close the door after her.

As I walk around the front of my truck, I replay what she just told me. I climb into my seat and face her. "You have a River Foxes jersey too?"

"What?" Rose's eyes go wide, and she sucks in a quick breath, as if she can't quite believe she let that fact slip out. "Oh…um…yeah."

I turn on the truck and get the heat blasting.

"I thought the Mobile jersey was the only one you owned," I say casually after a moment.

She shakes her head, pressing her lips together.

"Did the front office hook you up with my jersey after you started working on the feature piece, or what?"

"Not exactly," she hedges. "I guess I should have clarified that yours are the only jerseys I own. But I have multiple."

I run my gaze back and forth across her face. "When did you get the River Foxes jersey?"

She won't meet my eyes. "When I moved up here."

I do some quick mental math. "You've had my jersey for over a year?"

Rose squirms in her seat. "Yes."

The seed of hope in my chest has grown into a full-blown tree. There are lush leaves and sturdy branches, and look, there's a hammock where Rose and I can cuddle up together.

What I want out of my life hits me with the force of a linebacker barreling into me for a sack. I want Rose by my side. I want to make her smile. I want my last name to be hers. I want her wearing my jersey, or my shirt, or my sweatshirt, or whatever. I want her.

I'm about ready to tell her all that too. I've ticked off two of the suggestions the guys had for me: gift giving and quality time. The one that's left is communicating my feelings—or, in Del's words,

"Laying your heart on the line and being prepared to have it flame-fried again."

Quite the visual.

But not right now. It's been a long day, and I get the sense she's embarrassed about me finding out about her secret jersey stash. There will be a moment for the deep heart-to-heart, but right now, I want to keep things light, so I let her off the hook.

"Tell me about book club."

26

BOOK CLUB

Rose

Mood Reader is sparkling tonight. The flurrying snow from outside is making all the streetlights dance, and the reflection bouncing off the large front window of the bookstore is magical.

"You think we need more chairs?" Mia sets down a couple folding chairs and shoves her hair behind her ear.

"I'm going to grab a handful from the back." My spirits are high. I've given myself permission to turn off my undercover brain for tonight. I spoke with Lennox earlier, and he assured me that Anton is well looked after. I'm trying to trust that and take advantage of a night of peace.

This is my favorite night of the month. I started a romance book club as one of my first initiatives when Mia hired me on, and it's ballooned as interest has grown. My sisters started coming, at first to support me and so I wouldn't be the only one in attendance, but now I think they genuinely enjoy reading the books.

The jingle bell we've affixed above the door for the holiday season clangs, and Poppy and Noli tumble in, stomping their boots to rid them of snow. They slough off their jackets and hug me hello.

Poppy inhales. "Smells amazing in here."

"It's the books," I quip.

"No, it's cinnamon."

"Oh, right. I made homemade cider."

"Gram's recipe?" Noli licks her lips.

I nod. "Duh."

"Gimme." The two hurry toward the food and drink table we have set up in front of the check-out counter.

I smile as they stop to hug Mia before helping themselves to piping-hot mugs.

The jingle bell above the door starts jangling again in quick succession as the rest of our club members join us.

Inez, the owner of the Getaway Café in town, has a box in her hands. "I brought cookies and day-old pastries, in case anyone wants one."

"You're the best. Thank you." I point her to the food table, and she joins my sisters.

Willow Dunlap, a septuagenarian with the heart of a teenager, shuffles through the door followed by Collin's mom, Beverly. She makes a beeline for Noli, and the two women hug hello. I love that book club is multi-generational. We all bring our experiences to the stories we read and, subsequently, to the discussions we have.

And yes, we *do* actually discuss the books at this book club. And yes, romance novels *do* provide great fodder for discussion.

I'm willing and able to fight anyone who says something different.

I've heard my fair share of pushback from people who call them a waste of time. Folks who argue they aren't really literature. The same ones who'll never give a romance novel a five-star review because it's not, say, *War and Peace*.

To them I say, go away.

Romance novels do something for people's spirits. Romance is an outlet of hope. Believing in love is nothing to be ashamed of. This group functions as a safe space to enjoy this type of story. I'd like to think that we all go out and try to love the people in our real life better after reading and discussing these titles too. What more could you ask for out of a book?

The door whooshes open again, and Abner, who works for the Cashmere Cove Street Department walks in with his wife, Kelsey.

The two of them read our books out loud together, which, quite frankly, is the most adorable thing I've ever heard. If I don't find myself a partner who will read out loud with me, I don't want one.

My mind paints a mental picture of Anton sitting on the couch in The Downer with my feet in his lap. In my vision, I'm listening as his low voice bowls me over with text from a crisp paperback we've picked up from Mood Reader on a Sunday afternoon after one of his games. It's unreal how quickly I can conjure an image like this. It's torture, actually. Because I can see it so clearly. Anton would read books with me. I know he would. I know he's perfect for me. But how can I let myself be with him?

This is the mental tug of war I have going on.

I shut it down for now, turning my focus back to Abner and Kelsey. Ab is our only male book club member…so far. I'm holding out hope for more. Romance doesn't discriminate.

Mia breaks off from the group by the food table, a mug in her hands. She joins me near the front of the bookstore, taking a drink of the steaming liquid.

"I think we'll get started here shortly." I do a quick head count. "All our regulars are here, and I'm not expecting anyone else."

Mia nods.

The jingle bell rings behind me, and Mia and I spin toward the door.

Anton appears out of the snow, his broad shoulders filling the entire space between the door jambs. His gaze locks on me, and he smiles. It's a smile that's like my favorite book—beginning, middle, and ending all working together to tell a perfect story. There's a hint of mischief, a dash of anticipation, and a whole dollop of sweetness in that smile. The sight of it—of him—fills me with the warmth of mulled cider.

"Anton! What are you doing here?"

It's my night off from you.

Don't even act like you aren't happy to see him.

My brain is carrying on a back-and-forth conversation with itself.

Well, duh. But still. *This is not helping my effort to not fall for him.*

Just go with it.

"I came for book club. I hear it's the place to be on a Monday night."

My jaw is hanging half unhinged, but I'm helpless to control it. He asked me about book club yesterday, and I was so grateful to talk about something that wasn't me owning multiple versions of his jersey that I told him all about it. But...

"I didn't expect you to come," I squeak.

"Well, surprise." He winks at me before turning his gaze and gesturing around the store. "It looks great in here."

I survey Mood Reader, trying to see it through Anton's fresh eyes. We've got our holiday displays set up, with evergreen wreaths dangling from the shelf lights that are affixed to the tops of each bookcase. On each wreath, Mia and I have tied long red ribbons that dangle down. Above the shop's front window, icicle lights are hung from the ceiling, casting a warm glow on the glass panes. In the display case, we've created a Christmas tree out of books, stacking them in all directions, so they're fanned out like branches. I wound a string of multicolored lights around the spines and tucked the wires between the pages. The result is whimsical and charming and everything I want a bookstore to be. We've got cozy and Christmas-y displays on each of our free-standing tables throughout the store, and velvet table runners in different hues of reds and greens serve as a backdrop for the stacks of titles we're featuring. The gas fireplace along the side wall is festooned with an evergreen swag and snow-white, knit stockings are hung with care. A sign on the mantel encourages our patrons to drop off a pair of new socks in the basket on the hearth. I pitched it to Mia this morning, and we decided we'll collect socks and donate them to the local community shelter for those who could use them.

"Thank you." I'm proud of this store, but I remember myself then. Even Mood Reader, where I feel most at home, isn't mine to claim. It's another sobering reminder that I have nothing to my name. Not really. "It's Mia's place," I say, and I have to work to keep my tone even. "I just work here."

I tug my boss and friend forward. To her credit, Mia doesn't look as starry-eyed as most people do in the presence of a prince and a pro-football player. Then again, maybe she doesn't know who he is.

"Anton Bates." Mia steps forward and holds out her hand. "I have you on my fantasy team. You helped me crush my husband this week, and I thank you for that." She grins. "It's a pleasure to meet you. We spoke on the phone."

Anton grins and shakes her hand. "Thanks for having me. Happy to be of assistance with the fantasy team as long as you don't hold it against me and ban me from book club if I have an off week."

"Wouldn't dream of it. We're anti all things book banning around here. Right, Rosie?"

"Uh-huh." When Anton turns to hang his coat up, I hiss out of the corner of my mouth, "You knew he was coming?"

She cuts me with a look. "He called to make sure it was okay. I said all are welcome. Isn't that what you're always saying?"

"Of course." I frantically tug at the neckline of the ratty crewneck sweater I'm wearing. It says *Bookworm* across the chest in faded, varsity letters. Perfect for book club. Maybe not perfect when I'm standing in front of a man who's so far out of my league he may as well be on another planet.

I give myself a mental shake. I've never been self-conscious about my appearance or social standing around Anton before. I'm not going to start now.

He's not wearing a stocking hat, so there are snowflakes resting on his blond locks, slowly melting and turning strands of his hair darker. He gives his head a small shake, and a curl dips over his brow as he turns back in our direction.

"I hope it's okay. Me dropping in on you like this." His eyes are on me, and I feel like I'm a bird he's watching through binoculars. "I figured you've had to follow me around for the past week and a half. It's about time I spent some time in your space."

"That's..." *So thoughtful.* I don't even know what to say, and my throat feels like it's lodged with dough. "...good," I choke out.

"Yeah? You sure?"

"Mm-hmm." I glance up at him. "Thanks for coming."

My word, he's so good looking. Good looking and thoughtful. A lethal combination. I want to bull rush him, curl up in his arms, and ask him to hold me forever.

But I can't do that. I've got a book discussion to lead.

I curse. Because *of course* Anton is here—on the night we're discussing a Christmas romance. And not any Christmas romance. A royal one.

"What's that?" Anton says on a chuckle. "Everything okay?"

"Oh yeah. Fine. It's...nothing. I just said, 'S*hi*-ouldn't be long now.'"

His eyes are dancing the Macarena. "S*hi*-ouldn't be long now before what?"

"Before we get started. Come on in." I swallow and lead him toward the group.

I can do this. What's a little romantic book discussion between exes?

When one of them is an inch away from not wanting to be exes anymore?

With an audience of my sisters and my boss and half the town?

Piece of freaking cake.

• • • • • • • • •

"What I want to know," Mia says, "is how she found her way back through the palace in time when she was trying to stop Prince Augustine from marrying that other woman."

"My heart was pounding through that entire section." Willow Dunlap sits forward in her chair. "Like, was she going to make it? She had to make it, right? But boy did the author have me hooked, waiting to see how."

"I love that he was interrupting his own wedding before she had a chance to have her speak-now moment." Abner rubs his chin, and his wife nods.

Next to him, she adds, "If it would have only been Gianna giving her declaration of love, I wouldn't have bought in. I needed to see both characters choose each other. I love how it played out."

"And that kiss." Mia fans herself. "Worth the wait."

"Amen, sister." Bev holds up her mug in salute, and there's a general murmur of agreement.

I smile to myself. I don't know what I was worried about. Our discussion of A *Royal Christmas Wedding* has gone off without a hitch. Just like every book club, I'm tickled with the conversation, and I already want to read the book again to see if I agree with Abner about the foreshadowing the author laid down about the next book in the series.

"Anton, since you're here," Poppy pipes up from her seat on a stool near the stacks, "care to give us any insight into royal life? Did the author misconstrue anything?"

I hold my breath as every eye in the room turns and lasers in on Anton.

He takes this in stride, the only sign of any slight discomfort at the attention is the hint of pink that graces the tops of his cheek bones. He unfolds the leg he had draped over his opposite knee and sits back in his chair. I'm waiting for him to say he hasn't read the book, so he can't comment, but then he shocks me when he nods.

"I'd say the way Prince Augustine is described as being torn between his responsibility to the crown and the feelings of his heart is very accurate."

My own heart pinches. He's speaking from experience. I want to pull him into a hug, and stroke his hair, and protect him from the feeling of being pulled in two.

"But," Anton goes on, "there are obviously some stereotypes employed here. At least in Penwick, we don't eat the same breakfast every day. Though admittedly, Prince Augustine getting sick of hardboiled eggs made for some serious humor, didn't it?"

The whole group titters, and I think I might combust. If I thought Anton was attractive before, hearing him discuss a romance novel has taken him to the next level.

"And we aren't required to wear formal wear to dinner every night—though my mother would probably prefer that. I'm afraid she thinks I'm positively uncouth with my sportswear."

The circle chuckles again.

My goodness, the man dazzles.

"I wonder what it would be like to fall in love with a royal," Inez says on a sigh.

"Not all it's cracked up to be, I'm sure," Anton says with adorable self-deprecation.

"It is." The words tumble from my mouth before I can stop them, like a child's block tower knocked over with a chubby, baby arm.

"Oh, do tell." Noli has a Cheshire grin on her face. "Can you speak from experience?"

Anton's gaze has snapped to mine, and he's not taking his eyes off me. It's like he's a magnet, and I'm a collection of pencil shavings. Every part of me is flying toward him on a collision course. Everyone else is eyeing me with interest too. Great.

I scramble for something—anything—to say to appease the group, and to save face.

"I just mean that we shouldn't sell royals short."

Poppy rolls her eyes. "We're not selling them short, Rose. Everyone knows that with money and a title comes privileges. That's an added bonus."

I frown. "That's not really what I mean, though."

"Oh? What did you mean, hon?" Willow, bless her, is giving me an innocent look. Little does she know she's putting me on the hot seat.

I make an active effort not to look at Anton as I formulate my response. "Royals are regular people underneath their title," I begin carefully. "With anybody, royal or not, if the person is right, then dating them would just click. Take the title away from Augustine," I say, bringing us back to the book and hoping it takes some of the focus off of me, "and he's still the same person Gianna fell in love with. She likes him for him. Not for his title or the perks that come with it. And vice versa. Augustine fell for Gianna not because of what she could give him but because of who she is as a person."

"Well said." Mia nods. "On that note, we're almost out of time for this evening. But please grab an extra treat on your way out. We'll email out details about next month's book, so watch your inboxes for that."

I slump into my seat, letting out a breath of relief as the book club members stand and stretch, breaking off into small groups to continue the discussion or make small talk.

Anton gets swept up in a conversation with Abner and Kelsey, and I take advantage of the distraction to put some distance between myself and our resident prince.

Poppy and Noli are waiting for me by the cider.

"Good discussion, huh?" I speak first in an effort to head off any smart comments.

My efforts are in vain.

"It was delightful," Poppy agrees. "But let's not ignore the elephant in the room."

"What elephant?" I make a show of scanning the stacks and craning my neck this way and that. "I see no elephant."

"How about the prince in the room, then?" Noli deadpans. "Seriously, Rosie. What is your deal? Why are you not jumping his bones?"

"Hey now. No need to go *that* far," Poppy protests. "But the sentiment remains," she adds. "You two obviously have feelings for each other."

"Obviously? Who is that obvious to?"

"The entire room here, for starters," Noli scoffs. "He couldn't keep his eyes off of you the entire time we were discussing the book. The fact that he's even here should tell you all you need to know."

"That he likes romance novels?"

Noli sticks out her tongue at me, but Poppy tips her head to the side. "Wouldn't that be a point in his favor?"

She's got me there.

"That. And you know what I meant," Noli says sternly. "He's here for you. He wants to spend time with you. I know we don't know your history with him, but I'm telling you this because I love you, Rosie, and because I can speak from experience. Don't let what happened in the past dictate your present or future happiness. Sometimes you have to take a leap of faith."

I bite my lip, chancing a quick glance at where Abner and Kelsey are saying goodbye to Anton.

"You really think he likes me?" I hate how small I sound, how much I need to hear my sisters build me up. "Because I wasn't the greatest to him in Mobile."

Understatement of the century.

"He's into you, Rosie," Poppy says, and Noli nods. "Trust us."

I blow out a breath, my mind a tangled mess of what I want and what I should or shouldn't want. What I deserve and don't deserve. Nothing about this relationship—or potential relationship—with Anton will be easy. Then again, is anything worth having ever easy?

"We're here for you. You know that, right?" Poppy grabs my wrist and gives it a quick squeeze. "If there's something you want to talk about, you know where to find us."

"Just because we're partnered off doesn't mean we don't have time for you," Noli adds.

My throat is tight with emotion. "I know," I manage to croak out. "Thanks for saying it, though."

Poppy and Noli give me hugs and say goodbye to Mia. I wave as they head out into what's turned into a full-fledged blizzard.

The rest of the book club patrons take their leave shortly thereafter, and I get busy on my nightly checklist, tidying up the store and getting things back in order so we're ready to open tomorrow.

"You want these chairs somewhere special?" Anton appears with a folding chair under each arm and two more in each hand.

"You don't have to do that." I shake my head. "I got it."

"It's not a big deal. I'm happy to help."

Before I can answer, Mia joins us. She's covering her mouth with her hand. "Rosie, I'm not feeling the greatest all of a sudden."

"Oh no. What do you need?"

"My stomach is really off. I need to lie down. I hate to leave you with this mess."

"It's no problem. I've got—"

"Me." Anton shoots me a triumphant grin. "I'll stay and help her."

I roll my eyes at him before turning my attention to my boss, who, even in the twinkling lights of the dimly lit bookstore, looks a bit green. "Are you okay to drive home?"

Mia shakes her head. "I called Patrick. He's coming to get me. We'll worry about getting my car sometime tomorrow."

"Or later this week. I can cover the store if you want to rest."

"I'm sure I'll be fine. Just need a good night's sleep." Mia offers me a faint smile and grabs her coat and bookbag from behind the counter.

Patrick's truck appears through the front window a moment later, and I walk her out to him.

He hops out of the truck and circles the front of it. "Hey, babe. You okay?"

Mia leans into his hug. "I want our bed." She presses a hand to her stomach. "I feel so sick."

"Let's get you home, then." He helps her into her seat and closes the door. "Thanks for handling the shop, Rose."

"Of course. Take care of her, and let me know if you need anything. I hope she recovers quickly."

A look I can't quite place passes over Patrick's face, but then he smiles. "We will. Thanks again."

I hurry back to the store as he pulls away from the curb. My breath catches as I take in the scene of the whole road. All the businesses lining Main Street are done up for the holidays, and the oversized trees beyond the buildings are wound with small glittery lights. They peek out over the top of the cityscape and provide a warm, festive backdrop.

I love this place. I didn't set out to love it, but now that I do, the thought of leaving here for the foreign affairs job when I get promoted leaves a sour taste in my mouth.

I'm not sure how long I stand outside, lost in the maze of my own thoughts and feelings, when the door to Mood Reader opens inward, and Anton pops his head outside.

"Rose? What are you doing? You're going to catch pneumonia out here." He strides forward and grabs my hand, tugging me back inside.

It's only after the warmth of Mood Reader hits my skin that I realize I'm shaking.

"Are you okay?" Anton looks me up and down. He grabs a blanket that we have tossed over one of our comfy chairs and drapes it over my shoulders.

"I'm f-fine. I was admiring Main Street."

"Could you maybe do that in less inclement weather?" He's teasing me, but his eyes are kind. "What else do you need me to do?"

I tuck the blanket more firmly around my arms. I could protest his help. I could tell him to leave. But that's not what I want. Not really. He won't listen to me anyway. The man's heart is too big. Like, doctors should study it to see if it's actually oversized, because judging from the outpouring of his time and talents—with not only me but everyone around him—he's got more in the cardiac capacity department than most.

"If you wouldn't mind sweeping the floor. I've got to clean up the leftover cider."

He sets off, and we work quietly. It doesn't take long to get the bookstore back in order. I flip the overhead lights off so the twinkle lights are all that illuminate the space.

Anton comes to stand next to me. "You should be proud."

I side-eye him.

He catches my gaze. "Of what you built, I mean. Everyone here obviously loves book club as much as you do."

"I hope they do. But it's just book club. Nothing ground-breaking," I say, even if, for me, it's something to look forward to each month. I doubt everyone else, with their lives together and other things on their dockets, cares as much as I do.

I'm waiting for him to say goodnight and head out into the storm. But he seems content to stand next to me, staring out at the snow. The scent of cedar and cinnamon that's wafting off of him makes my brain feel sleepy and fuzzy, like someone spiked my cider. It's nice, this letting-loose feeling. I know I should fight it, but my reasons for doing so are becoming flimsier and flimsier by the minute.

"You should give yourself more credit." Anton's voice is low and kind.

"What do you mean?"

"You're undercutting your efforts and the work you put in to making something truly good. I wish you wouldn't."

I sigh. "Why are you doing this?"

He arches an eyebrow. "What? Standing here with you?"

I shake my head. "No. Being so nice to me. You didn't have to come here. You didn't have to stay and help me clean up. You don't have to tell me I should give myself more credit. I don't understand your motivations."

"My motivations?" Anton's eyes take on a hungry gleam, and I'm suddenly well-aware of the feeling his opponents get when he surveys the defense, ready to pick it apart play by play. I have a total-body feeling he's about to puncture a hole in every one of my arguments and shred my own personal defense.

"Yeah. I don't get you." I cross my arms and face him, ready for the onslaught but not really ready at all.

"Then let me make myself very clear. My motivation is you and you alone, Rose."

I tip my chin up at him. "Don't."

"Don't what?"

"Anton." I inhale. "You know what. I'm not the kind of girl you need. I was awful to you all those years ago. You...we...we shouldn't. You shouldn't fall for me."

"I can't," he says with a huff.

"You...can't?"

"Don't you get it?" He takes a step closer to me. "I can't help it. I can't stop myself. I can't *not* love you. I've tried. For years, I tried. Heck, you gave me every reason in the world back in Mobile to give up on us, and I took what you said at face value. But I've missed you every dang day. And now that you're here, and I'm here, and I've gotten a feel for you in my life again, I've reverted to all my old ways. I wake up in the morning and think about what you might be thinking about. I'm out there on the field, working my tail off on the off chance you might see me play and be impressed. I want to do it all for you and with you. You told me you didn't want me, Rose, but I don't believe you. Because you have my jersey. You brought my friends gifts. You told your book club that dating a royal wouldn't be so bad if it's the right royal. I think I'm the right royal for you. I'm the right man for you. And I don't want to try not to love you anymore. I want you. I want to love you. I think you want that too. So would you just let me?"

He sucks in a ragged breath, and I stare up at him. My mind is completely full of his words.

Of him.

How can I deny my feelings for him when he laid his feelings so bare? I can't. I won't.

I step toward him. Slowly, I place my hand on his chest. He's stock still, his gaze like lava fire, coursing over my skin.

"So, I guess the truth is finally out there, then?" I put my other hand at the nape of his neck, and his eyes flutter shut. "About your tattoo, that is."

He blinks and stares down at me. "My tattoo?"

"I'm guessing you don't have a thing for *Beauty and the Beast* after all."

He chuckles softly. It's low and throaty, and his gaze is even more determined now. "I only have a thing for you."

I pull his face down to mine, and I kiss him.

It's slow and sweet, both of us reacclimating ourselves to something that once felt as natural as breathing. My entire body hums to life, like I've grown a new set of nerve endings, and they're crackling to attention. Anton's fingers run up and down my back, and instinctively my spine tightens and I arch closer to him. His soft touches are tantalizing and careful. His hands find my waist, and he squeezes above my hips, holding me upright. It's a good thing, too, because even though in the grand scheme of kisses, this one's pretty chaste, it still has me feeling like my skeleton might liquify and leave the rest of me a pile of mush on the floor.

Anton spears his hands through my hair, his thumbs coming to rest on the hollow below my ears. He takes his time, and I whimper because I want more. He's warm and solid, and I can't get enough. I press my body closer to him.

He responds immediately, replacing gentleness with power as he scoops me into his arms, putting his hands under my thighs. I wrap my legs around his waist while he backs me to the nearest bookshelf. He sets me on my feet and proceeds to make me feel lit up all over, like I'm a human twinkling light. I've been asleep for the past five years, and now I'm awake and the sunrise is breath-stealing.

He's everywhere, all at once. His capable, commanding hands hold me like I'm precious and like I'm *his*. Like he won't let anything else touch me, because that's his job. He splays one palm on my back, pulling me close to him and then leaning in. He anchors us both to the bookcase with the delicious weight of his body. His other hand traces a scorching path along my ribcage, up to the column of my neck, and around the shell of my ear before he angles my jaw and continues to have his way with my mouth.

My hands are greedy as they fly over the contours of his arms and shoulders. The pads of my fingers connect with the exposed skin at the back of his neck, and it's hot to my touch. He groans into my mouth as I knead it tenderly before lacing my fingers through his hair. I relish the silky softness of it and then tighten my grip and use it to get the leverage I'm craving to tug his mouth harder to mine.

We go back and forth, a give-and-take kiss that encompasses everything I want in a partnership. It's playful and serious. Soft and strong. He's cherishing me. I'm treasuring him. It's a selfless kiss. A competition to see who can take better care of the other, and we're both winning.

We spend a long time, lost in each other, before Anton drags his lips from mine and starts trailing kisses along my jaw.

"I've missed you every single day, Sammy Rose." His mouth is dry ice, making me hot and shivery all at once. He's powerful and controlled and wholly focused on me. *Me.*

"I've longed for you," he scrapes out.

I wrap my arms around his neck, clinging to him as I whisper, "Yes."

He freezes for a moment before shifting and forcing me to look at him. His eyes are dilated to a point where I can't see any blue or green...only inky black pools of love and hope. He's fighting to get his breathing under control. I can feel his heart pounding.

"Yes what?"

"Yes. I want you to love me."

He exhales a shuddering breath and buries his head in the crook of my neck. I hold him as he holds me.

Somewhere in the back of my mind, I know this has the potential to be a terrible idea—to crash, burn, and implode spectacularly. Because doing this with Anton again means turning my back on my job with the agency and forfeiting the overseas career move. It means I'll need to stand up to my father—and Anton's mother, if it comes to it—and come clean with Anton about what I've been doing and who I've been working for. The only way it'll work between us is complete honesty. I owe him that. The thought is terrifying, but not as terrifying as living one more day without at least trying to make something work with the best man I've ever known.

I'll figure that all out tomorrow...or the next day. For now, I want to stay right here, in a bookstore bubble with Anton. Because for the first time in five years, I feel like I know who I am. I'm a woman in love with a man who happens to be a prince and a pro-football player, and he loves me back.

27

A GIRL TO SEE ABOUT

Anton

Practice runs long on Tuesday, and I'm scurrying around the locker room after my shower, trying to get my life organized so I can get the heck out of there.

"Someone's in a hurry." TJ comes out of the shower with a towel tied low on his waist.

"Didn't you hear?" Del pipes up from where he's lacing his shoes. "Our boy has himself a hot date."

TJ shoots me an affronted look. "Dude! When were you going to tell me?"

"I'm telling you right now." I fumble with my cologne. I can't get my finger to connect with the nozzle, and when it does, I accidentally spray myself much more directly than I intend. "Dang it."

Poe waves his hand in front of his face to redirect some of the smell. "Easy, killer. You don't want to singe her nose hairs."

The guys chuckle. I scowl at them. "Excuse me for being a little nervous. I want everything to be perfect. This is our second chance."

"Did she tell you what happened back in Mobile?" Del asks.

"Not yet. But I plan to talk it all out with her."

TJ slaps me on the back on his way to his locker before spinning around and dropping his towel, giving us all a full-frontal view of his birthday suit. "Open communication is the way to go, that's what I always say."

"A little less open communication from you would be appreciated." I cover my eyes with my hand. "And I agree. I'm going to talk to Rose about our past. But not today."

"Why not?" Del asks, worry pulling the skin of his forehead into three lines.

"Because today, I'm meeting her in Cashmere Cove so she can show me around her new hometown. It's a night to reconnect and get to know each other. There'll be time for honest conversations about the past and the future. Today, I want to live in the present."

"Too bad your present smells like an overeager pine forest." Poe plugs his nose.

I shove him into the nearest locker and swing my duffel over my shoulder. I exit the locker room to the heckles of the guys, but I can't stop grinning.

I've got a girl to see about.

I make the scenic drive to Cashmere Cove. Last night's blizzard left the tree limbs that form the canopy over the winding peninsula roads coated with snow, like salt on the rim of a spicy margarita glass.

Rose texted me the address to a Mexican restaurant where I'm meeting her for dinner, so the analogy feels applicable, if not particularly seasonal.

Then again, do margaritas ever go out of season? I think not.

I follow my GPS to the address, which, as it turns out, isn't far from Mood Reader. I ease my way down Main Street, slick with ice and slush beneath the weighty wheels of my truck. Cashmere Cove glows in the evening twilight. The town is small, and yet I don't feel closed in here. It feels more like a resting spot. A place to come home and recover before going back out into the world and doing the work.

It's contrary to how I feel about Penwick, which has always felt more like a jail cell.

I mentally brush off all thoughts about my home country, the responsibilities awaiting me there, and my feelings about it all. I want my sole focus to be on Rose.

I snag a parking spot on the street outside Lupe's. The restaurant is set in a long narrow building, and when I walk through the front door, the smell of homemade tortilla chips tickles my nose. It's heavenly. I glance around the dimly lit space and spot Rose immediately. She's tucked into a small table for two in the corner, her nose pressed into a book.

I take a minute to study her here. Her short hair is draped over one eye, and she shoves her hand up to keep it out of her face, resting her elbow on the table in the process. Her posture is terrible as she hunches forward, so engrossed in the story it's like she can't be bothered to consider her spine's alignment. She nibbles her lip as her eyes scan the words on the page.

I could watch her like this all night. That's always been how I am with Rose. She could be doing the most mundane thing in the world—washing the dishes, flossing, talking about the weather—and I'd be content to be in her presence.

Her head snaps up when the hostess greets me, and she presses the book closed, a tentative smile seeping over her face. She's wearing red lipstick, which is a change. I like it. A lot. I want to ruin it with another mind-bending kiss like the one we shared at the bookstore, which I haven't been able to stop replaying in my mind. But there'll be time for that.

Time.

What a happy thought. All I've ever wanted is more time with Rose, and now I've got it. I feel like a kid on Christmas morning.

I tell the hostess I'm all set and hurry across the restaurant. Rose stands from her table, and I wrap my arms around her, drawing her as close to me as possible and holding her to my chest.

She lets loose a surprised laugh and then a content hum. She places her arms around my midsection, and we stand there, embracing each other. It's the best hug of my life.

I didn't get a lot of hugs from my mother—the queen of air kisses—and I never really thought much about what I was missing, but there's something tender and sweet about the simple gesture of holding and being held. Like two people are both in it just because they want to be close—no ulterior motives, no presumptions, no strings, no expectations.

Rose leans away slightly and smiles up at me. "What was that for?"

Her skin shimmers in the lights of the restaurant, and I drag my thumb across the angle of her jaw. "Honestly, I don't know," I admit. "I hope it's okay."

She nods quickly. "I'll never say no to a hug from you. You're a good hugger."

I'm inordinately proud to hear her say that. "Good hugger." I beam down at her as I pull out her chair for her. "Put it on my tombstone."

28
SNOW GLOBE REDEMPTION

Rose

Anton and I shared a filet mignon fajita and a platter of grilled shrimp tacos, and all the while, he stared at me with such hunger in his eyes it made it nearly impossible for me to eat. He insists on paying, and when we stand, he helps me slide into my jacket. I wore the one that he got for me. Maybe it's overkill, but it's the warmest piece of clothing I own. And I love having his name on my back.

"This jacket is the coolest," he says, as I zip it up. "And it's good luck, so I think you should wear it again to our next home game."

"You think I'm going to show up to all your home games now, do you?" I'm feeling feisty and high on his attention.

His forehead puckers. "I wouldn't want to assume. I figured for the article...I don't know. I'd never force you to come and watch me play. I—"

"Anton." I grab his forearm. "I'm kidding. Of course I'll be there. And not for the article." I pause, the reality of my situation threatening to press in and ruin this perfect evening, but I kick it away with a firm boot. "I want to be there. Can I tell you a secret?"

"Yes."

We step out onto Main Street, and he stands next to me. I can't believe I'm about to admit this, but I tell myself it's the first step toward total honesty with a guy I want a future with.

"You know how I have your jersey? Well, jerseys, multiple," I add with a chagrinned smile.

"Uh-huh." He's staring at me with the full force of his gaze.

"And you know how I told you I bought the River Foxes one when I moved to Wisconsin?"

"Mm-hmm." He shifts to tuck a strand of hair behind my ear. The wind kicks it immediately back into my face, and he repeats the gesture.

"I got the jersey because I planned to go to some River Foxes games. To watch you. And I needed something to wear."

His eyes widen and then narrow, a slow smile sauntering across his face. "How many games have you been to, Rosie?"

"A few." I bite my lip.

He touches my elbow. "What's a few?"

"All the home games."

"Rose!"

"It's not a big deal."

"It's a big deal to me."

"Well…okay, then. Now you know." I grab for his hand. "I don't want you to think I wouldn't want to show up for you. Because I do."

He gazes down at me, and I can see the carousel of questions flickering through his eyes. He's probably wondering why I would follow his career. Why I would support him from the nosebleeds when I forfeited the chance to have a front-row seat to his life.

I can't answer those questions for him. Not right now. I need to talk to my dad. I need to figure out a game plan. So, I do the one thing I've wanted to do since he walked into the restaurant looking more delicious than the fish tacos.

I grab the lapels of his peacoat, pull myself flush with his chest, and kiss him.

And suddenly, I'm changing my tune about being inside a snow globe. Because this…here…in his arms, with my lips against his, and the snow falling down around us, and the lights from the streetlamps glistening…it's actually pretty darn spectacular.

I'm not even cold.

Someone whistles at us from across the street, bursting our bubble. We lean back, both chuckling. I get a good look at Anton's mouth and gasp. "I got lipstick all over you."

I reach up to rub the red stain from around his lips.

He catches my fingers with his hand and presses them to his lips in an achingly sweet movement. "I'm not too worried. I've been thinking about messing up your lipstick since I walked into the restaurant."

My stomach swoops. "Do you have to get back to Green Bay right away?"

"I'm not in any hurry."

I smile to myself at that. "Want to walk?"

"With you? Always. But it's freezing out here. You sure you're okay being out in the elements?"

"Yeah. It's funny. It's like when I'm with you, my body heat skyrockets. Wonder why?"

"I'm going to take that as the highest of all compliments from my favorite ice queen."

I laugh as we stroll down Main Street. "I want to show you Wool Beach. It's not really the season for it, but in the summer months, it's one of our favorite spots."

Anton nods. "I want to see it all."

I nuzzle closer to him, feeling at once like I could fly and, at the same time, be completely grounded. Being here, next to him, is like curling up in front of a warm fireplace with a book that'll take me to a far-off land.

In a word, perfection.

29
ABDICATING

Anton

As Rose starts pointing out her favorite spots in Cashmere Cove, I can't help but imagine our life here...together. I know I'm about fifteen steps ahead, but now that I've got Rose back, I want to keep her forever. I'm thinking engagement. Marriage. A family. The whole deal.

Looking around this quaint town, even in the dead of winter, I can see it now. This is everything I've ever wanted in a home base.

Bonus points for it being less than a half hour's drive from Green Bay, so as long as my football career lasts—and I have every intention of retiring as a River Fox—I'll be close to work during the season.

There's just one tiny detail I need to work out. I'm a prince, and there are...expectations of where I'll live and work and spend my time.

"I feel like I've been doing all the talking." Rose squeezes my bicep, drawing me out of my thoughts. "Tell me something about you."

"What would you like to know?"

She hums next to me. "Plans for Christmas?"

I tense involuntarily, and she notices. "Is that a sore subject? We don't have to go there if you don't want. I thought—"

"No. It's fine, Rosie. Not your fault." I sigh.

She stays silent, waiting on me.

"My mother is coming into town."

Rose's foot catches on the lip in the sidewalk, and I reach out and steady her.

"Yeah, the thought of having her around makes me want to face plant too."

She lets out a strangled laugh. "Sorry. I know we shouldn't joke about it, but…yeah."

I blow out a breath. "My mother has a way of ruining everything."

"Well, now, that's not fair." Rose is trying to be politically correct, but she doesn't need to.

"It's the truth."

She's quiet for a beat before admitting, "She's intimidating."

"And domineering, bossy, narcissistic, and stuck in her ways." I hold up my fingers, counting off. "To name a few of her charming qualities."

Rose winces. "When does she get here?"

"This weekend. I'll be at our away game when she arrives. But then we'll do an early Christmas in the States. She has to be back in Penwick for the actual holiday celebrations at the end of December. Heaven forbid her own family would take precedence over the country." I sigh. "I don't mean to sound bitter. I'm mostly okay with it. But every once in a while, it gets under my skin. Especially because I'm expected to do the same. I'm mad at myself because for all of my life, I *have* done the same. I've said yes to whatever was asked of me by my country, no matter the personal detriment or my true feelings about it."

Rose looks up at me, and there's no pity in her gaze, nor do I see any annoyance. There's just understanding, and if I'm not mistaken, respect. "I'll be there for you—if you want me to be. Or if not, I'll make myself scarce."

I bend toward her and capture her lips with mine. It's an awkward kiss because we're walking side by side, but the fact that she offered, that she understands how challenging it is for me to face my mother alone, means the world.

"Don't ever make yourself scarce around me. I want all of you, all the time. The good. The bad. The snarky. I want your best days and your worst ones, and if you'll have mine, I'll share them all with you too."

Rose holds out her hand. I stare down at it and then ping my gaze up questioningly.

"It's a deal." Rose wiggles her fingers. "I thought we should shake on it to make it official."

"Right. Of course." I take her proffered hand in mine and give it a firm shake.

I bend and kiss her again.

"It's way more fun to seal something with a kiss than a handshake," I tell her when she pulls back.

"Fair." She turns us down a side road. "Wool Beach is right up this way."

I hear the scrape of the water hitting the shore as we approach, and when we crest the edge of the cove, the sight before me steals my breath.

The water is coal black near the shore with some patches of solid ice. The moon shines off of it, reflecting a creamy glow across the wide expanse. The trees creak beneath the weight of the fresh snow, and it smells like earthy, cold air and pine.

"This place is incredible."

Rose bobs her head and shivers.

"You're cold. Come here." I pull her in front of me and wrap my arms around her, holding her back to my chest.

She burrows in. "This is a favorite local spot. We keep it secret from the tourists so it doesn't get overrun. We have bonfires out here and cool off in the summer months. There's a great view of the fireworks over the lake too."

"I can picture it."

"We can come back this summer if you want." Her voice holds all the hope I feel in my chest.

I bend and kiss her behind the ear. "Promise?" I whisper.

She shivers, but I don't think it's from the cold this time. "You have my word."

I tip my chin up and stare out over the water. We stand in silence for a while. My head is full of all things Rose, and I can't help but long to unload a secret I've been carrying around.

She's someone I would trust this with. It's a big thing. But if not her, then who?

"Can I tell you something? Off the record?" I ask.

She scooches more deeply into my embrace. "Go ahead."

I exhale. "I'm thinking of abdicating."

Rose freezes in my arms before she slowly swivels her head and stares at me. I keep my eyes straight ahead for an extra second before glancing down and meeting her gaze.

"Abdicating?" she probes.

"Yeah." My tongue is thick in my mouth as I try to figure out a way to explain. The weight of failure that I associate with it presses painfully down upon my shoulders.

"Like forfeiting your position as prince of Penwick?"

"Pretty much. But I don't know if I'm brave enough."

"You are," she says without hesitation. "How long have you been thinking about this?"

"Years, I think," I admit. "My whole life maybe. Even before I knew there was a word for it or that it was an option. But I've been looking into it more recently. Since I'm only twenty-eight, I could give my mom and the palace some forewarning so they could get things arranged for succession. I'd like to still work for Penwick, behind the scenes, but not as the king."

"Have you told anyone?" Rose asks.

I shake my head. "Not yet. Does that make me cowardly?"

"Not at all. It's a big decision."

"It is."

"You want to talk me through it? Or not. Either way."

I blow out a breath, grateful for the space she's holding for me. "I've always felt suffocated in Penwick. Getting out and coming here was the best thing I've ever done. I love my life and getting to play the sport I love. I think I can make a difference here. I know I could make a difference in Penwick too, but not on my own terms. Everything is dictated to me, and I'm expected to fall in line. I don't love my life as a prince. That's what it comes down to."

Rose chews on her lip. "It seems like you've made your decision."

"Yes and no. I can't help but think I'm acting selfishly. I'm not someone who walks away when there's a job to do. But I'm already a miserable prince. I'd be an even more unhappy king. I'm sure of it. So, I don't know what to do."

Rose blows out a breath. "You're not selfish, Anton. You are the least selfish person I know. Maybe it'll be difficult for some people to swallow the change in their expectations, but you've been forging your own path for as long as I've known you. I admire that about you. You know who you are and what you want. I wish I could say the same."

"Hey now." I'm not about to let her diss herself.

She spins in my arms and puts a hand against my lips to silence my protest. "I know. I know. I'm working on it, okay?"

I blow out a breath and nod.

"It's not easy to push against expectations, but if you do that here, you'd be doing it not in an unappreciative or untasteful way, but with integrity and your focus on the greater good."

I nod slowly. "Truthfully, Duke would make a better king than I would."

Rose freezes and cocks her head to the side. "Duke? Really?"

"He loves our country. He's a better fit that I am."

Rose looks thoughtful, and we lapse into silence. She rests her head against my shoulder and wraps her arms around my waist. It's a simple hug but incredibly intimate. I feel safe in her arms. It's a gift.

"You don't think I'm crazy?" I say after a couple minutes. "Wanting to give it all away? To stay here in the States?"

"I don't think you're crazy. Your mom might," she adds ruefully. "You should talk to her about all of this. You may as well get out in front of it."

"I know." I sigh. "I'm dreading it."

"Don't blame you there."

"She'll consider me a blight on her good name and her legacy. If I go through with this, I will be the single greatest letdown of her life. I don't know if I can handle that."

Rose cups my face in her hands, her eyes flashing blue flames. "You are anything but a letdown, and if your mom makes you feel that way, then that's her issue, not yours."

I close my eyes. "Thanks for letting me unload all that on you...off the record."

She chuckles softly, her warm breath caressing my jaw. "I'm glad to listen. And"—she pauses, and I blink my eyes open—"I'm here for you."

I believe her, and it feels so good to have someone in my corner. I drop a kiss on the top of her head and hold her tighter.

I don't remember the last time I was this content. For the first time in a long time, I feel like I know what I want out of my life...mostly because I know who I want by my side.

30

WHO I AM

Rose

"Lennox... Sir... DAD."

My dad's head snaps up from the computer screen he's been staring at for the last five minutes.

"What is it, Rose?" His voice is snippy.

I want to roll my eyes, but I keep it professional. "I have something to tell you about Bates, and I think you should hear it...without distractions."

He clicks around but then finally swivels his chair toward me. "Fine. I'm listening."

I shift on my feet, suddenly nervous. I drove from Cashmere Cove to the outskirts of Green Bay, where our temporary offices are located, to say this in person. But now...

"I'm waiting, Rose. What's so important that you needed this meeting? I've got a lot on my plate."

I clasp my hands behind my back. *Just say it, Rose.* "I'm in love with Anton."

My dad doesn't blink. He holds my gaze—blue eyes staring back at mine. He doesn't speak, and I know he's calculating his next words carefully.

When the silence turns so loud I'm afraid my ear drums are going to burst, he cracks and barks out a laugh. "No, you're not." He swivels his chair back to his computer screen. "Is that all?"

I step forward, nerves replaced by annoyance and resolve. I use my foot to move his chair back in my direction. "No. That's not all. And yes, I am."

My dad's shoulders slump, and he gives me a pitying look. "Rose, honey—"

"Don't 'honey' me." Fury rises up in my chest. He lost that right a long time ago.

He holds up his hands, at least having the decency to look sheepish. "Sorry. Sorry. But I don't see why we're even having this conversation. You're not in love with Anton."

"Yes, I am."

He shakes his head. "You can't be. Not in your role as his security—someone assigned to protect him. And not really ever. We've been down this road."

I grit my teeth. We haven't exactly been down this road, because when I told my dad I loved Anton five years ago, he told me I wasn't allowed to love him—or anyone, really—if I wanted to do this job well, and then he told me the palace in Penwick no longer needed my services, and I was being sent on an overseas assignment, so I needed to end things with Anton.

And I did. I didn't push back. I didn't fight.

But I'm going to fight this time around. I'm choosing a different path. Robert Frost would be proud.

"You can't tell me how I feel. That's up to me."

He rolls his eyes. "Fine. I guess that's true. But what's also true is that you're under contract to do your job. There's no room for a relationship in our line of work. What about the overseas promotion? It's all you've ever wanted."

"What I want changed." It's as simple as that. I'm still figuring out exactly what I want in place of that position. I'm still finding my footing. But wherever I land, I want Anton in the picture. I want to come clean with him about my feelings and about my assignment. I'm sick and tired of keeping secrets—from him and everyone else. "I want to tell him the truth about the threat on his life and about the role I've been playing in protecting him."

My dad narrows his gaze at me. "That's absolutely out of the question."

"Why?"

"Because you'd be in breach of your contract with Penwick. They could sue you until you didn't have a dime left to your name. They could make your life absolutely miserable. Your credibility, the good name and reputation that you've spent years building...all of it would be gone. I won't let you ruin your life for some man you're infatuated with."

The blood rises to my face, and I feel my cheeks flush. I know that I'm bound by my contract, but I want my dad to fight for me. To see my side for once. To help me figure out how to get out of it and to recognize that this is in the best interest of our client as well.

"But—"

"No, that's it. Conversation over."

"What if there was a good reason for coming clean with Anton?" I hurry to say. "What if it could actually help keep him safe?"

My dad scoffs. "The man has never once accepted security or extra protection. That's the whole reason we've had to go about all this undercover business. Coming clean would do nothing but irritate him and put his life more in jeopardy."

"Not necessarily." I've been weighing my options, trying to figure out how much of what Anton told me last night I can disclose without completely betraying his confidence. I want him to have the chance to talk to his mom about his plans to abdicate, but I also want to keep him safe. If this news gets out, and Duke finds out that there's no one in his way on his quest for the throne, then the threat against Anton's life all but disintegrates.

I like the sound of that.

My dad is watching me closely. "What do you know, Rose? You better not be withholding information. We're counting on your reports to be complete and accurate. That's what Queen Della hired us for, and if you're falling down on the job or concealing information, we're going to have issues."

It's my turn to roll my eyes. "Give me a break, Lennox. You know I'm good at my job. I have been for almost a decade."

"Things change. People change." My dad's eyes flash, and he points at me. "Clearly. Look at you, leading with emotion. You're usually so clinical and detached."

He's not wrong. I've become so much like him over the past several years, keeping those closest to me at a distance, because I thought all I had was this job. It was something I was good at, and it was a connection to the father who abandoned me. This job has become my identity. As a result, I've shuttered everything else of meaning.

But the thought of my whole life as a security agent going up in flames doesn't freak me out like it would have last month. Then, I didn't know what I'd be without it. But now? I kind of can't wait to figure out what I could be...what comes next for me.

In order to get to what's next, I need to keep Anton safe, so...

"There might be a change in the line of succession in Penwick." I cross my arms and wait for my words to land.

My dad's eyes widen a fraction of an inch before he schools his features into the same perpetually even expression I've come to associate with him. I swear the man has completely suppressed all his emotions.

"I'm listening."

"It's not my place to say more."

"It darn well is. Tell us what you've found out." He motions to the room, where one of our colleagues has now joined us.

I hate that I'm about to betray Anton's confidence, but I'm doing it for his safety and for the greater good of coming out from the shadows. I pray he'll understand when everything comes to light.

"Anton is planning to abdicate."

My dad flinches so hard his rolling chair moves backward and bumps into the desk. "He told you that?"

I nod.

"When?"

"Last night. I told you, I'm not withholding information, Lennox."

Terry, our colleague, immediately starts typing on the computer, but my dad stares me down. "You think this changes the threat against him?"

"If the threat is coming from someone within the Penwick palace or the royal line, then wouldn't this massive change-up affect their plans?"

"But nobody knows?"

I shake my head. "He said I was the first person he told."

I keep my expression even because I can play my dad's game too, but my lips tingle from where I kissed Anton last night. I absently bring my fingers up and touch them because they feel like they're on fire even now. I don't take it lightly that Anton trusted me enough to share his plans. I'm going to earn that trust with honesty.

My dad squares his shoulders. "We need to alert—"

"Nobody's alerting anyone." My tone is firm.

My dad's eyebrows arch. "You literally said that this information could have a massive impact on Anton's safety, and now what? You're telling me to sit on it?"

"Not forever. Just until Anton has a chance to tell his family on his terms. We owe it to him."

"We don't owe him anything but his safety. That's what we were hired to ensure."

I wet my lips, trying not to let my creeping fear about whether or not this is the right call show. I don't know that I'd ever forgive myself if waiting to share this information somehow put Anton in greater danger.

"We're doing that. We're protecting him. We've done a good job. His mom is coming into town this weekend. He'll tell her then. I can even encourage it." I shake off the icky feeling of being a puppet master and press on. "I'm sure Duke will lay off whatever he's planning once he realizes that Anton will be out of his way."

"You can't know that for sure."

"None of us can know anything for sure, but I'd say it's a logical bet. We can assess more after this information gets through the Penwick channels." I glance to Terry, looking for some backup.

His gaze pings between me and Lennox, and he looks like a deer in the headlights.

"Rose has a point," he says after a beat, and I want to cheer. Instead, I keep my face placid and make a mental note to buy Terry an extra-nice Christmas present. "Letting Anton spill the beans about his plans doesn't really hurt us or him, does it? In fact, it may protect our position here. If word got out, he'd know Rose was behind the leak, and he might start asking questions. Better for it all to happen organically."

"Exactly." I shoot Terry a grateful smile.

My dad's mouth is set in a firm line. "Fine, but if we get any new intelligence, I reserve the right to change my mind."

I dip my chin in acknowledgement and change the subject. "Do we have any other intel about what Duke is planning? Did Charles report in yesterday or today?"

Seriously, I'd like to know if that guy gets as much crap as I do, because I doubt it.

Lennox shakes his head. "Per Charles, Duke has been stowed away in his hotel room, working. He's acting pretty unassuming, I'll give him that."

I weigh this. "I don't like it. I feel like we're missing something. Why hasn't Duke made his move?"

"He could be lulling Anton into a false sense of security," my dad suggests.

"But why would he need to do that at all? Anton doesn't suspect him. Anton doesn't know what we know. He'd have no reason to question Duke. Why not get in and get out? Get it all over with."

"Who knows why criminals do what they do?" Lennox shrugs. "It's not our job to understand them. It's our job to prevent their plans from going through."

I can't argue with him there. Still, I don't like it. "What are Duke's plans for the rest of the week?"

"According to Charles, Duke wants to go sightseeing. He does have a meeting blocked out on his calendar for Thursday evening. There're no details listed, and Charles hasn't been able to get any information out of him about who it's with or what it's about."

I square my shoulders. "Charles will be there, though?"

"As far as I know, yes."

"As far as you know?"

"Rose, you are not point on this case. I agreed to let you have your way about sharing Anton's news, but I'd appreciate if you let me do my job without the condescension," Lennox snaps.

I hold up my hands. "I'm not trying to make trouble. I want to ensure Anton's safety, that's all. That's my job."

My dad hits me with a hard look. "Because it's your job or because you love him?" He ends his statement with a scoff.

"Can't it be both?"

"No. You're a liability if your feelings are involved."

"I disagree. I can use my feelings to my advantage."

My dad shakes his head. "You say that, but in practice, it never works."

"I'll make it work."

Terry continues to watch us like he's ready to pull out a bowl of popcorn and settle in for the show. My father notices his keen interest and sets his jaw. There's nothing he dislikes more than making a scene. "We'll table this discussion for the time being, but think long and hard about your *feelings* of *love*." He uses air quotes. "Because you're going to have to choose. Him or the job. And this job is all you have. It's who you are. I'd hate to see you give that up for a man."

I don't react. I don't let on that my heart pounds in each and every one of my fingertips and even down in my toes. I refuse to believe that what he's said is true. I think about Anton's list.

About his belief in me. I can be more than who the agency—who my father—tells me to be. I *am* more than that.

31
SUSPICIOUS WITH a CAPITAL S
Rose

I force myself to sit up straighter in my chair at the upscale restaurant in a suburb of Green Bay and take a sip of wine. I'm at this bougie restaurant tonight because Charles told the team Duke is dining here. It's all he's been able to find out about the meeting on his calendar. That, and Duke told Charles, in no uncertain terms, that he is not needed or welcomed to join him for dinner.

Suspicious with a capital S if you ask me.

Enter me.

I'm here to observe Duke and report back.

Too bad I've been sitting here for two hours, and Duke has been alone the entire time. He's typing on his laptop. I can't get any closer to see if I can see what he's writing, or I'll risk blowing my cover. I can't get up, period, because I'll have to cross in front of his table, and I'm not sure my different shade of lipstick, heavier eye make-up, and updo will really hide my identity.

I catch sight of my reflection in the shiny silver spoon at my table, and I grimace. My stretched-thin-ness is showing in the bags under my eyes that even four layers of concealer didn't conceal. I worked a full shift at Mood Reader today. Mia is still under the weather, poor thing, so I'm trying to cover for her as much as possible.

I slide my phone out of my pocketbook and peer at the time. It's almost nine o'clock. I shift in my seat, and my mind wanders to Anton. I've been around the stadium—and him—every day this week. I've observed practices, talked to his coaches and the

River Foxes staff, building out background information for my article. We've kept things strictly professional there. But at night, after practice is done for him and my shifts at Mood Reader are over, we have dinner together and talk and kiss and keep things decadently unprofessional.

He asked me to hang out tonight, and it felt like a sword to my Achilles tendon to lie to him. I told him I had promised Noli and Poppy that we could do our annual Christmas cookie baking night. We aren't doing that until next week, and now I'm going to have to come up with another excuse when we actually are baking cookies.

See how the lies add up?

I'm slipping on the sludge of my deceit.

I'd much rather be with him, curled up in sweatpants, watching the movie he proposed: *Miss Congeniality*—my favorite. But instead, I'm here. With Duke.

The door to my right whooshes open, and my heart rate increases as my eyes bounce up to take in the new arrival. Maybe this is—finally—Duke's guest.

It's Anton.

I scream a long sequence of curse words in my mind and immediately drop my gaze and shove my chair back, ducking my head under the table and pretending to mess with the clasp on my high-heeled shoe.

What is he doing here?

Is he who Duke was planning to meet all along?

Why?

My dress goes from uncomfortable to suffocating as a layer of nervous sweat prickles my skin.

I sense Anton move toward Duke's table, and I wait an extra moment before I inch up from my position. Anton takes his seat, and mercifully, he's got his back to me.

But now what do I do?

My phone buzzes, and I scramble to grab it, nearly sending it clanking to the ground in my haste. I've got a new message from my dad.

> **Lennox:** Report in. What's going on there?

I tap out a response.

> **Rose:** Anton is here now. With Duke. Not sure what to make of that. You?

Bubbles pop up on my screen, and then another message follows.

> **Lennox:** Interesting. Sit tight and wait and see what happens.

> **Rose:** What if Anton sees me?

> **Lennox:** Why would that be an issue?

> **Rose:** Because I told him I had other plans tonight.

> **Lennox:** Tell him your plans changed. Get creative. Don't make a big deal out of a non-issue.

I grind my teeth. This is what irks me about my dad and this whole gig. My personal thoughts, feelings, and opinions are secondary to the job and the principal. Though, in this case, my personal thoughts, feelings, and opinions are directly tied to the principal, so I've really gone and made things extremely convoluted, haven't I?

I sigh and toss my phone down on the table.

I get out my compact mirror and use it to look over my shoulder at Duke and Anton. They're at ease with each other, laughing and talking. A waiter approaches, and I hold my breath, thinking maybe he's some sort of courier for a missive or some type of secondary attacker. But nothing happens. The pair places drink orders, and a couple minutes later, the waiter returns with a large stout glass filled with amber liquid and sets it in front of Duke. Anton is drinking ice water.

I allow myself a smile. My guy is in season, and he's too committed to his team and teammates and their performance to put something into his body on a Thursday night that could have any sort of negative effect on his game play this weekend.

I'm so lost in my thoughts of Anton that I don't immediately register when he stands from the table. He says something to Duke, and then he turns in my direction.

I'm across the restaurant, so I have maybe fifteen seconds before he passes my table. I snap my compact shut, stowing it in my purse and reaching for my wine glass. If only it was one of those large goblet-style glasses. Maybe it would cover more of my face. As it is, I make a show of leaning over the drink and sniffing it. All I can do is pray that Anton doesn't look this way.

I know the moment he skirts past my table. I don't look in his direction, keeping my focus on my wine glass and pretending to read the book I've brought along. But I can smell him. I think I could recognize his woodsy scent in a crowded room, even if I didn't know he was there.

He disappears into the restroom at the back of the restaurant, and I let out the breath I'm holding. I should get out of here while I have the chance. Screw the instructions from Lennox. But I waffle.

What if Duke is planning something tonight...here at the restaurant? What if Anton is in danger, and I'm so worried about saving face in my relationship with him that I fail to do my job and actually keep him safe?

I down the rest of my wine. I hate everything about this. My phone buzzes again, and I reluctantly grab it from my purse, expecting another message from my dad. Instead, my heart lifts and hammers.

Anton

> How's cookie baking? Missing you and wanted to check in. I promise I'm not clingy or desperate.

I smile so wide my cheeks hurt.

Rose

> Too bad. I have a thing for clingy, desperate men…

He types back immediately.

Anton

> In that case, can I see you tonight?

I let out a soft chuckle. I want to see him too. Really see him. Not covertly while I'm trying to do reconnaissance work. But I don't know how to respond, because anything I say will be a bold-faced lie. I mull it over for a couple seconds and then type out my answer, staying as close to half-truths as possible.

Rose

> I'm sorry I'm tied up.

Not a total lie. I'm just not tied up with my sisters like he thinks I am. And then, because I'm dying to tell him something real, I add:

Rose

> I miss you too, for the record.

I'm staring at my phone, so I don't see the movement in my periphery until it's too late.

"Rose?"

I jolt upright and find Duke giving me a questioning look.

"Uh, yeah. Hi." I stand, sliding my phone back into my purse. I need to get out of here.

"What are you doing?"

I cast a quick glance at the bathroom door, hoping Anton takes a minute longer in there.

"I was having a drink." I motion to my empty wine glass. "I was just leaving."

"I thought you were with your sisters tonight. That's what Anton said. He's here."

"Is he really?" My words come out sounding all pitchy.

"You didn't see him?" Duke points to the bathroom door. "He walked right past you."

I let out a pretend chuckle. "I must've been really absorbed in my book."

Duke doesn't look like he believes me.

I collect my purse and book. "I'm going to get going."

"You don't want to wait and say hi to Anton? I'm sure he'd be glad to see you."

Not after he knows I lied to him.

I feel like the walls are closing in on me, and there's no way out of this. Either way, Duke is going to tell Anton he saw me.

This is bad. This is really, really—

"Rose?" Anton's voice sounds close, and I spin around to find him directly behind me.

—bad.

There are two different emotions swirling around in his eyes. One I'd catalog as delight. He's happy to see me. The other is confusion. He can't understand why I'm here.

Honestly, fair.

"Hi." My voice is weak.

"What are you doing here? I thought you were at cookie night?"

I blow out a breath and make a split-second decision. I'm going to tell him the truth about everything. Right now. I'll deal with the fallout, but he deserves to have the whole picture. I can't wait one more minute, and I refuse to spin one more falsity to his face. Oh gosh, he's going to be mad. And hurt. I hate myself for it already. But I shove the thought aside. If I tell him the truth, he'll understand. He has to. He's Anton. He's the most understanding man I know.

Right?

Right.

"I, uh...didn't go to cookie night."

"Why not?" Anton looks bewildered. "Did you know I was going to be here?"

I glance between Anton and Duke. "I need to talk to you." I offer Duke an apologetic look. "Alone, if that's okay. But I don't want to interrupt your dinner."

Anton shakes his head. "It's okay. Right, Duke?"

"I'm going to head back to my hotel. You two have a good rest of your evening." Duke stares me down before turning and leaving me alone with Anton.

All at once, my legs can't support my body weight, so I drop back into my seat at the table.

Anton sits across from me, his shoulders fighting against the seams of his sport coat.

"What's going on, Rose? Did you come here to talk to me?" He glances at my empty wine glass, likely realizing that I've been seated at the table for a while. "Or were you here with Duke? Did you have an interview lined up that you didn't want to tell me about?"

"No. It's not like that at all. I mean, I wouldn't go behind your back about the article."

"Then what?"

I close my eyes for a second, gathering my strength and fortitude. This is Anton. He'll appreciate me being upfront and honest with him.

"I don't even know where to begin," I admit.

"You're kind of freaking me out, not gonna lie."

"Okay. I'm just going to tell you this."

He leans back. "Please do."

"I'm not actually writing an article on you. It's a cover story."

His eyebrows hitch up. "I'm going to be on the cover?"

I wince. "No. Sorry. Bad word choice." I try again. "It's a cover story for what I've actually been hired to do."

He stares at me blankly, and I plug ahead.

"Which is to stay close to you as a personal protection agent."

"A personal protection what now?"

Here we go. For better or worse. Being honest starts now.

"I'm a security agent, Anton. Kind of like a mix between a bodyguard and a spy."

32
SO MUCH FOR MY HAPPY ENDING...AGAIN

Anton

I blink. Rose is biting her lip, waiting for me to say something, but my mind and mouth are refusing to work together. Maybe it's ridiculous, but the first words out of my lips are, "No, you're not."

"I am, actually." She winces. "I was hired by the palace in Penwick to keep you safe. There's been a threat made against you."

I hold up my hands because *that* gets my attention. "Wait. What?"

"I know. This is a lot. But I need you to hear the truth from me. You've got nothing to worry about. We're doing everything we can to keep you safe, and we will keep you safe. You have my word."

I shake my head. "That's not what I'm focusing on here."

Rose sits up straighter and cocks her head to one side, like she can't figure out what I mean.

"You said you were hired by Penwick," I say slowly.

She nods.

I try my best to keep my voice even, but inside, my blood feels like it's rushing through my veins like whitewater rapids. "Nobody cared to inform me about this?"

"It was written into my contract that I'm not allowed to disclose any details about this arrangement to you. You've always rejected security in the past."

I press my hands against the table and jut my chin at her. "You're darn right I did, for good reason."

"I know you don't like to feel confined, and you want to live a normal life. This was Penwick's solution. They put me undercover with you in an effort to allow you to live life normally while also having an extra layer of protection in place."

"So, this was, what, some sort of service to me? Done for my benefit." I let out a mirthless laugh. "Please. Let's not pretend either of us believes that. I was lied to, by the palace and by"—my voice cracks—"you."

Rose's face falls. "I wanted to tell you. I tried to get them to let me, but they refused. I'm going against every protocol put in place by my agency by coming clean with you tonight. I'm probably going to lose my job."

Maybe I should care more about that, but right now, all I can see is red. "How could you do this to me?"

"I—"

"I trusted you, and you took advantage of that…and of me." My mind is reeling.

"No!" Rose shakes her head. There's a frantic look in her eyes. "You have to understand. I wanted to tell you the truth about everything, but since I couldn't, the only thing I could do was try to keep you safe. I didn't want anything to happen to you, so I kept my mouth shut and did my job."

"But you didn't care about me enough to be honest."

Rose's shoulders slump. "I do care about you."

"Really? Because from where I'm sitting, it doesn't feel like it. You've basically been spying on me."

"No! Well, yes. But it's for your own good. Your safety."

"I don't feel safe. I feel completely violated."

Rose straightens her spine. "You have to believe me. Don't you see? It's different this time. I'm telling you the truth now. I—"

I hold up my hand, and she falls silent. "This time?" I whisper. My stomach is in knots. "You mean I was a job to you all those years ago too?"

Rose's expression contorts into one of anguish. Her eyes are frantically searching my gaze. "Hear me out."

"No. Tell me the truth—if you're even capable of that. Were you hired back in Mobile too?"

She drops her gaze, and I have my answer.

"So, when I ran into you in the bar, that wasn't serendipitous? It wasn't providence. When you told me you didn't know who I was and sat there shucking peanuts with me, you knew the whole time I was Anton Bates, Prince of Penwick, because you were assigned to protect me?"

"Yes." Rose's voice is so low I almost don't hear her.

"You lied to me." I push back off the table. I need more space from her, but now that we've come this far, I have to know. "So tonight? You're here spying on me? How did you even know I'd be here?"

"I was here to watch Duke." Her voice sounds small.

"Why?"

"Because we're afraid he may be behind the threats against you."

I let out a strangled laugh at that. "That's absolutely ridiculous."

"Maybe." Rose tips her head to the side, like she knows best. "Maybe not."

I snap. I'm so angry at her that I can barely breathe. "Don't patronize me, Rose. Not after everything you've done."

She shakes her head quickly, holding up her hands. "I'm not trying to. I'm so sorry. About all of it." Her eyes are watery. "I did what I thought was best." She reaches out and places her fingers over my hand. She grabs my wrist and holds me in place, forcing me to look at her. "They made me break things off when the job was done back then, and they sent me overseas. I hated myself for how I ended things with you. I refuse to let that happen again, which is why I'm telling you all this now. I need you to know my feelings are real. They were back then, and they are now."

I shake my head and peel her fingers off my arm. "How am I supposed to believe anything you say?"

"Because. It's me, Anton. You have to believe me. You mean so much to me." She sounds desperate.

"And I'm supposed to trust you? I let you in—twice—and all you did was act out a role and keep secrets from me. Who even is the real you? How am I supposed to know?"

"Don't you see?" She's crying now. "I've felt so lost because of this job and the way it forces me to fit into the next role and be a chameleon. The real me all but disappeared. But then I started spending time with you, and you helped me realize who I want to be. Who I can be. I'm the most myself around you."

I stare at her, and I can tell she means it. I can tell she's contrite and that she probably didn't want to hurt me. But none of that matters, does it? What matters is how she acted. How she withheld information. How she was deceitful.

"You chose the palace over me—on more than one occasion. You knew about my complicated relationship with my mother. You knew more than anyone. You still acted the way you did. I can't overlook that. You know how much I value honesty. How rarely I trust." My voice sounds hard, and I don't try to soften it. "You're another in a long line of people who were play acting around me."

"You can't believe that."

"You don't get to tell me what I can and can't believe. You lost that right the second you lied to me. Since our entire relationship, then and now, has been built on a lie, you never had a right in the first place." I push back from the table. "I need to get out of here."

"Anton. Wait. Please." Rose follows me out into the parking lot, but I don't break my stride. She jogs impressively fast in heels, I'll give her that.

She gets in front of me and holds up her hands. "Stop. Stop! We're not finished here."

"That's the thing, Rose. I am finished. You're fired."

She crosses her arms over her chest. "You can't fire me."

She's right. Because I didn't hire her. Which is the entire issue here. But as I stare at her, a face I love—a woman I love—I feel my heart crack open, because I know what I need to say next.

"Maybe not, but I can tell you that our relationship...our friendship...our...whatever it is we were doing...it's over for me. I don't want to see you again. Please, if you have any real feelings for me at all, leave me alone."

I side-step her and get into my truck. I start the ignition and pull away. I look in the rearview mirror once before leaving the parking lot. Rose is standing in her dress, shoulders slumped, looking completely defeated.

My heart tugs. It wants to go back to her. To wrap her in my arms and warm her up. But my heart doesn't know what's good for it. My head is screaming at me to put my foot on the gas and leave her and her deceit behind.

That's what I do.

33
Sisters and Secrets

Rose

I don't know how I make it from the restaurant where everything exploded with Anton to the office building, but I do. From there, everything goes from bad to worse.

My dad fires me.

In front of the whole team.

And in front of Queen Della, who is there via video conference.

By the time I pull into the driveway of The Downer, there's a trail of teardrops and snot running from my eyes and nose and dripping off my chin. I didn't think it was possible for one person to produce so many facial secretions, but I'm about to set a world record.

I fumble with my keys at the front door. My fingers are freezing, and the snot on my face turns frozen in the sub-zero temperature. I finally get the door open and tumble inside. It's pitch black, and I don't bother with the lights. I drop my bag of stuff and walk aimlessly toward the couch. I flop down, grab a throw pillow that Poppy picked out when she lived here and cling to it as a fresh wave of emotions crashes over me.

The front door bangs open, and I scream.

"Rosie. It's us." Poppy's voice slices through my haze, and when one of them hits the lights, I make out the forms of both my sisters. "We were next door and saw you come in."

They flank me on the couch. Poppy immediately puts her arms around me and holds me to her in a motherly hug. Noli holds out a tissue, making me cry even harder.

I don't know how long I go on for, but they sit there with me, holding me, rubbing my back, not asking me what's going on. I love them so much for it that there's a deep ache in my chest.

When I finally come up from my tears for air, they stare at me with concerned expressions. Their blue eyes, so similar to mine, search my face for answers to unasked questions.

"Do you want to talk about it?" Poppy asks quietly.

"I really don't." My voice is hoarse from the sobbing.

"It might help," Noli says after a second. "It's something I'm learning in therapy. Naming my anxieties and issues takes some of the power out of them and puts it back in my hands."

I let my head rest back on the couch. "I've ruined everything."

"What do you mean?" Poppy asks.

"Everything with Anton," I begin. "And with my job."

Noli frowns. "What happened at Mood Reader?"

I shake my head. "Not that job."

Poppy cocks her head to the side. "What are you talking about?"

I scrub my hands over my face. "I haven't been honest with you both. When I tell you this, you're going to hate me too...like everyone else."

"Not true," Noli says at the same time Poppy says, "We would never."

"What if I told you I've been in touch with Dad for the past decade?" I blurt.

My sisters go still. The only sound in The Downer is the hum of the furnace.

"You've...been in touch with Dad?" Poppy asks slowly. "Our dad?"

I nod once. "Not just in touch with him. I've been working for him."

Noli leans back. "What are you talking about?"

"Dad is the head of a private security and intelligence agency. I've been one of his agents since I graduated high school."

Now that the truth is out there, I plow ahead. I tell them everything. How our father recruited me after I graduated high school. How he trained me in self-defense, intelligence gathering, and undercover work. How I moved up the chain from small, odd jobs to more significant ops.

"Anton was a job back in Mobile. I was tasked with gathering information on his life and patterns of behavior and reporting them back to the palace in Penwick," I explain. As I spell it all out for them, what I did to him sounds manipulative and sketchy, and I hate myself all over again. He has every right to hate me too.

"I fell for him then, but I shouldn't have," I press on. "He was a job, and when the job was done, I was told I needed to remove myself from his life. I broke up with him." I suck in a breath. "It nearly wrecked me, but I stayed busy. That was when I went overseas. I was assigned to another protection detail there."

"You weren't teaching English abroad?" Poppy asks, dumbfounded.

I shake my head. "That was my cover."

"Oh my gosh, Rosie," Noli breathes.

"Were you in danger?" Poppy squeaks.

"Not really. Not directly." I hedge. "I'm very good at my job—or what was my job. I was fired tonight."

I tell them about Anton and coming clean. About how that put me in breach of our contract. About how Dad was livid and so was the queen. And most of all, so was Anton.

"He doesn't want anything to do with me." My voice cracks. "I don't blame him. I was dishonest. For his whole life, people have been telling him what he wants to hear or telling him what he needs to do. He never knows anyone's motives and whether or not they're pure. He trusted me, and I turned out to be everything he feared. I went from being someone he cared about to his worst nightmare."

"You're no one's nightmare, Rosie." Poppy starts stroking my hair.

I shake my head. "How can you even say that? I lied to you too."

"Yeah. About that," Noli huffs. "What the heck?"

Poppy reaches across me and swats her. "Not. The. Time."

"Sorry," Noli mumbles.

"No. I'*m* sorry." I start crying again. "I just…when Dad reached out, I was so hopeful for a connection with him. I thought he'd come around eventually and want to have a role in our family again. He got into the business because he was a loner. He didn't have anything holding him back, and that worked to his advantage. I was the same way, so he taught me everything he knew. The whole time, I was waiting for an opening to try to get our family reconciliation going, but it never came. By that point, I was so far in the weeds of my secret life with his agency that I didn't know how to get out. I've completely lost myself. I just morph into whatever my assignments require of me, and I don't know which way is up anymore. But it doesn't matter. I don't deserve to be found."

"Alright, let's get one thing straight." Noli's calm voice pierces through the fog of my self-loathing and grief. "That is absolutely not true."

"One hundred percent false," Poppy puts in.

I start shaking my head, but Poppy reaches up and squeezes my cheeks between her hands, cutting me off. "You do, Rosie. You unquestionably deserve to be found."

"Thank you," I whisper. "I really went and ruined everything, but you guys are being so nice."

"It doesn't matter what you did," Poppy shushes me. "With the whole secret-double-life thing, or with Anton, or with our father, or any of it."

"Although, we're definitely going to circle back to all of that because *wow*, I'm going to need details." Noli's droll tone makes me chuckle in spite of myself.

Poppy shoots her a look. "Right now, you need to understand that your worth, who you are as a person, isn't tied up in what you've done. You are inherently good. You have value because you're a human being. That doesn't go away because you got messed up in a job or a relationship."

I want to believe her, but it's going to take a lot of soul searching to regain a semblance of my own identity—and the belief that I'm not a complete screw-up and the worst person in the world.

"It feels a little like it does. I'm scared," I whisper. "Who even am I?"

"That's the beautiful thing, Rosie. You get to decide that," Noli says.

"For starters," Poppy leans in and hugs me, "remember that you are Rose Marie Kasper, and you are loved."

She holds me close, and Noli strokes my hair, and I fall apart again. I don't remember the last time someone took care of me. I've always felt like the outlier in our sister group. I love Poppy and Noli more than anything, but I've intentionally kept myself distanced from them because of my job. Now I don't have to. Everything imploded, and honestly? It's a relief.

Another bout of my tears makes me shake. I feel empty, but at the same time, in my emptiness, there's a levity I haven't felt in years. It's like I cried out all the secrets, broke through the web of deception that had been shrouding my soul, and while all that's left is open space, at least I'm finally clean.

34

For The Team

Anton

My teammates are eyeing me with varying levels of concern. For good reason. I was a complete space cadet during our Friday walk-through. I wouldn't make eye contact, wouldn't talk to anyone beyond one-word responses during our entire flight to our away game. Instead of using my free time on Saturday afternoon to explore the city and grab dinner with the guys like I usually would, I holed up in my hotel room alone. I got room service and only came out for team meetings. When those were finished at a little after eight, I came straight back to my room. I've gone through the motions of the warm-up today on autopilot.

We're waiting in the tunnel to take the field, and most of the guys are giving me doleful looks that say, *Get your head out of your butt. We've got a game to play.*

They're right. Of course they're right. I need to flip the switch and turn off all thoughts of facing my mother, which I'll do when we get home to Wisconsin later this evening. I need to stop thinking about Rose too. About her betrayal and how she treated me like she did—not once, but twice.

About the way she looked in my rearview mirror on Thursday night.

I need to block it all out. I *will* block it all out. Because I'm a professional.

I slap my helmet a couple times and catch Poe's eye. He's flanking me on the left. TJ is on my right, and I sense Del behind me with the rest of the offensive line.

"You good?" Poe knocks his shoulder pad into mine.

"Yep. Let's do this."

We storm onto the field, and the home team crowd heckles us with a barrage of boos. I'm used to it, and I let their animosity penetrate my skin and seep into my bloodstream. I'll use it as fuel.

We lose the coin toss, so the ball is in my hands first. Our offense runs three consecutive running plays—likely the offensive coordinator's conservative decision based on my total lack of focus the past few days. I can't blame the guy, but when we don't get the first down, I stomp off the field, heated. The more time I spend on the bench this afternoon, the more time my brain will have to wander, and I don't need that.

"Let me do my thing, Coach," I mutter as I walk past him.

He reaches for my arm and stops my progress, yanking me back for a conversation. "Can I trust you?"

I look him in the eye. "Yes."

He stares back at me and nods. "We're counting on you."

He's right. My own family may have betrayed me, and these guys may not be my blood relatives, but they've had my back numerous times over the years. I'm more firmly resolved than ever to play for them and to finish out this game—this season—strong. "I won't let the team down."

"Good." He slaps my shoulder. "You'll get your chance to prove yourself."

He's right again.

Our defense is a bunch of man-eaters, and they force a three and out. Philadelphia's punter shanks his kick, so we get excellent field position. I run into the offensive huddle, and through my earpiece, my coordinator calls a four verts deep pass play. Basically, our fastest wide receivers are all going to run vertically down the field and get open. I relay the play to the guys, and I can see them salivating.

We break with a clap, and I settle in behind Del. I run through my cadence, and he snaps the ball. I drop back, and the offensive line protects beautifully, giving my receivers a chance to get all the way down the field and putting stress on the safeties, who can't keep up with the speed of my guys.

I air out of a throw and feel good about it from the moment it leaves my arm. It drops perfectly into Kennedy's outstretched hands, in stride, and he high-steps into the end zone.

My adrenaline pumps through my veins as I sprint down the field to celebrate with the team. I glance over to the sidelines, and point at my coach, a wordless thank you for giving me a chance even though I've been a complete diva. He points back, and for the first time since Thursday, I feel like I have control over one aspect of my life.

· · · · ●·●· · ·

After a blow-out victory in Philly, I'm in much better spirits on the team's flight home. I can tell that Del, Poe, and TJ want to talk to me about what happened that sent me spiraling, and even though I'm not ready to hash it out yet, I owe them an explanation. We huddle up toward the front of the plane, and I unload everything, from Rose's official position as a security specialist, to the way she lied to me, to my mother's manipulation, and the threat on my life.

"Dude, holy crap." TJ whistles.

"I'm sorry, man," Poe says.

"There's a lot to unpack there." Del has got tears in the corners of his eyes.

"Delly, don't blubber," I warn him.

"I know. I'm not trying to. I just want you to be alright, emotionally and physically. Don't need a crazed attacker taking out my QB."

I offer him a wry smile. "I've had threats like this before, and they all amount to nothing. I'm not that important. I'll be fine—physically, at least."

"And emotionally?" he prods.

I shake my head. "I don't know honestly. The betrayal is still too raw to even process."

The guys nod, and we fall into silence. I'm zoning out, and my eyes are about to fall closed when I register my teammates whispering amongst themselves.

"What?" I open my eyes and stare them down. They all hesitate, shooting looks at each other. "Just say it."

"We would never take Rose's side over yours," Poe begins.

"Obviously." TJ nods.

I tip my head to the side. "But?"

"But when you're ready...when you take some time to do the processing that you need to do...it might be worth another conversation with her," Del says. "There's something special about what you two had."

I clench my jaw. "I don't know if I can trust her."

"I get that." Del nods. "She messed up with the lying and the secrets for sure."

"But I give her credit for owning it," Poe adds. "She did what she thought was right under the circumstances, and it sounds like she was only ever trying to protect you."

I digest his words. They echo what Rose told me herself.

"We're here for you, man." TJ slaps my back. "No matter what."

"I appreciate that." I lean back in my seat and close my eyes.

It's all too much to think about right now, especially when I know I have to face my mother when I get home to Green Bay.

• • • • • • • • •

My mom is perched on the edge of my couch when I arrive home.

She rises and sashays toward me. "Anton, darling. Good to see you."

"Mother." My voice sounds mechanical. I drop my bag inside the door and give her air kisses—our usual, stupid form of greeting.

"How was your little game?"

This is so typical of my mom. I'm the star quarterback for a professional football team, but to her, what I do equates to some silly game.

"Good. We won."

"How nice for you." She sounds bored. "I hope you don't mind, but I ordered food for us." She flips her gaze to the corner, and it's only then that I realize Duke's assistant, Charles, is here. That's weird, but whatever. "Charles will pick it up. We have a lot to discuss."

I walk into my kitchen and open the fridge, pulling out an electrolyte drink and taking a long slug. "Sure. Let's start with how you've lied to me. Continuously. For my entire life."

"For your own safety and good. I won't apologize."

I grunt.

"You are my only son, Anton." She doubles down. "The heir to the Penwick crown. I'm going to do anything and everything to safeguard you and your future."

"What do you want me to say to that? Thank you?"

"A bit of appreciation would be nice, yes." My mom stands up straighter. "After all, what would you have done if I'd told you about the threats? Not a darn thing, that's what. You're way too flippant with your security. You have an entire country that's counting on you, and you can't be bothered to take any precautions. It's selfish."

The blood rushes to my cheeks, and I feel my face turn hot. "I'm a lot of things, Mother, but I've worked every day not to be selfish. Don't accuse me of that."

My mother rolls her eyes. "You've had no problems being a model citizen here in the United States, but you've completely failed your home country. What am I supposed to say to the press when they ask me why you haven't returned? That my son chooses a life away from his family—shirking his responsibilities in favor of some sport? How do you think that looks?"

"It's all about my image and the optics for you, isn't it?" I lean on the counter between us. "It always has been."

"I don't know what you mean."

"You care about me to the extent that I do what I'm told and step into my role for Penwick. But if I swerve out of the line you've drawn for me and my life—even if it's for a good reason—you do whatever you can to snatch back control. In this case, it was to stick Rose on me as your spy."

My mom crosses her arms over her chest, her forehead creasing in grave offense. "I don't appreciate your tone."

"You weaponized a woman who I loved against me. How do you expect me to sound, Mother? Like I'm happy about that?"

"Oh, Anton, get over yourself." My mom flicks her wrist as if I'm being dramatic. "You never loved her. Not really. She was acting. You fell in love with a façade. I did you a favor the first time, demanding that she get pulled from your detail when I did. I could see it was headed for a train wreck. This time, the girl cooked her own goose. She never should have been allowed to work with you again if she couldn't have been trusted to keep confidential information confidential."

I turn my back and chug my drink. Discussing Rose like this feels like someone is cutting into my skin and peeling it back in sheets. I thought she was on my side, but she was working for my mother this whole time.

And yet...

Was she really that good of an actress?

The memory of Rose's pleas at the restaurant mingles with the perspective of my teammates.

Is it possible that she got herself stuck between a rock and a hard place and couldn't figure out a way out? And hadn't she tried to get out when she told me the truth? Against all the rules and stipulations that had been put on her?

My heart starts to hammer, but I need to put a pin in these thoughts, at least for now. Because there's something I have to get off my chest. Ironically, it's Rose's voice I hear in my head, reminding me I can be brave.

The door to my apartment opens. Charles must've stepped out for the food when I wasn't paying attention. He's returned now, and he places two large takeout bags on the counter before resuming his position in the corner.

I suck in a deep breath and face my mom. "I'm stepping away."

She claps her hands. "Finally. Good. You've come to your senses. I'll help with your transition, of course, in any way I can. Let's set up a press conference. You can let your fans know you're taking your rightful place back in Penwick."

I hold up my hand. "You misunderstand. I'm not stepping away from football. I'm stepping away from Penwick. I'm abdicating."

My mom stares blankly at me. "No, you're not."

"I've made my decision."

"Don't be ridiculous. You can't abdicate."

"I can. It's in the bylaws. I've already spoken to Duke about it. I wanted to give him fair warning that the royal duties will fall to him."

Granted, our meeting got interrupted by Rose and her admission, but he got the gist of things.

"I don't believe this." My mom's voice is low with an undercurrent of fury building at the edges. "How could you?"

"I can't live within the confines of Penwick. I'm sorry if that hurts you, but it's the truth, and I need to be true to myself. I've got to go my own way."

Her mouth opens and shuts like a fish, and she sways on her feet like she might pass out. I take a step toward her, but she holds up her hands in the universal *stop* sign. "So what? You're staying here, in America? With your silly ball team?"

I nod. "This team is my family."

My mother pulls herself up to her full height. "How dare you insult me like that? Family is blood."

I shake my head. "Not always, Mother."

She swallows, and I can practically see the way the wheels in her head turn as she adjusts her argument. "What about when your career is over? Then what? You won't be on this team forever."

I blow out a full breath. "Honestly, I don't know." I don't like to think about football ending. I know my time in the league is finite, but that's a bridge to cross another day.

"This is a big mistake." My mother grabs her bag. "You'll be sorry. Mark my words. Football is temporary. But your family...your country...that's who you are. This is not the end of this conversation." She collects her things and storms out of my condo. Charles gives me a brisk nod and follows her out.

I stare into space for who knows how long, trying to come to terms with everything that's happened in the past few days.

To recap, there's a threat on my life, which means I need to coordinate a security detail and figure out what the heck is going on. I just made that way more challenging when I told my mom I'm abdicating. I don't really want to deal with her or tap into my usual Penwick resources at the moment. So I'm on my own.

On top of that minor (read: major) issue, I've got a football team counting on me to lead us on a deep playoff run. I refuse to let the guys down, so I need to keep my focus.

And that's already nearly impossible because I've got a broken heart.

I grab the bag of takeout and bring it to my couch. Stuffing your face with sweet-and-sour chicken is a decent coping mechanism, right? It'll have to be...for now.

35
New Chapters

Rose

The December rush is here at Mood Reader, and I am dead on my feet. Mia and I have worked in tandem all day. She's been perched on the stool behind the counter, checking out our customers, while I've circled the floor, doling out book recommendations and gift ideas. The Christmas music tinkling over the speakers is cheerful, and the glistening twinkle lights make the space feel extra cozy now that the sun has set.

It's been one whole week since I came clean with Anton. One week since my dad fired me. One week since I've taken what my sisters told me to heart and had a good, hard look at myself and who I want to be.

I've cried. A lot. I'm telling myself it's good and healthy to feel my feelings. It's also a reminder that I'm a human, and my emotions are valid, even if I feel so messy it makes me itchy.

I've also started my own list. Anton was on to something with his notes about me, I think, and I've taken it a step further. My list is a compilation of things I want to be. Promises to myself. At the top of the list, I've written *honest* and *faithful*. If nothing else, I've vowed not to succumb to the secrets any longer. I want to live my life in the light.

Also included on my list are things that bring me joy like *reading*, *working out*, and *spending time with family*.

I couldn't put a finger on another aspect of my identity, but I eventually settled on *helping people*. In any form, I like to help out. It's why I love it here at the bookstore so much. It combines my love of books with my love of helping people. When I can match a book to a person, I feel a shot of happiness zip up my spine.

Earlier this week, I typed up my article about Anton, which felt like a dagger to the heart for all three thousand words. I emailed it to my dad, and then, after a moment's thought, I also fired it off to Ned.

When I finished the article, I stared at a blank Word document for about thirty seconds before letting my fingers fly across the keys again, a new story pouring out onto the page. I'd all but given up on writing fiction, but now I figure I have nothing to lose.

You know what? Writing is oddly therapeutic. I've typed myself to sleep every night this week. All those tropes I thought I'd never include because they're too painful? They're in there. Go figure.

I feel good when I'm writing, like I'm piecing myself back together as I'm piecing together a story. I don't know if I'll do anything with this manuscript, but that's not really the point right now.

Anyway, it's a start.

I'm doing okay. Not great. But okay.

The fact that Mood Reader has been swamped is helpful. The less time I have to dwell on how much I miss Anton, the better.

On the other hand, Mia keeps shooting me furtive glances and worrying her bottom lip. All day, I've felt like she has something she wants to say to me, but she keeps chickening out. I'm half terrified she's going to fire me too.

When I finally close and lock the door behind our final patron, it's 9:07. Mia shuffles to the comfy seating area, dropping into one of the overstuffed chairs.

"What a day." She motions me to the chair opposite her. "Sit."

I do as I'm told. She's got dark circles under her eyes, and she looks like she could fall asleep right here.

She catches me staring and offers me a wry grin. "I'm exhausted."

"Is everything okay? You seem a little"—I search for the word—"off. Anything I can do?"

Mia shifts her jaw and her gaze before meeting my eye. "Actually, that's what I want to talk to you about."

Here we go.

I brace for the worst while also giving myself a pep talk. If she's going in another direction with Mood Reader and doesn't need me anymore, I'll be okay. I'll be devastated, but I'll be okay.

"You've obviously noticed I haven't been myself lately," she hedges. "I've been waiting as long as possible to tell you because I didn't want you to worry. I was hoping to bounce back quicker."

Oh gosh, it's happening.

I bite my lip and try to keep the corners of my mouth from dropping into a frown, but it's tough.

"Apparently," Mia continues, "I'm not one of those women whose morning sickness goes away after the first trimester."

I blink. "Wait. *What?*"

Mia's face splits into a grin.

"You're *pregnant?*" I leap up off the couch and charge her, slowing only to make sure I don't maul her in a bear hug that could hurt the baby. "Oh my gosh, Mia. Congratulations!"

When Mia leans out of my hug, she's got tears in the corners of her eyes. "Thank you." She swallows a watery laugh. "We've been trying for a while, and we're so excited it finally happened for us."

I grab her hand and give it a squeeze. "I'm so happy for you and Patrick." I think back over the signs I missed the past few weeks. "Everything makes so much sense now."

"Right?" she chuckles. "Not only is my morning sickness not going away but it's also not limited to the morning. I've felt pretty miserable twenty-four seven. The only thing that helps is eating Granny Smith apples, of all things."

I shake my head in awe of her. "Why are you here? You should rest. I can handle the store."

Mia squeezes my hand. "I can't not work for the entirety of my pregnancy," she argues.

"Well, tell me what to do so I can help you, then."

Mia presses her lips together. "That's what I want to talk to you about."

I nod at her to continue.

"Patrick and I have talked about what we want our family life to look like after the baby comes. I'd really like to stay home with our little one—at least part time."

"Of course."

"I can't do that in good conscious as the sole owner of this place." She glances around the now quiet book shop before taking a deep breath and looking me dead in the eyes. "I want to take on a business partner, and I want you to be that person."

My jaw drops open. "Are you serious?"

She nods. "You don't have to make a decision immediately. We would obviously get lawyers involved to draw up a fair business contract before you buy in. I don't know your financial situation, and I don't need to know," she hurries to add. "But I want to make sure our plans are solid, because I want this store to thrive for years to come."

My heart is thumping out of control, and my head spins with possibility. My savings from my undercover work will go a long way in helping me to cover the buy-in, and I'm sure I could get a loan. The prospect of putting down roots in Cashmere Cove—of doing something that's my choice—makes me feel like I could fly. Here I thought she was going to fire me or tell me the shop was closing, and instead, she's handing me an opportunity to have a stake in a business I love dearly and continue doing a job I enjoy…right when I felt like my prospects were dwindling.

I reach out and hug Mia again.

She squeaks out a laugh. "I'm guessing you're interested."

"So interested. You have no idea how much this means to me." My throat is thick. I haven't told Mia everything that went down in the last week, but she knows something is up.

She smiles. "I'm thinking we'll get through the busy season, and then when the calendar turns, we can figure out what this business looks like between the two of us going forward. How does that sound?"

"Amazing. Thank you so much."

She grins. "Thank *you*. I'm going to be able to enjoy this pregnancy a whole lot more, knowing things will be taken care of after the baby arrives."

"You got it." I stand and hold out a hand to hoist her up. "Let me take care of shutting down. You head home."

She stifles a yawn. "Are you sure?"

"Yes, I'm sure. Get outta here."

"Thank you." She grabs her bag and coat from behind the counter and leaves through the back entrance.

I take my time getting things in order, stopping to spin in circles every so often. I have big dreams for the store. I've been wanting to pitch an idea to Mia for a while now about linking up with some independent authors to see if we could sell signed copies of their books and handle the shipping and logistics of the sales for them. I've dragged my feet because I haven't wanted to overstep, but now? Now I'll be able to take ownership of this idea and then some.

I can't wait.

I dance around the comfy chairs, wiping away our customers' coffee rings on the end tables and singing a Christmas carol about sleigh bells, when a knock on the front window makes me scream.

I clutch my chest and whirl around, squinting into the darkness outside. Because of the lights of the store, it takes a minute for me to register who I'm seeing.

36
Die Trying

Rose

My heart lurches because, at first, I think Anton is standing outside, waving at me. But that's wishful thinking at its finest. Upon further inspection, I clearly see it's Duke.

He points to the door, beckoning me to let him in.

I hesitate, weighing my options. He appears to be alone. I could take him if I had to, though I don't know if he's armed. I could keep the door locked and not let him in, but that would give away that I'm wary of him and could potentially bring more danger to Anton's door. That's the last thing I want.

I decide to play it cool and see why Duke is here—if for no other reason than to satisfy my own curiosity. I'm anxious for any update from Anton's world. It's been a whole week, and other than catching part of his away game on Sunday, I haven't heard anything from my father or my former team about where the threat level is at.

I flip the lock on the door and pull it open. "Duke. What are you doing here?"

He peers beyond me into the empty bookstore. "Can I come in? I need to talk to you. Alone," he adds.

I hold the door wider in response, and he walks in, stomping his shoes on our entry rug.

"What's going on?" I swing the door shut and lock it again. If anything goes sideways with Duke, I have definite homefield advantage.

"Anton told me you were hired to protect him from a security threat." He watches me closely.

I swallow and nod. "That's right."

"What kind of security threat?"

Your kind. I stop myself from saying as much...but barely. Instead, I choose my words carefully. "Why do you ask?"

"Because I'm worried about my cousin."

I stare him down. The stress lines bracketing his mouth make him look incredibly genuine. Still, I keep my guard up.

"I'm sorry, I can't help you. I was released from the security firm where I used to work, and we were informed that Penwick Palace didn't have need of our services anymore." Queen Della made that *very* clear over the video call on the night I was fired.

Duke starts pacing.

"None of this makes sense," he mutters.

"What are you talking about?"

"The threat against Anton. I've done some digging this week, after Anton told me about it."

I arch an eyebrow.

"I have a background in cyber tech."

"What kind of background?"

He just stares at me.

I connect the dots. "You're a hacker?"

"On the record, absolutely not." Duke tips his head side to side. "Off the record, I could shock you with the information I'm able to find."

I nod slowly. I may have underestimated the man standing in front of me. "And?"

"And all of the chatter, the little bread crumbs being dropped online that your people and the Penwick security force are scooping up and using as evidence about this threat to Anton, is coming from one source."

"That makes sense. It's likely one organization or person who wants to harm him."

Duke shakes his head. "I know, but the organization that seems to have it out for Anton is the palace in Penwick."

I squint at him. "That can't be right."

"My thoughts exactly." Duke rubs the back of his neck. "Worse even—especially if you're me—is that whoever is behind the threats is trying to make it seem like they're coming from one person in particular. Me."

"What?" I suck in a breath. "You're being framed?"

"I think so. Nothing's happened yet, obviously, but it's like someone is planting seeds so that when something *does* happen, they can go back and point to all these instances where I supposedly hinted at taking Anton out to secure my path to the crown."

My mind is spinning, but I ask the first question that comes to mind. "Who's framing you? Can you tell?"

He gives his head a rueful shake. "Not entirely. The IP address is one within the palace's infrastructure, but there's no way I can know who's behind the screen."

"Do you have a guess?"

He cuts me with a look. "If I tell you what I think, can I count on your help?"

I'm nodding immediately. "I hurt Anton, but all I want to do is protect him. If there's anything I can do, say the word."

He studies me for a long moment. I let my face show every emotion that's pummeling my heart—determination, love, hurt, and, if I'm being honest, a little fear.

Eventually, Duke nods. "We need to figure out what's going on with Charles."

"Your assistant?" I frown.

Duke shakes his head. "He's not my assistant. He was assigned to me before I traveled to the U.S., but I don't trust him. I think he may be a pawn for whoever is trying to hurt Anton."

Something tickles the back of my mind—a conversation I had with my father when I found out about Charles for the first time. *He works for Queen Della directly.*

"What's with that face?" Duke points at me. "What do you know?"

I feel sick. "That the person who put Charles on you to 'keep an eye on you' is the queen. If you're saying Charles is actually around to cause Anton harm, then I think it's at Queen Della's hand."

Duke pulls himself up to his full height, and I'm terrified he's going to call me out for accusing his queen of regicide. But instead, he gets a steely glint in his eyes.

"We need to protect him."

I nod, familiar adrenaline coursing through my body with renewed intensity. Anton may not want me anymore, but I will do everything in my power to protect him. Or die trying.

37
Pre-Game Fit Check
Anton

I brush the front of my sport coat and flick the lint off my trousers before stepping out of the team bus. I'm in the first bus. We come to the stadium from the hotel in three waves ahead of home games. I like to get here early to pray, run through my visualizations, stretch, warm up, and not feel rushed.

The pre-game walk into the locker room is a media frenzy. They love to capture our game-day fits. Some of the guys, like TJ, go all out in wacky combinations and patterns. Earlier this year, he actually wore cargo shorts made solely from cerulean blue duct tape and a blue-and-white striped sweater vest. It was...something.

I keep it simple and classy. Today, I'm wearing a custom-tailored navy suit and a plain white shirt underneath.

I'm focused on the game, and I have my Bluetooth headphones on so I can't hear anything as I walk the tunnel of reporters on my way to the locker room. I keep my eyes straight ahead and avoid meeting anyone's gaze, not because I don't want to be friendly but because I'm on a strict timeline. Out of the corner of my eye, I spot one of my new security guys. Good. See? I did my due diligence, and now I'm putting the threat on my life out of my mind. Erin is standing nearby. If all goes well, I'll have another interview with her after a win this afternoon.

A flash of dark hair catches my attention, and my heart catapults to the back of my throat. Is that Rose? The woman is with Ned, and she disappears through an *Employees Only* door before I can tell for sure.

I shake my head slightly, resuming my trek to the locker room and trying to quell my hammering heart. It probably wasn't her. This woman was in a black jacket, not the custom one I had made. Though, would Rose wear my jacket after I told her I never wanted to see her again? Probably not.

A twinge of sadness prickles behind my eyes, and I have to swallow down a surge of emotions. Because here's the thing. In spite of it all—in spite of the way Rose lied and was working for my mother all this time—I still wish she were here.

After my conversation with my teammates last week and my meeting with my mother, I have mentally gone over every second of Rose's and my relationship, past and present, and knowing what I know now, I can see there was more going on than I understood. Which means Rose's actions were more nuanced than I allowed for when I was losing it in the restaurant. Yes, she hurt me with her deceit, but with a little distance and perspective, I can see her side of things.

I need to talk to her.

I wish she *was* here.

But I doubt she actually is. I'll ask Ned later.

I keep my face neutral. I've got a game to win.

• • • • • • • • • •

By the second quarter, our offense is firing on all cylinders. We scored on an eight play, eighty-seven-yard drive during which I went five for five on passing completions and put the cherry on top with a twenty-yard touchdown to Poe on a crossing route in the end zone.

"Heck of a ball, 4." Poe taps his helmet to mine as we jog to the sidelines after the on-field celebration.

"You make me look good, man," I return the compliment.

Del runs by and screams something incoherent, making us both laugh.

I'm feeling good, and not even catching sight of my mother in my box can sink my spirits. She's been on my case all week, trying to—in her words—"talk some sense into me" about the whole idea of abdication. She keeps reminding me that football isn't forever. I'm so sick of it, but I can hardly put her on a plane and send her back to Penwick.

Duke, for his part, has been kept out of our family conversations. I keep trying to get my mom to sit down, the three of us, but she refuses. She's called him some nasty names, and she's accused him of brainwashing me into giving up my position for him.

"You're enough of a people pleaser to do it!" she yelled during one particularly scintillating conversation.

Her words landed, but they had the opposite of her intended effect. I *have* been a people pleaser, and I do like it when everyone around me is happy. So much so that I've considered ruining my own life and happiness for the sake of serving Penwick. But I drew a hard line, and I'm sticking to it. Is it awful to feel like I'm letting her down? Yes. It chafes. But I know it's for the best. I'm well on my way to being a *former* people pleaser.

My gaze lingers on my mom. She's not paying attention to me or the game. She's talking to Charles. As if they can sense me watching them, they both look up, and our gazes connect. I bob my head in acknowledgement, and Charles returns the gesture. I don't get so much as a quirk of the lips from my own mother.

I swing my gaze over the rest of the stands. It's stupid, but I'm looking for Rose. I have a weird sense that she's close by. I don't get a chance to dwell on the idea because I'm called into a meeting with my QB coach and Jones, my backup. We go over the defense we saw on the last drive and prep for the next one.

We manage to convert a field goal just before half. We only had fifty seconds with the ball. I would have liked to score another touchdown, but points are points, and we head into the locker room up twenty-four to three.

I'll take it.

The second half is more of the same, and once again, by mid-way through the fourth quarter, the coach has Jones in, and he's resting my arm.

I shouldn't complain. It's good to be winning by such huge margins that I can afford the time off the field, but it makes me antsy. Fortunately, the guys on the sideline keep things interesting. We've got friendly bets placed on which second stringers are going to score. We're each pulling for our own player, and that helps pass the time.

"If Jones QB-sneaks this and scores, y'all owe me dinner," Kennedy drawls. He points at me because my guy is our backup running back, and I wagered at the start of the drive that if he wasn't the one to score, I would buy whoever did dinner.

"You're on. It's play action. He's going to hand it off." I'm ninety-five percent confident. Although… "Then again, the defense is playing soft on the weak side. If he fakes the hand off, he could roll out and…"

We watch the play unfold, and sure enough, Jones rolls out and sprints to the goal line. The defenders come up and try to stuff him. We all cringe at the contact, but after the refs confer at the goal line, they signal a touchdown.

"My boy!" Kennedy starts leaping around like a maniac. "Steak dinner, sucker. One hundred fifty dollars a plate."

I can't even be mad. It was a great play call, and I'm happy to see Jones do well. Not that I want competition for my job, per se. But iron sharpens iron. And Roy Jones is a good man. He deserves all the success in the world.

When the time on the clock reads zero, our second-string offense has notched two more touchdowns. Our second-string defense has given up three scores, so the final score makes it look like a closer game than it really was, but still. We'll take a 38-24 victory at this juncture in the season, no questions asked.

Erin wants to interview Poe instead of me, so I'm free to head back to the locker room with the rest of the team.

"There's a new steakhouse on the far side of town, 4. I say we try it out." Kennedy jogs off the field next to me.

"Deal. I'm taking you and Roy. He's the one who really earned it."

Kennedy whoops and sprints ahead. "Roy Boy! Wait up. I've got good news."

I chuckle as I slow to a walk. There are staff, trainers, and logistic team members lining the walkway. I nod my head in appreciation as several of them call out, "Good game, Bates!" and "Go River Foxes!" And then I do a double-take, because Rose is standing not four paces ahead of me.

I freeze as our eyes lock. It *was* her with Ned. She's wearing all black and an unreadable expression. What is she doing here? I change courses ever so slightly so I'm walking toward her, but her gaze bounces up and over my shoulder, and the look on her face goes from pensive to one of pure panic.

38

SHOTS FIRED

Rose

I'm so caught up in the sight of Anton and the fact that his expression isn't completely closed off when he sees me that I almost miss the figure that slides into view from around the corner. Before my mind can wonder what Anton might be thinking—or get my hopes up that maybe it's not, *Get the heck out of here. I don't ever want to see you again*—I catch movement out of the corner of my eye. It's Charles. He's got a bandanna wrapped around his mouth, but I watch in slow motion as he raises his Penwick-issued handgun and points it directly at Anton. My intuition and training kick in.

"Anton! Get down!" I launch myself at him.

Everything happens in slow motion. I collide with Anton's shoulder, taking him so much by surprise that I knock him off balance. I topple to the ground on top of him as I register the searing pain in my leg.

Here's the thing. Long ago, I reconciled the fact that I may have to take a bullet for one of my clients. Anton isn't technically a client. Not anymore. But there's no one I'm more willing to take a bullet for than him.

I press my full body into him, covering him with my person. He's yelling at me, but I can't make out the words. There's a ringing in my ears and all sorts of whooshing light as people sprint past me in both directions. There's a distant reverberation of a siren that seems to wail over the loudspeakers at the stadium, and then a voice comes through on the intercom. It's all a cacophony of distant noise. I'm using all my energy—all my focus—to keep Anton safe.

But then, all of a sudden, I'm being rolled over, and Anton appears above me. He's cradling my head in his arms, and the expression on his face is one of fear. His mouth is moving, and I blink up at him. It takes a couple seconds, but then my senses roar back, flooding my system with sounds and smells.

The blaring of an emergency siren rings in the background. Anton's face is so close to mine I can see the lines of dried sweat running down his jaw line.

"Rose. Rose! Answer me." His voice is rough and demanding, and though there are people moving everywhere, Anton keeps his gaze lasered on me.

"I...I'm sorry," I croak. "For everything." I wince. "My head feels fuzzy."

"Hey. Hey!" Anton's grip tightens, and it's weird that I can feel that, but I can't feel my right leg. It's like the nerve endings along my neckline, where we've got skin-to-skin contact, are exposed. "Rosie, I need you to keep your eyes open for me."

"I'll try." I search his gaze. "Are you hurt?"

He shakes his head. "No. I'm fine. You jumped in the way."

"I guess I did." I dart a glance to my lower body, but the blood on the floor beneath me makes my stomach roll, so I look away and pinch my eyes shut. "Oh boy. I did."

Even with my eyes closed, I can tell when one of the medical personnel from the River Foxes starts evaluating me.

"Gunshot wound. Vitals stable. Signs of shock. I need an ambulance to the south end zone tunnel." There's movement, and then another voice speaks. "Bates, we gotta get you out of here. Let's go."

"I'm not leaving her." Anton's voice is firm, and even in my post-gunshot-wound fog, hope flutters in my chest.

I feel pressure on my leg and burning pain. I hiss.

"It's okay, Rosie. Hey. Look at me."

I glance up and into Anton's worried eyes.

"I'll be fine," I tell him through gritted teeth.

His gaze flits to my leg and then back to my face. "I thought I saw you before the game. With Ned. But I didn't think that could be right. Your assignment was called off, right? And yet, here you are…somehow still on the job."

"Unofficially, if anyone asks," I whisper.

Anton arches a brow.

"No one believed us that you were still in danger."

"Who's us?"

"Me and Duke. Is he around here? He was trailing Charles."

"Charles?" Anton darts a glance away from me. "Why?"

"Because Charles was trying to take you out." I grimace. "I'm sorry. I should have figured it out sooner. I…I failed."

"You didn't." Anton looks down at me, and there's anguish in his gaze.

Tears are pooling in my eyes and leaking out the corners. I'm trying to take deep, slow breaths, but my chest feels tight, like someone's sitting on my lungs. "It's never supposed to get to this point."

"You did your job," he says, his tone firm. "You did a good job."

I shake my head. The pain radiating through my entire body is acting like truth serum, but I don't even care. I want him to know. Yes, I was trained to keep him safe, but that's not the only reason I did what I did.

"You're not my job." I choke on my spit and start coughing.

"I know. Because you were fired." Anton nods. "It doesn't matter. It's okay."

I'm panicky, and I can't catch my breath, and the room is at once spinning and closing in on me, but I force myself to speak. He has to know what I mean—before it's too late. "You're more than my job. Always have been," I murmur.

The medical people who are working on my leg are talking, and I focus on them and what they're saying. I'd like to try to figure out what the damage is. I have no concept of anything. I could have been barely grazed, or I could be bleeding out. It's all relative.

Someone yells, "Keep her talking. Keep her awake."

"Hey!"

I start and open my eyes, which I didn't realize I'd let fall closed. Anton has his hands on my cheeks and his face hanging over mine.

He's breathing heavily. "I didn't recognize you before because you aren't wearing your jacket."

I frown. Why is he talking to me about a coat right now?

"The one you gave me?" My voice sounds hollow in my ears.

He nods. Even in my haze, I can tell how earnestly and intently he's staring at me.

The edges of my vision are tunneling, but I swallow and try to focus on the conversation. "I didn't think you'd want me to wear your name on my back...after everything I did."

Anton's voice sounds farther away, and I can tell I'm slipping out of consciousness. "Hey! No. Rosie! Listen to me. Stay with me." He sounds like he's at the other end of a tunnel. Before I close my eyes, I hear him say, from what feels like one hundred miles away, "I always want my name on your back. No matter what."

Then everything goes dark.

39
NO HUGS FOR YOU

Anton

The tension in this cramped waiting room at the hospital in Green Bay is thicker than a seven-layer, dark-chocolate cake and not nearly as sweet.

I'm sitting in the corner, in a chair that's three sizes too small for me, listening as Rose's sisters verbally decimate their father. I don't know all the details, but suffice it to say, I'm glad I'm not the one on the receiving end of their ire.

They stormed into the hospital, took one look at me—still in my gameday pants and football cleats—and Poppy said, "You're here. Good."

That's been it as far as I'm concerned.

Lennox Kasper has not been so lucky.

The tongue-lashing the Kasper sisters are giving their father has been unrelenting.

From what I've gathered, this is some sort of unplanned family reunion. He walked out on them a decade or more ago, and this is the first time he's shown his face since. Apparently, Rose has been working for her father's agency without her sisters' knowledge. I don't blame them for unloading.

Rose must've come clean with Poppy and Noli, because they aren't acting miffed at her, but they are being downright chilly to their father. That's an understatement. They're beyond chilly. They're arctic.

For his part, Lennox has dug his heels in, which isn't helping his cause. He'd get further if he apologized, but I'm not about to put myself in the middle of the family drama—not when I have no say in any of it.

"You shouldn't be here," Poppy starts in on Lennox again.

"Poppy, give it a rest." He crosses his arms. "Rose works for me. She was injured in the line of duty. I'm not going to *not* follow up. I'm a good boss."

"Can't say the same about being a father, can you?" Poppy mutters.

"Amen." Noli stands up straighter. "And Rosie *worked* for you. Past tense. You fired her. She told us."

Collin, who is Noli's husband, if I'm remembering correctly—or maybe her boyfriend? I forget the details—is standing close at hand, as if ready to jump in and back up his girl if she needs him to. But so far, she's been completely capable.

Poppy too. She's gripping Mack's hand in such a way that I'm sure is cutting off circulation. But the two of them haven't wavered.

"It's so freaking fitting," Poppy takes up the argument. "You fired her, Dad. Left her out on her own. Where have I heard that before?" The bitterness is back. Scratch that. It never left.

"Because she's so dang good at her job," Noli says, "she went and did what you weren't smart enough to do and put herself in between the bad guys and Anton."

My heart pops into the back of my throat. I still can't believe that Rose took a bullet for me, without even thinking. She saw the gunman and jumped into action. No hesitation. I wish it would have been me taking the bullet for her.

I feel like climbing the walls. All I want to do is talk to her. She's out of surgery. Her surgeon came and talked to us a bit ago. Said everything went as well as could be expected in the operating room, and she's lucky the bullet missed her bone, only nicked her femoral artery, and that the medical staff on site reacted immediately. A couple millimeters in a different direction and without the quick thinking of our team's doctors, and the bullet could have caused her to bleed out.

I will not be thinking about that. I say another prayer of thanksgiving as I half-listen to Poppy and Noli unload years of pent-up anger on their dad.

"She probably could have used some back up, huh?" Poppy spits out. "You couldn't even give her that. You have no right to be here. You did nothing."

Lennox doesn't argue. He sets his jaw in a firm line.

The standoff is broken when a nurse walks into the waiting room. She glances around at the crowd of us. Her eyes widen when they land on me, but she turns her gaze to Poppy. "Your sister is awake and asking for you."

The Kasper sisters sprint down the hallway after the nurse, leaving me with Lennox, Collin, and Mack.

My phone buzzes, and I check my messages. I've got a pile-up of texts from my mother, but I haven't looked at one of them. I don't have the bandwidth to deal with her right now. She's only going to use this attempt on my life as ammunition to try to convince me to come back to Penwick.

My teammates have blown up my phone, making sure I'm okay and asking about Rose. Poe has her on the prayer chain at his church already. Del has offered to coordinate meals for her after she gets home. TJ is ribbing me for the fact that I needed her to protect me—all in jest, of course.

Duke has been reaching out as well, asking for updates. I gather he and Rose got pretty close over the course of the past week. I try not to be jealous, but I'm a weak man.

But this message isn't from the guys or Duke or my mom. It's from my new security team.

> The guy who shot at you cracked in interrogation. He says he was working for a man named Duke.

I blink. That can't be right. Duke was working with Rose to protect me. Isn't that what she said?

I pick up the phone and call Duke. He answers on the first ring.

"Is everything okay? Is Rose alright?" His voice is hurried.

"I think so. Her sisters went in to see her. I haven't seen her yet." I step out of the waiting room and into the privacy of the nearby hallway. I relay the message I got from my security. "What's going on?"

Duke is quiet, and then I hear him sigh. "I was afraid of this. It's a good thing Rose and I have our ducks in a row. Anton, I don't know how to say this to you…"

"Just say it."

"We think your mom is behind your attack and all the threats against you. She's been trying to frame me. I've documented it all, and I can make a case to prove my innocence."

I'm stunned speechless.

"I'm sorry," Duke goes on. "I…I don't understand her."

I shake my head, even though he can't see me. I shouldn't so readily believe him. I mean, it's my mother. But somehow, I'm not even surprised. "Where is she now? What do I do?"

"I don't know. I'm guessing I'm going to be called in to speak to authorities soon."

"You're sure you're okay? You don't need anything? I can vouch for you."

"I appreciate that. I appreciate you trusting me—more than you know." Duke blows out an audible breath. "I'll be good, though. I'll let you know where things are at."

There's a kerfuffle down the hall near where my security is positioned, and I say a quick goodbye to Duke, thanking him profusely for what he did to help me and promising to be in touch.

My mother comes around the corner at that very moment. She's got a police escort. Because of course she does. Everything's always a production with her, even though she could walk around America and no one would know her from the next sixty-something-year-old.

"Anton, there you are. Thank goodness you're safe." She reaches out her arms, the picture of a doting mother.

I hold up my hands, preventing her from embracing me. I catch the look the cops shoot each other. I nod at them and make eye contact with my security over my mother's shoulder. I have a feeling I'm going to need their services here shortly.

She furrows her brow. "What's going on?"

"You tell me." I cross my arms.

"What are you talking about?"

"I've just been informed that Charles was working for you."

"Charles? Where is he?" My mom peers around.

"Don't play dumb, Mother. Charles is in custody."

My mom balks, but her eye twitches. It's the only tell I need. "Why?"

"Because he tried to shoot me."

"You think I had something to do with that? Charles was working with Duke. If anyone from Penwick is behind this attack, I should think we would look to him first."

"Funny. That's what he told me you'd say. He's got proof that it wasn't him. It was you this whole time. Charles was working for *you*."

My mother pulls herself up to her full height. "You're clearly not thinking straight. Why would I hire someone to shoot my own son?"

"I can think of a couple reasons. For starters, maybe you were so put out that I wouldn't return to Penwick with you that you tried to scare me into compliance. Or perhaps you actually wanted to kill me rather than risk the social disgrace of having a son abdicate."

My mom's eye keeps twitching as she shoots a covert look at the police, who are shifting on their feet. "This is the most absurd thing I've ever heard." She waves me off. "You've obviously had a long and emotional day. I'm going to go and let you cool off."

"You're not going anywhere but to jail." I motion to the police and wave my security forward. I don't really know how this works in America and with a foreign dignitary, but I'm hoping they do.

"I can assist with that." Lennox steps up from behind me.

I whirl around. I'm not sure how long he's been standing there. He nods at me. "Duke and Rose looped me in earlier today. I didn't pay their notes much attention, which was my mistake, but I have the evidence necessary to prove this was Queen Della's doing."

I turn to my mom, who looks a bit like a caged animal. She glares back at me. "This is all your fault."

"My fault? That you tried to kill me and injured Rose in the process? Yeah, I don't really think so."

"We weren't trying to kill you!" My mom stomps her foot. "Charles was supposed to blow out your knee. If football wasn't an option anymore, then what would be left for you here? Nothing! You'd come home. That's all I've ever wanted. It's your rightful place."

"I think we've heard enough." Lennox grabs my mother's arm and, with the help of the police, ushers her out of the hospital wing. "Give Rose my best," he calls over his shoulder.

I nod. I'm completely at a loss as I stare after them. My brain keeps starting and stopping, but what I'm hung up on is the fact that my mom really doesn't know me at all. Just because my time on the team may come to an end one day—hopefully not for several years yet, but it will end—my friendships with my teammates and the relationships I've built here won't disappear.

"There you are." Poppy's voice sounds from behind me. I spin around. She's standing in the doorway at the end of the hallway, smiling. "Rose wants to see you."

40
The Do-Over

Anton

I pause outside the door to Rose's room, trying to collect myself. Poppy left me to, as she said, "kiss and make up."

Bold of her to assume that's what I want.

Bold. But correct.

Still, I'm timid. Because what does Rose want? Where do we even begin with each other?

"I see your shadow under the door." Rose's voice sounds hoarse and distant from behind the partition. "Why don't you come in here?"

So much for getting my bearings before I face her. I open the door, and the sight of her in the hospital bed steals my breath. She looks small and frail—two words I have never once associated with the tough-as-nails woman I know.

That's when the truth hits me. I *do* know her. In spite of the deception, I know who Rose is. I like who she is. I think she likes me too. I take a tentative step forward.

As if reading my mind, Rose waves a hand through the air. "I look like I got run over by a truck. Feel about the same."

I nod. "How's the leg?"

"I get to keep it." She pauses. "It'll be a while before I'm back in the weight room, though," she adds quietly.

"You'll be back. There's a rack with your name on it at the River Foxes stadium when you're ready."

Her eyes zing to mine, and I relish the flicker of determination I see in their blue depths. "Really?"

"After what you did today, the whole organization is bowing down to you."

Rose presses her lips together and dips her chin. "What about you?"

"What about me? You want me to bow down to you?"

"No!" She rolls her eyes, and I'm grateful to see them spark with humor before she turns serious again. "Are you alright?"

This is so typical of Rose. She's laid up, nursing a gunshot wound, and yet she's concerned about me.

"I will be. I just confronted my mom."

Rose pales further.

"I'd rather not talk about it right now, if that's okay."

"Very much okay." She nods hurriedly, and then she studies me. "What is it?"

Her hands fist the sheets, as if she's trying to quell her worries about something. "Before either of us say anything else, I'm wondering if I can have a do-over."

"A do-over? How would that look?"

She waves me back toward the door. "I'll show you. Go into the hallway, and when I say it's okay, come inside again."

I do as I'm told, not sure what her end game is but willing to play along. There's not much Rose could ask of me that I won't do. It's how it's always been, and if I have my way, it's how it'll always be.

She doesn't make me wait long before I hear her call, "Ready!"

I walk through the door again. She's cued up an old Faith Hill song on her cell phone. When I come to a stop by her bedside, she hands me a package of vending machine peanuts.

My eyes dart to hers, and she shrugs. "It was the best Poppy could do under the circumstances. You'll have to imagine the scent of spilled beer."

My heart is pumping faster than it does when we're down by a score and I have the ball in my hands with less than two minutes to play.

She holds out her hand. When I don't immediately take it, she wiggles her fingers. "Come on."

"What?" I grin. "Can't a man try to memorize a moment?"

She sucks in a breath as I clasp her hand and bring it to my lips. Two can play at this do-over.

"Okay. Here goes." She clears her throat. "Hi. I'm Rose Kasper. I love books and lists, and I've recently started writing again."

I cock a brow.

She fights a smile. "I'm figuring out who I want to be and working on being her, unapologetically. I also love Mexican food, being warm, and watching football. Well, one football player in particular."

My pulse pounds and my whole body feels light, fizzy. Like my blood is fifty percent carbonated water.

"My family dynamics are complicated. My mom is dead. My relationship with my dad is rocky at best. But my sisters mean everything to me." She shifts in the bed. "I'm a trained security operative, and I like keeping people safe. You are"—she pauses—"you *were* my assignment. I would do anything in my power to protect you." She gestures to her leg. "Exhibit A. But I also value honesty and transparency. I'm sorry I didn't give that to you before. I'm sorry I didn't tell you I knew you were a football player prince the moment I met you." She takes another breath. "I knew then, like I know now, that our backgrounds are worlds apart, but what I also know, what's always been true, from that first night in the bar, is that when I'm with you, I feel like I'm who I want to be."

She stares up at me with vulnerability and hope splashed in the pools of her eyes.

I'm still gripping her hand. I squeeze it.

"I'm Anton Bates. Football player and soon-to-be former prince. You know a lot about me from our past, and I can't wait to teach you a lot more about me in the future. But what I need you to know right here, right now, in the present, is that I loved you back then. I love you now. I'm going to keep loving you as long as you'll let me."

Rose blows out a breath. "You're sure?"

"One hundred percent." I motion to the side of her bed. "May I?"

She nods, and I sit down, brushing a tear from her cheek. I'm careful not to jostle her as I wrap my arms around her and hold her to my chest.

"Thanks for the do-over," she murmurs. "I'm so sorry I wasn't honest with you upfront."

I kiss her forehead. "No more apologies. Besides, I didn't know what I didn't know when I didn't know it. But if I did know it, I might have lost what I gained by not knowing."

She tips her chin up at me and looks thoughtful, digesting my words before slowly nodding. "What did you gain?"

"Time with you. The opportunity to lay the foundation of a relationship. I wouldn't change a thing, Sammy Rose. Everything led me here. To you. There's nowhere else I'd rather be."

She kisses my collar bone. "Ditto. Kind of."

I freeze and glance down at her.

She shrugs. "I mean, actually I'd rather not be shot and in a hospital bed. I'd rather be at the book store, or the football stadium, or out to dinner with you, but the sentiment is nice, and I know what you meant."

She's teasing me, and I love it. Because nobody, save for my teammates and Rose, has ever felt comfortable enough around me to give me a hard time. It makes me feel normal. It makes me feel safe, and I love her all the more for it.

"Look who's got jokes along with her gunshot wound." I readjust her in my arms.

"What can I say? I'm a woman of many talents."

"Yes, you are." I kiss her forehead. "I have something for you."

She perks up. "What is it?"

"I've got to go grab it."

She wilts. "You're leaving me?"

"Not for long. You're going to be sick of me in no time, you wait. It's right outside. Hang on." I sprint out to where Poppy, Mack, Noli, and Collin are waiting.

Noli arches her brow at me. "Everything okay?"

"Better than okay." I grab the rolled-up ball of fabric in the corner where I'd wedged it with my shoulder pads. I jog back down the hall to Rose's room. Before I open the door again, I hear Poppy say, "No way she's ending up an old cat lady."

I push open the door to Rose's room and hold out the wad of fabric for her. It reeks, and I second-guess myself. It seemed charming in the moment, but now I realize I'm presenting her with smelly football player germs.

She takes it from me and opens up my jersey.

I'm suddenly bashful.

But then she clutches it to her chest. "Your gameday jersey?"

"I'll wash it. Or get you a better one at the pro shop. But let this be a sign for now. Never, ever show up to one of my games without my name on your back. You got that?"

Rose's cheeks pinken. There's fire in her eyes, and yes, I hope she's reading into what I'm not saying. I'll give her my actual last name soon. If she'll let me. I was ready to do so five years ago, and I'm still ready now. But for the time being, a jersey will have to do.

"Understood," she says.

"Good." I stride toward her and capture her lips with mine.

41
THE TROPHY

Rose

Much like during the regular season, the River Foxes are dominant, and as I sit here in Anton's box at the Super Bowl, I can't help but marvel at how far I've come—we've come. From our time in Mobile to sitting in the nosebleeds in Green Bay, watching him without his knowledge. I glance down at my jersey. It's not the one Anton gave me in the post-op room at the hospital two months ago, but the sentiment is the same. I'm wearing his name, and my guy is leading his team to a Super Bowl victory.

There's only two minutes left in the game. We have the ball, and we're up by two touchdowns. It's not officially in the bag, but it feels pretty much like it's in the bag. Poppy, Mack, Noli, and Collin are with me in the box, along with Duke, who flew back from Penwick so he could be here for Anton.

The two have kept in close contact since everything went down with Queen Della. They put out a joint statement to the Penwickian people, explaining the circumstances. Duke stepped up sooner than anticipated. He and Anton have worked out a plan where Anton can still work on behalf of his charities and the causes he's passionate about in Penwick, but behind the scenes. He won't be an acting prince, but he'll maintain his ties to his cousin and his countrymen. It's the best of both worlds for him, and Duke has been nothing but gracious in working it out. I really like the guy, and I'm grateful Anton has him. It's hard to feel the betrayal of a family member. I know that well.

We've both got baggage where our parents are concerned, but we're working through it. My dad, to his credit, helped in getting charges brought to the queen after she had Charles shoot me. There was no way Anton was letting his mother get away with that. She's currently being held in a high-security prison in Penwick, where she was extradited. Both she and Charles will stand trial there for regicide and then here in the US for attempted murder. It'll be a long road to justice, but we'll walk it together, Anton and me. Or he'll walk it. I'll hobble.

My leg is healing nicely, according to my team of doctors and physical therapists. It's nearly killed me having to modify my workout regimen, but I'm channeling all my pent-up energy into doing exactly what my PT tells me to hopefully expedite the healing process. Poppy and Noli have been slightly smothering in their care for me, but I can't blame them. I secretly love them for it, even if I sometimes want to strangle them.

Anton has been a huge cheerleader, coming to my appointments when his schedule allows and listening to me grumble through my exercises. He wasn't kidding when he said the River Foxes' facilities would be made available to me. I've been having therapy there once a week, and his teammates keep me cackling with their antics before Anton shoos them away and leaves me breathless with his kisses.

I should be mostly back on my feet in time to take over Mood Reader this summer and give Mia a nice, relaxing maternity leave.

In the meantime, she's insisting I rest and not worry about working. But I'm going stir-crazy at home. I've been coming into the book store to be around people during the day. When we're quiet, I write my book. I'm getting close to finishing the first draft. Anton surprised me at Christmas with two tickets to South Carolina, where he's taking me for a writing retreat in a couple months. Ten whole days to work on my story and have him all to myself? Dream. Come. True.

I stare down at the field where he's under center. He calls out the play and hands the ball off to TJ, who pushes the pile forward enough to get a first down.

"That does it." Collin claps next to me. "The River Foxes are Super Bowl Champs!"

Poppy and Noli whistle, and I throw my hands over my head and scream.

"Let's get you downstairs." Mack offers me his arm. I can walk, but it doesn't feel great yet. Poppy, Noli, Collin, and Duke follow us out into the hallway and toward the elevator. We ride down to turf level and arrive with enough time to watch from the end zone as Anton takes a knee to end the game.

Confetti rains down from the ceiling. Everyone is screaming and hugging. Ned has his cell phone out. He's got a massive grin on his face, and he's spinning around in circles, capturing the moment. He spots me and waves, a giddy open-mouthed smile on his face. He's become one of my new best friends, ever since I sent him the article on Anton. After I recovered from my surgery, we ended up working together to edit and revise it, and then Ned sent it to his contacts in the sports world. With Anton's sign-off, we used my feature piece to explain how his role in Penwick was changing and what his hopes are for the future. The article went semi-viral, mostly because Anton is in high demand, but also because Ned insisted we include my role in saving him from Charles's bullet and a bit about our love story too. Readers gobbled it up, and while the attention makes me slightly uncomfortable, I also think it's really cool that my name is in the byline of the story about Anton's life and future. If I ever decide to take my fiction writing public, I'll already have some writing credits.

I grin at the scene in front of me, imagining exactly how I'd describe it in a manuscript. There's a pile-up of players in the center of the field as River Foxes teammates embrace and shake hands with the team from Denver, who stuck with us in the first half and played well, but in the end were no match for our offense.

My chest is so full of pride I feel like my rib cage could crack open.

I stand gingerly, careful not to do anything to my leg that could set me back. My crew has formed a protective circle around me so no one accidentally jostles me.

Poppy is on her tiptoes. "I don't see Anton."

"I think he's on the far side of the field." Noli points into the mass of oversized men.

"It's alright." I smile. "He'll find me."

The TV network people bustle by as the stage where they'll do the awards ceremony is being erected in our end zone. I spot Erin Thomas holding a clipboard and microphone.

I recognize the River Foxes' GM from my initial meeting. That feels like a lifetime ago. The circumstances surrounding it weren't ideal, but I wouldn't change a thing. It led me back to Anton, and there's nowhere else I want to be than with him, right here. Right now.

The crowd of players, their families, coaches, and reporters surge toward us, but then, in what feels like slow motion, the people part, and there's Anton. He's across the field, probably still fifty yards away, but his gaze is completely focused on me. He takes off jogging in our direction.

I've got a huge, goofy grin on my face, and Anton does too.

People are reaching out like they're hoping to pat him on the back and trying to talk to him as he makes his way over, but he ignores them and continues running to me.

"Incoming," Poppy squeals, but I barely register it.

He slows down only enough to scoop me into his arms without hurting me, and he spins me around in a circle, burying his head in the crook of my neck. I can't do the old *wrap-the-legs-around-your-man's-waist* trick, what with a gunshot wound and all, so my legs hang straight down, dangling off the ground as I savor Anton's embrace.

"You did it!" I lean back and look into his eyes. "You're incredible. I'm so proud of you."

"Wouldn't be here without you." He places a featherlight kiss on my lips. "How's the leg? Stiff?"

"It's perfect. I feel like I could run a mile on adrenaline alone. I can't imagine how you feel!"

He shifts so he's cradling me like a little baby. "Pretty darn good at the moment."

"You can put me down." I'm saying the words even as I'm nuzzling in. "You've got team stuff to do."

"Nope." He hugs me to him, and my heart warms. "Be prepared to have a very attentive boyfriend now that it's the off season."

"Sounds good to me." I peek over his shoulder, where he's still holding me off the ground. "Where's the Lombardi Trophy? I've always wanted to see that thing up close. It looks so shiny on TV."

He holds me closer and gazes into my eyes. "It's right here as far as I'm concerned."

I suck in a breath and laugh, because how is this my life?

Here we are. A prince and a spy. Or rather, an ex-prince and an ex-spy.

Somehow, we fit together perfectly.

This is the stuff they write books about.

42
EPILOGUE
Holland

I stare at the happy couple in front of me—the way they keep shooting each other secret glances that aren't secret at all, the way their hands are intertwined and their shoulders are curved toward each other—and I feel an unfamiliar longing in my chest.

Not *just* for female contact—as a popular pro-golfer, I could snap my fingers, and socialites and drop-dead-gorgeous women would be lining up to go out with me—but for true companionship. To spend time with someone who sees me as more than just a no-strings-attached good time.

I don't know what's gotten into me.

I *am* a famous golf pro and a guy who likes to have a good time. Nothing wrong with that.

But lately, I've been feeling…I don't know. Unmoored? Juvenile? Like maybe I'm ready for something more than casual flings with pretty women.

I blink, bringing my thoughts back to Rose and Anton. "Everything should be all set up for you here. Make yourselves at home."

"We can't thank you enough for this, Holland." Rose's gaze sweeps around the mansion. "I'm so excited."

I step out of the way so they can move inside. Anton reached out to me about using some of my contacts in the golf world to secure a house right near the course here in South Carolina. They've got the fairway on one side of the property, and it's a quick drive to the ocean in the opposite direction. It's a tranquil place that I hope will be the perfect getaway for the two of them.

Rose isn't back to full strength after getting shot this past winter, but she's moving pretty well.

"This is perfect, man. Thanks again." Anton shakes my hand and follows Rose inside.

"Call if you need anything, but otherwise, I'll let you two be."

I slip out the front door but not before I hear Rose squeal, "Anton, put me down!"

I smirk, but the tugging in my chest tightens. Maybe it would be nice to have a true partner...

My phone lights up with a call from my agent. I answer it as I walk to my car. "What's up, Noah?"

"Holland, how's it going? Look, I know you're busy, but I've got a big offer to talk through with you. You got a sec?"

My chest puffs out, and a rush of satisfaction makes me stand up straighter. My career is on the upswing. Endorsement deals are rolling in. I'm the golf world's darling. Basically, I'm living the dream.

"Sure. Go ahead." I ease behind the wheel of my car but don't start it. I check my watch. I'm late, but whatever.

"You know how we talked about the benefit of getting more face time in the mainstream, like beyond your sports deals?"

"Yep."

"Well, I've been working my contacts within the TV world, and I hit pay dirt."

"I'm listening."

"How would you like to be the star of the next season of *Most Eligible Mister*?"

Whoa.

"Are you serious?" I don't watch a lot of TV that's not sports-related, but everyone knows about *Most Eligible Mister*. It's the longest-running reality dating show on network television. My mom has been watching it religiously since I was eight years old.

"Would I joke with you about something like this? It's huge, man. A massive opportunity. But only if you want it," Noah adds.

God bless him. Noah is a really good agent. He has my best interests in mind at all times, and he cares about me as a person.

"I know you're enjoying your singlehood," he says, "so no pressure. But if you're at all interested, tell me, and I'll get to work hammering out some details."

I glance out the window of my car to where I left Anton and Rose, blissfully happy, and the feeling of want returns in my chest, humming a bit louder. I *do* want to find my person. That's always been part of my plan. I've just had so many women lining up for a chance to spend a night out on the town with me. It's great for my ego, not gonna lie, and I've leaned into it and enjoyed the attention for all it's worth. But I have no intention of being a playboy for the rest of my life.

"How would it work with my tournament schedule?" I ask, starting the car.

"Filming takes six weeks. Producers would want to squeeze you in this spring so they could air the show at the end of summer and have it coincide with the Tour Championship in late August. Added exposure for you and the show with follow-ups of you and the lucky lady during that tournament. It would be like your coming out party."

I grin. This is sounding better and better. Find a nice lady in a fun way—being surrounded by twenty beautiful women—and draw more attention to my golf game?

Sounds like a win on all fronts.

My Bluetooth connects to the car, and Noah's voice sounds through the speakers. "What do you say?"

"I'm liking what I'm hearing. We'd have to work it around my golf schedule, though. I'll need to practice, especially if we're filming this spring, with the Grandmasters and the PGO Championship."

The fiery face of my coach pops into my head. She's going to hate this.

"I'll need to stay in one place to film, except the travel I'd be doing otherwise for tournaments," I tell Noah. "My training can't be affected."

"I'm sure we could work that all out," Noah says. "You let me handle the details. I'll talk to the producers and loop you back in when I have something solid. You good with that?"

"Yeah, man. Thanks. You're the best."

"I know," Noah says on a chuckle. "Later."

No sooner does our call disconnect than my phone rings again. Speaking of my coach...

"What now?" I let my eye roll color my tone.

The at once silky-smooth and hard-as-a-rock voice of Mallory Walsh comes through my car's speakers. "Where are you?"

"Aw, did you miss me?"

"Not even a little bit."

"Ouch."

"You were supposed to meet me at the driving range twenty minutes ago, Holland."

I sigh. I owe most of my success to Mallory. She's a year older than I am and a heck of a golfer in her own right. But she's an even better coach.

Still, I wish she would lay off. I've put in the work. I'm reaping the benefits.

"I'm on my way. I had something to do."

"It's always something." She scolds me like I'm five years old. "What did I tell you about not taking this seriously?"

"I was helping out some friends. Give me a break."

"What about this weekend? I saw the pictures online. You were out both nights. When did you get home? Did you get any sleep?"

"Jeez, Mom." She hates when I call her that. "Lay off. I've got plenty of time to recover."

"You say that, but you'd be surprised. Hurry up and get your butt over here."

"I always knew you liked my butt."

"It's good for kicking, I'll give you that."

"Looking forward to it."

In response, she ends the call.

I huff out a laugh. This is how our relationship works. She pushes me. I push back. She gets the best out of me in the process. But it always seems like she hates my guts.

If she's unhappy with me for being late, she's going to be totally rage-y when I tell her about the *Most Eligible Mister* opportunity. She'll consider it an unnecessary distraction, tell me it is completely ludicrous to even consider it. Basically make me feel like an idiot.

Mallory is all golf, all the time. She's the most driven, focused person I know. But sometimes I wonder if she has a life outside of the sport. I mean, what good is all of this if I don't get to enjoy the perks of the hard work?

I spend the next few precious minutes bracing for the totality of her wrath.

When I park, I bypass the clubhouse and head straight to the range. No use poking the beast any more by making her wait while I yuk it up with the guys inside.

She's standing at a tee box, hands on her trim hips. She's wearing her usual ensemble: a snug-fitting white polo shirt, a black baseball cap over her copper hair, and a black golf skirt.

Her eyes are narrowed at me.

I hold up my hands. "I'm sorry."

Best to get out ahead of it.

"You will be sorry if your stupidity translates to the links this weekend," she says coolly.

"Not going to happen." It's easy to be cocky when you're as good as I am. "Now let's not waste time standing around."

Her nostrils flare.

Gosh, it's fun messing with her.

"I've got something to run by you." I smirk. "But first, put me to work, Coach."

· · · ● · ● ● · · ·

Need more of Holland and Mallory? Read *Pros Don't*, the fourth book in the Fall In Love series.

Acknowledgements

All glory to God, now and forever.

Thank you, readers, for loving the Kasper sisters! I have had the most fun writing this series. Cashmere Cove has become my happy place, and I am thrilled you love visiting, as well. Your support for me and my books is so very appreciated. I love writing stories for you.

Thank you to Melody Jeffries for bringing the characters of Rose and Anton to life so perfectly with your cover design and illustration. You nailed it! I can't say enough good things about working with you. Let's get started on the next book, yeah?!

A huge shout out to Jenn Lockwood for being a mastermind editor. I always know my books are in the best hands with you, Jenn, and I'm grateful for all your time and attention. Thanks, too, to Heather Pine for her critique and feedback. So helpful!

My beta readers, once again, came through for me with clutch commentary, support, and ideas. Moni, Heather, Amanda, and Sam, I appreciate you more than you know. Thank you! To my ARC readers who hyped me up ahead of release, you have no idea how much your kind words meant to me as I was anxiously waiting to take this book live. Huge thanks for your enthusiasm and help in spreading the word about *Exes Don't*.

To all the book people, near and far, who have shared my excitement for this release, thank you! Librarians, booksellers, bookstagrammers...everything you do to get books into the hands of readers means the world. You make this indie author's dreams cover true with every share, promotion, and kind word.

Thank you to my family for your unwavering support. We watched a lot of football growing up. A big thanks to my mom and dad for teaching me the rules of the game. It was always a great party trick to be the girl who knew about and could call out an illegal block in the back from a mile away. Shout out to my brothers, too. I have so many fond memories of Sundays spent together watching the Packers play. Luke, thanks for naming my team the River Foxes! It's my favorite. And to my cousins and extended family for all your team name suggestions, thank you! The team could have just as easily been the Gingerbreadmen or the Stink Bugs. I'm still laughing about that text string. You guys are my favorites, and I can't even explain how much your love and support means.

Thank you to my kids, for putting up with me being a full time mom and a part time author. I hope I inspire you to keep telling your stories and to love big. I love you so much.

To Nick. Always, always, always. If Joe Burrow was the inspiration for the look of Anton, you're the inspiration for all the good things about all the good guys I make up to put in these books. Thanks for the second chance. I love you madly.

About the Author

LEAH DOBRINSKA is the author of the Fall In Love series, the Larkspur Library Mysteries, a cozy mystery series set in the Wisconsin Northwoods, and the Mapleton novels, a series of award-winning standalone small town romances. She earned her degree in English Literature from UW-Madison where she was awarded the Dean's Prize and served as a Writing Fellow. She has since worked as a freelance writer, editor, and content marketer. Leah lives in Wisconsin with her husband and their gaggle of kids. When she's not writing, handing out snacks, or visiting the local library, Leah enjoys reading and running.

www.leahdobrinska.com
Instagram: @whatleahwrote

www.ingramcontent.com/pod-product-compliance
Lightning Source LLC
LaVergne TN
LVHW091719070526
838199LV00050B/2463